"We belong together."

"No!" Jennifer told him, shaking her head. "Just shut up. I don't want to hear one more word. Keep your wonderful lies for somebody else. We don't belong together. You belong in *The Guinness Book of World Records* for... for... for most pathological lover, and—"

"Most pathological lover?" Race interrupted, trying not to laugh.

"It's a perfect description of you. You lie every time you touch me, every time you open your mouth and start telling your pretty stories." She walked to the door, opened it and gazed pointedly at him, a pained expression in her eyes. "Go away, Race."

He touched her cheek on his way out. "I'll leave for now. But since you can't trust a pathological lover, I won't bother making any promises you know I won't keep...."

Dear Reader,

If you're looking for an extra-special reading experience—something rich and memorable, something deeply emotional, something totally romantic—your search is over! For in your hands you hold one of Silhouette's extremely **Special Editions**.

Dedicated to the proposition that *not* all romances are created equal, Silhouette **Special Edition** aims to deliver the best and the brightest in women's fiction—six books each month by such stellar authors as Nora Roberts, Lynda Trent, Tracy Sinclair and Ginna Gray, along with some dazzling new writers destined to become tomorrow's romance stars.

Pick and choose among titles if you must—we hope you'll soon equate all Silhouette **Special Editions** with consistently gratifying romance reading.

And don't forget the two Silhouette *Classics* at your bookseller's each month—reissues of the most beloved Silhouette **Special Editions** and Silhouette *Intimate Moments* of yesteryear.

Today's bestsellers, tomorrow's *Classics*—that's Silhouette **Special Edition**. We hope you'll stay with us in the months to come, because month after month, we intend to become more special than ever.

From all the authors and editors of Silhouette **Special Edition**,
Warmest wishes,

Leslie Kazanjian
Senior Editor

KANDI BROOKS
The Real World

Silhouette Special Edition

Published by Silhouette Books New York

America's Publisher of Contemporary Romance

To Marty Robinson,
who started it all

SILHOUETTE BOOKS
300 East 42nd St., New York, N.Y. 10017

Copyright © 1988 by Kandius Brooks

ISBN: 0-373-09471-X

First Silhouette Books printing August 1988

Printed in the U.S.A.

KANDI BROOKS

says reading has been an obsession since grade school and romance is one of her favorite addictions. A former social worker and teacher of psychology, she is also the author of a computerized science-fiction trivia game. Originally from Michigan, Kandi now calls South Carolina home, where she lives with her university-professor husband, their two children and a bull terrier named Agatha.

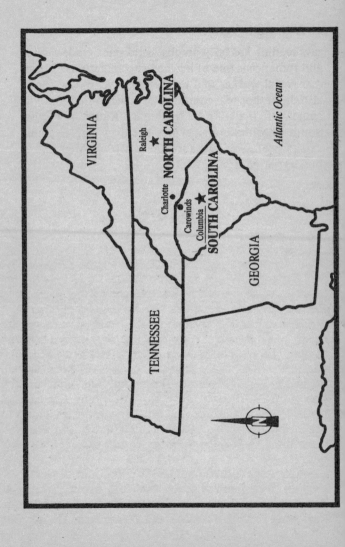

Prologue

When was the first time she'd seen Racine Huntington? Jennifer Grange knew exactly when and where she'd seen him *last*, but she couldn't recall the precise moment she'd *first* seen his gray eyes or his now-famous crooked smile.

She must have been nine or ten when Racine and his family had moved next door. The tall, dark-haired boy had instantly become her older brother Mike's best friend and part of her life. Even at thirteen, Racine—or Race, as he'd insisted the neighborhood kids call him—had been a knockout. He'd been born with something special that made people notice him, and he'd certainly learned how to use it. Everybody now knew Race Hunter, country-and-western singer. Few knew Racine Huntington, the boy next door.

Sitting back in her chair in the newsroom of the Charlotte Sentinel, Jennifer thought ruefully about the changes that had taken place since those carefree childhood days. Reviewing tonight's concert and seeing Race Hunter was not going to be easy. Standing up, she grabbed her purse and walked to her editor's desk. It was two-thirty, and her column for tomorrow's edition was finished. There was no point in sitting at her desk and reminiscing. She was a professional reporter, and personal memories had nothing to do with her assignment to cover Race Hunter's concert, nothing at all.

"I'll see you later," she called to her editor as she headed out of the newsroom. When he turned and gave her a hard look, she smiled reassuringly, knowing he was still uneasy about her initial negative reaction to the Hunter concert assignment.

She'd expected a more experienced reporter to get the job, but her editor had told her gruffly that since she was the entertainment reviewer, it was her story. It had taken her a few seconds to regain her composure, long enough for the man to wonder why she wasn't eager for the assignment. "Don't worry. I'll have the review on the night editor's desk by midnight. I realize that having Race Hunter in town is a big deal. It's the first time he's been back in Charlotte in eight years." Eight years and five months, to be exact, Jenni thought to herself as she got in her car and started to drive home.

Without planning to, Jenni found herself detouring through the old neighborhood where she, Racine and Mike had grown up. Modest by any standard, the brick homes now seemed smaller and shabbier, but they were still full of memories. Sighing, she pulled to a stop in front of her old house and recalled her childhood. Racine was a part of her past, and she had to accept the past—all of it, the good and the bad.

Mike and Racine had been inseparable all those long years ago, with Jenni a tagalong younger sister. She'd shagged balls for them, kept score when they'd played basketball, done anything she could to spend time with them. With both his parents working full-time at a local mill, it had often seemed as if Racine spent more time at the

Grange home than his own. He was the youngest of four children, born seven years after the youngest of his three sisters. Once his youngest sister had moved out, Racine had been mostly on his own. Though his parents had loved him, they had been so overwhelmed by their daily routine that they had had little time for their fourth and last child. Racine had never had enough of their time; or their love. And money had seldom been available for any extras. In fact, Jenni strongly suspected that Race's trademark faded blue jeans had not been so much a deliberate choice as a necessity at the beginning of his career. She could hardly recall him wearing anything else during his high school years. Maybe his childhood poverty explained his driving need for fame and success as an adult. All that Jenni knew for sure was that for years Racine had been Mike's constant companion and her other brother.

Things would have been fine if Racine had remained her brother, but he hadn't. Somewhere along the line, the affection she'd felt for him had changed and deepened. It had all started, Jenni had long ago decided, the day that Racine had saved her schoolbooks from the neighborhood bully. After he'd forced the other boy to return Jenni's book bag, Racine had grabbed him by his shirt and promised to beat him up if he ever bothered Jenni again. Never mind that the bully was a year older and ten pounds heavier than Race, they had all known that he meant it. That was the year that seventeen-year-old Racine Huntington had decided that he wanted to be called Race Hunter. That was the year that he had decided to be a country singer; and the year that Jenni had started to fall in love.

Nothing had happened to crystallize her feelings until one day shortly after her fourteenth birthday. She would never forget that day. Race had been a senior in high school, all of eighteen. He'd been ready to leave the house for an appearance with his band when he'd leaned over to kiss her goodbye. The brotherly kiss had changed suddenly; for a brief moment. She recalled Race looking totally horrified, and then he was gone. It had been Jenni's first kiss, and her last one from Racine Huntington. He'd turned into Race Hunter before he'd kissed her again. The rest of the year he'd been somewhat distant, though he'd never treated her with anything less than warm affection.

Then he'd won a music scholarship at a university in Tennessee. The rest was history. Everyone knew how the persistent singer-songwriter had made the rounds in Nashville, dropping out of college in his senior year to start touring as an opening act. He'd grown a beard to make himself look older and continued to wear the faded blue jeans that still marked his image. Everyone remembered his first record, his gravelly, sexy voice stirring waves that were so wide they crossed over from the country music business into the mainstream of popular music. Everybody knew Race Hunter, the country superstar who'd even made a few movies that proved he could act as well as sing.

How different her life would have been if their history had ended there, Jennifer mused two hours later as she sat alone in her bedroom, getting ready to attend Race's concert. If Racine hadn't come back to town after he'd moved his parents to Florida. Unable to resist the pull of memory, Jennifer was drawn to the scrapbooks she'd kept about Race. She'd started the first one as a young girl, thrilled to death that her Racine was making his dream come true. There was a clip from the first review; and a battered autographed copy of his first record cover. She touched the faded letter that Race had sent to Mike and his college sweetheart, Stephanie, with their wedding gift, wishing Mike and his fiancée all the best. Race had been on tour when Mike had been married, and he hadn't been able to attend the wedding. He had, however, sent a fantastic stereo system to the newlyweds, as well as airplane tickets so that they could "visit" him in Miami, where he was the opening act for a female country singer. It had been his way of providing Mike and Stephie a honeymoon they couldn't afford, and Jenni would be forever grateful they'd had that special time to share.

Knowing it was inevitable, Jenni turned the pages and forced herself to recall the very last time she'd seen Racine Huntington in person. It had been early evening when the doorbell had rung and Jenni, then a twenty-year-old college student, had answered the door. Her parents had been staying with Mike and Stephanie in their Raleigh home, helping out after the birth of their first grandchild. It was only natural for Jennifer to invite Racine into the house and share her good news with him. She was an aunt and Race was an adopted uncle. He'd been in town to close the sale of his parents' house and had stopped by the Grange house on his way out of town. The movers had taken everything from the house except his first battered guitar, given to him by Jenni's mother one Christmas.

After Racine had called and congratulated Mike and Stephie in person, he'd insisted on going out to buy a bottle of champagne to celebrate. Jenni and Racine sat in the living room for hours as they slowly drank the wine, discussing Race's career and Jenni's college courses, then reminiscing about their childhood days.

Finally Racine had fallen silent and taken the empty glass out of Jenni's hands. "Do you remember that day when I kissed you? You were so young and so sweet. I always wanted to do that again, always wondered what you'd taste like," he'd whispered as he'd leaned over to brush his lips against hers. "You were too young then, lovely Jenni," he'd added, running his hands through her thick golden red hair. "Are you too young now?"

She had been too young, but of course Jennifer hadn't realized that at the time. All she'd known was the taste and feel of Racine. Her body burning with need for that first passion, Jennifer had surrendered to Racine, offering up herself to the boy-man she'd loved for as long as she could remember. Their lovemaking had been fiercely exciting, youthful desire burning all rational thought from the world.

Shaking her head, Jennifer stood up and put the scrapbooks rapidly aside. She selected a jumpsuit from her closet and began looking for the matching shoes. It would not do to remember that night, the first rush of passion and the wonder that Race had shown her. If she insisted on remembering that night, she should recall what had happened after they'd made love.

"Jennifer," Race had finally choked out as he'd moved gently away from her warm, still-quivering body: "You were a virgin! Why didn't you tell me? Or stop me? I never imagined. You must be nineteen by now."

"I just turned twenty," Jennifer had told him in a hurt voice. "Why are you upset? What's wrong?" she asked, looking at him with eyes full of love and trust. "Did I do something wrong?"

Race had stood up and pulled on his blue jeans before answering her. "Nothing's wrong. You're wonderful. I'm just surprised. I never expected you to be—I thought you told me you weren't too young."

"I'm not, Racine. I'm old enough to know that I want you, that I love—"

Race interrupted her. "Don't say that, Jenni. You can't want anything serious with me. You know this is just for now, don't you?" he asked, his voice unsure. "I never meant this to happen," he whispered, looking away from Jennifer's now-pale face. "You know I'm on tour, only here for one night. And you're in school. I like you a lot, Jennifer, maybe I— Look, you know I care about you, but I never meant to get involved, not like this. Damn," he swore, "Why did you let this happen? I never thought you were a virgin, not from how you kissed me, how you melted. I thought you knew what you were doing."

"I'm sorry, Race," Jenni told him softly as numbness set in, giving her the ability to appear more controlled than she felt. "I didn't realize that I was required to announce my condition to you before—'' Standing up, she pulled her shirt back on, covering her nudity, and asked Race to excuse her. "I'll take a shower, if you don't mind," Jennifer told him, and walked out with what dignity she could muster.

She came back a half hour later, not sure what to expect, not sure if Race would be there or not. He was. Holding his old guitar, he was strumming a song, lost in his music. Quietly Jenni came up beside him and asked him to sing to her. With a flash of the smile that she so loved, Racine sat her down and said, "This is for you. Maybe it'll say what I don't know how to say."

Sadly Jenni listened to his song, knowing that he'd be gone soon. The bittersweet tune told her that although he felt something for her, something good and true, youth called, his new life beckoned him. He was pleased, honored, grateful that he was her first lover, and he hoped that she'd always remember him fondly. He told her he'd named his song "The Sweetest Gift," and she listened with tears in her eyes.

It was then that Jenni understood the truth about Racine Huntington. It was then that she began to grow up. He was gone. She had made love with Race Hunter, up-and-coming country singer. A man who was driven to seek fame and fortune. A man not ready, or even able, to commit himself to anything but his music.

With a maturity that she had not known she possessed, Jenni stood up and told Race it was time for him to go. "I hope you find what you're looking for, Race Hunter," she added, using his shortened name deliberately. "And that it makes you happy."

Race kissed her goodbye, a sweetly gentle kiss, and when he pulled back to look at her his eyes darkened with some sort of emotion Jenni couldn't interpret. Then he turned and walked out the door.

But before Jennifer could close the door, he stopped and turned.

"Look," he began, but stopped again, seeming unsure of what he wanted to say. "I'll call you, Jen, soon," he said finally. "Maybe you can come and visit me or something."

Those were the last words Jennifer heard from Race Hunter. He hadn't called. She did hear from her sister-in-law that he'd sent a huge stuffed bear for their new son along with a thousand-dollar savings bond, but that was the end of it. He hadn't given her a thought, probably, since that day so long ago.

Well, Jennifer decided as she checked her reflection in the mirror, tightening her belt and firmly grasping her leather purse, she'd find out just how good a performer Race Hunter was onstage and then write a fair review. She wasn't going to concern herself with what had drawn the man back to his hometown after so many years. She simply didn't care anymore.

Chapter One

The noise drifted over Jennifer like a huge wave, the clapping and shouting of the crowd blending with the country music to form an earsplitting backdrop for her memories. The mixed crowd of teenagers and adults was dressed in everything from preppy sophistication to the most extreme cowboy style. Some were swaying their bodies in time to the music; some were dancing in their seats. Many sat quietly like Jenni, appreciating the bluegrass music.

Looking less out of place than she felt, Jenni sat alone in the audience, the sound of the opening act band throbbing in and out of her consciousness. Part of her mind was busy analyzing the crowd and the music, taking notes for the review that she would write later. Another part, perhaps the greater part, was reliving her own teenage years and dreading the moment when she would see Race in person.

Suddenly the opening act was finished and, though it seemed impossible, the crowd grew louder. Jennifer fleetingly noted that she'd probably be deaf for at least a day when she heard the amplified twang of a guitar strike, and then the sound of his voice filled the auditorium. After so many years, she would see and hear him in person. Forcing herself, she looked up; past the spotlights, past the screaming crowd, and saw him exposed on a giant high-tech screen above the crowd. Hand-held minicams guaranteed that all who paid their money could see his face. The great Race Hunter, megastar, owner of ten Grammy awards and five platinum albums, the man three times voted country entertainer of the year, was here in Charlotte, North Carolina, to give a concert in his own hometown for the first time in eight years.

Unable to resist, Jennifer stared up at the big screen, scrutinizing the larger-than-life face of the legendary hometown hero. Race's dark good looks had improved over the years. His cheeks had lost the trace of baby fat that they'd had in high school. His elegant nose was now slightly crooked, adding to the air of rough sexuality that smoldered even on the screen. Race now wore his thick, curly black hair in a wildly undisciplined style that fell just to his shoulders. A mustache covered the top of his sensuous mouth, drawing attention to the white teeth that flashed as he sang. His lean cheeks were covered by a well-trimmed beard. The only times he'd appeared clean-shaven in public, Jenni recalled, had been for a part in a movie. When it was done, the dark black beard had returned. His gray eyes smoked, and, as always, he looked as though he alone knew the forbidden secrets that every female wanted to know.

If she closed her eyes, Jenni could imagine him just as he had been eight years ago; in his soft denim jeans and black leather jacket. His hair had been somewhat shorter then, his face still fresh, his eyes still kind. She would never forget that one evening, the evening that had changed her life forever. Taking a deep breath, Jennifer ordered herself to stop. She'd spent the last few hours remembering Race. That was enough.

After a long minute of staring at the screen, Jennifer closed her eyes and pushed her memories out of her mind. It was going to be all right. She would be able to maintain her calm and do her job objectively. No one would ever know that Race was more to her than just another country singer passing through town or that this review was more difficult than the others she routinely handled.

Jennifer gazed at his face curiously and decided that the years had been generous to Race. Some of the pictures she had seen in the last year or two in the fan magazines and gossip sheets had made her think that Race might be slowing down, fatigued by his jet-set life-style. Jennifer secretly had convinced herself that he'd aged and that he looked as dissipated as he deserved to look, but she'd been wrong. Then again, maybe not. It could all be a lot of stage makeup, though the Racine she'd known wouldn't have been caught dead wearing makeup. But that had been years ago; a time long past.

Then the auditorium grew quiet and the girls in front of her sat down. Race was talking slowly to the audience, telling them that he was pleased to be home in Charlotte. He held a plain guitar, ready to accompany himself as he let his North Carolina accent come through, dedicating his next song to young lovers everywhere. When he started singing the ballad, to be released on his next album, Jennifer felt as though she'd been doused with a bucket of cold water. Clenching her hands into tight fists, she closed her eyes and ordered herself to calm down. She hadn't realized that he'd recorded that particular song. If she had, she would have been better prepared to cope with the shock of hearing it. It was "The Sweetest Gift," the song he'd written for her years ago. She'd assumed it was long forgotten, pressed into the back pages of his music. He had no right to sing the ballad. Not here, not now, not after eight long years.

Deliberately Jenni forced herself to block out the past and concentrate solely on her job. Moments later Jennifer

Grange, entertainment reviewer for the Charlotte Sentinel, was back. All traces of the younger Jenni were ruthlessly banished, to be dealt with at another time, in another place. As Jenni watched the performance with a reviewer's eye, she forced herself to forget the one enchanted night that had changed her life forever. She doubted if Race even remembered it.

She had given herself to the boy next door, only to find that she'd surrendered to a stranger. The up-and-coming country singer had scored one more time, making her feel in retrospect like one of his many groupies. She had believed that he cared, believed that he'd be back for her, but his tender concern, his seemingly genuine regret, must have been part of a practiced line. He had left, never to call again, never knowing the consequences of his casual impulse, never caring what he'd done to her or her life. She didn't regret the twins; or the way her life was now arranged, but she could not forgive Race Hunter, the famous country singer, for his careless disregard of her affection.

Shoulders straight, she pulled her thick reddish-blond hair back from her face and took a deep breath. The concert was over, but the worst was yet to come. Showing her press credentials to the guard, she headed backstage, waiting for the promised press conference at the very back of the crowded room. With some luck, she would be able to hear his interview and not get within ten feet of him. Her readers would be content with her review of the concert without ever knowing she hadn't personally talked to the man.

Fifteen minutes later, she was not upset to be pressed back against the wall by an eclectic mix of reporters, photographers, local celebrities, disc jockeys and radio contest winners as Race made his entrance. The earthy scent of hot masculinity entered with him. He was dressed in his trademark skintight faded blue jeans and a wet white cotton shirt. That was all. It was too much; or not enough.

Somehow the vitality of the man, still high on adrenaline from his concert, was overpowering in a closed room. Sexuality seemed to ooze from his body, and every woman in the room swayed toward him, drawn despite themselves.

All except me, Jennifer swore, though she, too, was unable to draw her eyes away from his sweat drenched body. A large white-haired man spoke up, saying that Race was going to his dressing room and would be back outside to give an interview in ten minutes. With a smile, Race shouted to the crowd that it was good to be back home and that he expected some good old home cooking at the mayor's party that night.

Leaning against the closed door, Race grabbed the soda that was offered to him as he wiped the perspiration from his face and chest. He heard the murmur of his staff around him, but he'd long ago learned to ignore their comments as irrelevant. They always said he was great, whether it was one of his best performances or one of his worst.

His stomach was tied up in knots as he wondered if Jennifer Grange was out in the audience. He hoped she was, because whether he'd wanted to admit it before tonight or not, one of the major reasons that he'd finally consented to return to Charlotte was to see her. For some reason she had haunted him lately, ever since he'd found that old song he'd written for her. He remembered her as he did no other. Ever since he'd found that song, Race had been compelled to return home. Perhaps it was the pull of his childhood, the lost innocence of his high school days, that drew him back to Charlotte. Maybe it was more. Now that he was here, he knew that it was Jennifer whom he wanted to see.

While Race slipped into a clean set of clothes, he asked Jameson, his personal assistant, to track down a Jennifer Grange. Race hadn't kept in touch with any of his high school or college friends. His career had demanded every ounce of time and energy he possessed, especially in the beginning.

When his manager reminded him that it was time to start his press conference, Race took a deep breath and walked out. Suddenly Race Hunter, superstar, was back, ready to meet the crowd.

A teenage girl standing next to Jennifer sighed as she watched him disappear into the back door. Looking overcome with emotion, she commented to Jennifer, "He's the sexiest thing I've ever seen in all my life."

"He's certainly something," Jennifer quipped dryly, thinking her personal opinion would not be well received in this crowd. Whatever she might think of his moral character—or lack thereof—Jennifer had to admit that Race had come a long way musically. When she had known him he had been a talented writer and singer, but the polish and charisma were new to her. Now, at thirty-two years of age, he was an experienced entertainer. A top star for the past five years, he was one of the acknowledged leaders of country music, country all the way but accepted in all the various worlds of entertainment. Race was truly talented. If his moral character was no different from those of the rest of his kind, who was she to question him? In the end it had been her choice to believe that she was special.

Jennifer was in control by the time Race reappeared, now clad in a fresh pair of blue jeans and a loose silk shirt of pure white that was unbuttoned far enough to show the dense black curls that covered his chest. She saw only the country singer, not the man who had been her next-door neighbor and idol for years. With professional aplomb, she held her notebook ready and jotted down her impressions of him and the style with which he worked the crowd. He answered all the questions with clever wit, never revealing very much of himself. When he was asked about Patti Silk, the singer-actress he'd lived with on and off for the past two years, his lips tightened, but he managed to keep the same light note in his voice. They were involved in a rather public lawsuit—some were even calling it a palimony suit—centering around the ownership of Race's ranch in California. The press was naturally fascinated by their stormy relationship and frequent public outbursts.

"No comment, folks. You know how it is when people get to fightin'. Nothing is as unhappy as the end of a love affair."

"Mr. Hunter," one of the more strident members of the national press demanded, "has Patti talked to you recently? She's been hinting that you two would reconcile after this tour is over."

"I'm really not going to say anything about that," Race drawled. "Now, why don't we go over to the hotel and have that party that y'all promised me?" He whispered something to the man standing next to him, and suddenly all the doors were open and the crowd was starting to move.

Jennifer stayed by the wall, barely moving as the crowd began to inch its way out of the room. She was folding up her pad and fumbling in her purse for her car keys when a hand touched her shoulder. Looking up, she was dumbfounded to see Race's face in front of hers.

"Jenni, is that you?" Race questioned hoarsely, stunned at his good luck. "I thought I saw you before, but I couldn't believe my eyes. Nobody else has that great gold-red hair."

Taking a deep breath, Jennifer looked up into Race's gray eyes and forced herself to remain impassive. "Hello, Race. I enjoyed your concert."

"What are you doing back here with the press? Are you coming to the party?" he asked as he edged her out of the crowd.

"I wasn't planning on it. I need to go."

"Come on, Jenni. Please. Just for a few minutes? It's been a while since we've seen each other," Race went on, his eyes raking her face and then her figure. She had changed in the past eight years, gaining polish and sophistication. Her reddish-blond hair was now shoulder-length and slightly curled, a perfect frame for her oval face and those smoky, incredible green eyes. Her fair skin was still sprinkled lightly with freckles, and he was pleased, some-how, that she wore no makeup to cover them. Memories of their last night flashed through his eyes as he glanced slowly down over her high breasts, past her waist and down to her slim legs.

"You're looking good, honey," he whispered in her ear. He was surprised that she'd come to him, but then women came to him all the time. At least he was glad to see this one. "You've turned into a beautiful woman. I'm so glad that you came down to see me again. How did you manage to get press credentials?"

Jennifer went from studied indifference to anger at that last comment. Did he have the colossal ego to think that she had come to see him on purpose? He surely could not think that she was ready to fall back into his arms as though eight years hadn't passed. As she opened her mouth to tell him that she would not be within ten feet of him were it not for her job, he smiled down at her and kissed her.

The moment his lips touched hers, Race realized this was not the friendly showbusiness kiss he was used to giving. His tongue insinuated itself into her mouth with ease as his expertise demanded her compliance. Race hadn't planned on kissing her, but when she had looked up at him and her mouth had opened, instinct had taken over. He went with his impulse, unable to resist.

For a few abandoned seconds, Jenni felt herself respond to his warm lips. The remembered taste and feel of her first love were all too soon replaced by the practiced technique of the famous country singer. His hands came up to touch her hair and, she opened her eyes in time to see him mo-tion to his manager. She saw Race's eyes signaling to him to head off other people. Suddenly hot and cold at the same time, Jennifer pulled back from Race, looking up at him in disbelief, stunned at just how very angry she was. At both herself and at Race.

"How are you, Jennifer?" Race whispered, pulling back and looking down into her eyes. "It's been a long time.

You're all grown up this time," he added, edging in front of her to keep her from leaving the room.

Using her elbows to push him away, Jennifer swallowed her first sharp retort and took a deep breath before she spoke. After all, it was partly her own fault. She had kissed him back, at least for the first few seconds before she could control her body's traitorous reaction. "Eight years, Race, it's been eight years," she said. "And before you say another word, let me clear up something. I am not here to see you personally. I'm the entertainment reviewer for the *Charlotte Sentinel*. This is my job, nothing more. Now, if you'll excuse me, I'll let you go to your party."

"I suppose I should go, since they've sold tickets for the thing. Won't you come, too? I'd like to hear how you are." Suddenly he pulled back and her old friend was looking out of his eyes again. "So you're a reporter now? What else have you been doing in the past seven, eight years?"

"Nothing you'd be interested in, Race," Jennifer told him truthfully. "I finished college and got a job at the paper."

"Come with me, pretty Jenni. You must have to include this charity thing in your review, and I—"

He was interrupted by his manager as they walked toward the door. "Race, get a move on. Bring the broad if you must, just move it." The man's gaze raked Jennifer impersonally as though she were a mannequin, and he smirked slightly as he added, "You can do all the partying you want after you've made your appearance."

Race grabbed her hand and pulled her out the back door of the hotel, toward a waiting car, before she could answer him. "Come on, Jen. You heard the man. I have to make an appearance. We can talk in the limo."

"I need to get my car, Race." Jennifer insisted quietly. "Call me in the morning at the paper if you want to talk."

"Come with me, Jenni," Race insisted, ignoring everything she was saying as they walked out of the auditorium together. "It's been years. You can catch me up on all the local news. I'll send someone back for your car, or you can get it in the morning," he said casually as he pulled her toward the open door of the waiting car.

"In the morning?" Jennifer asked him carefully, allowing herself to settle down in the car. She couldn't believe that she'd heard him correctly.

"In case we decide that we should renew old times," Race said with a crooked smile as he brushed the side of her cheek with a callused finger, surprised at how intensely he reacted to her. One kiss and he wanted her more than he'd wanted anyone or anything in a very long time.

"Aren't you going to ask me if I'm married or engaged, or doesn't even that mean anything to you anymore?"

Surprisingly, Race looked sheepish. For a second, the famous singer was gone and her old friend looked out at her. "Jennifer, I'm sorry. Sometimes I forget who I am and—hey. It was a dumb thing to assume." Then arrogance edged into his voice again and the superstar was back, saying, "I assumed you wouldn't have come to me if you didn't want me, too."

Jennifer looked at him and wondered if there was any trace of her old Racine left. Even his apology sounded fake, just like the rest of him. As he leaned forward to speak to his manager for a moment, she was confused. Part of her wanted to slap his face and get out of the car. Another portion of her mind traitorously wanted him again, regardless, foolishly remembering his touch, foolishly wanting him to be someone he wasn't. Anger won out, and she found herself wishing someone would teach this arrogant womanizer a much-needed lesson in humility.

As he reached for her again, placing a familiar hand on her thigh, she clenched her fist to avoid striking out at his confident face. No one could treat her the same way twice. The first time she had forgiven herself and him for being too young and too eager. The timing had been wrong for them both. Eight years later she could not, would not, give him the benefit of the doubt. Racine Huntington, the tender, sensitive man who had been her next-door neighbor and her first lover, was gone forever. *Race Hunter* was a womanizing swine.

Smiling at him with clenched teeth, she pulled out all the stops. She would play along with his game and see just how arrogant he truly was. If nothing else came of this evening, Jennifer was sure it would wipe out all the magical memories that she'd secretly cherished of their one and only night together. Those memories had held her captive over the years, and she was determined to exorcise them, and Race, from her life. Holding his hand, she gradually tugged him back toward her and admitted truthfully, "I'd just love to talk over old times."

When he gave her a look of genuine gratitude, Jennifer wondered exactly who Race was and what he was trying to prove with this on-again, off-again macho image. Had he been teasing her? Blushing, she started to stammer when he took her hand kindly and told her, this time with a great deal of feeling, "I would like that more than I can say." Puzzled by his changing moods, she looked deeply into his gray eyes and, for a moment, saw the loving, tender friend from her past.

The limo pulled up to the front door of a major local hotel, and there was no further time to talk. Jennifer pulled back, but Race insisted that she accompany him into the party. Surprisingly enough, he kept an eye on her all night, even though women and girls from fifteen through fifty were draping themselves all over him, offering him anything and everything he could possibly want. Race was polite to each and every one but steadfastly told them that he already had plans for the evening.

In one sense, Jennifer wished that were true. Never had another man so appealed to her. Across the room, with his eyes alone, he could arouse her more fully than any other man ever had. No other had ever come close. That was the entire problem. If she hadn't known that it was all an act and that she was just one of an endless parade of women who were similarly affected by Race, she would have felt something other than sorrow for the past and contempt for her own reaction to him.

As she stood watching Race charm the entire roomful of people, Jenni abruptly realized it was time for her to leave. There was nothing to be gained. Nothing she could do to Race that would turn him back into the man she had loved. There was no way to erase his memory. As the evening passed, she knew with a deep certainty that every second she stayed around him would only make things worse. Instead of exorcising his memory, she was reviving it. Instead of getting him out of her system, she was wanting him again. Only a masochistic fool would even stay in the same room with him.

She had more than enough information to write up her morning's column. It was time for her to get back to work. Avoiding his gaze, she edged out of the room. She had just reached the lobby when a tall, muscular man placed his arm on her shoulder.

"Excuse me," Jennifer said, turning to stare into the black eyes of a large man with no neck and several inches of impressive muscles. "Let go of my arm."

"Race said you were to stay, lady," he told her in a deep voice. "So you stay."

"What did you say?" Jennifer asked in a loud voice, unable to believe what she'd heard. "Let go of me or I'll scream."

"Race wants you, lady, and what he wants I get for him."

"You gorilla," Jennifer snarled through clenched teeth. Turning to face him, she kicked him right in the shin, twisting away at the same time. "Touch me again and I'll have you arrested for assault. You tell Mr. Hunter that I've got a deadline. One doesn't always get everything they want in this world—at least not in the real world!"

With that, Jennifer turned and stalked out of the hotel lobby. A doorman quickly hailed her a cab, and she had the driver take her back to the auditorium, where she reclaimed her car. Unable to believe that even Race could have sunk so low as to sic a guard on her, Jennifer fumed all the way back to the paper.

Sitting at her computer keyboard, she quickly rapped out her article. She was objective about the man and his performance and gave Race a deservedly excellent review. He was good, even great, in the world of music, but he was a rat in his personal life.

As she sat proofing her copy, her phone rang, echoing hollowly in the semideserted office. "Hello, Mom?" she answered automatically, because her mother was the only one who ever called her at the office this late. "Is everything all right?"

"No, pretty Jennifer," she heard Race say over the sounds of the party in the background. "Everything's not all right. Why did you run away? I thought we had a date."

"A date?" Jennifer ground out. "Is that what you call it when a goon tries to grab me?"

"Hey, Jen, he was just trying to do his job. I panicked when I saw you leaving and told him to find out why."

"Don't call me Jen," she said, tightening her hand around the phone. "Nobody calls me that anymore."

"Why not?"

"It's really none of your business. Look, I have to go."

As she prepared to hang up, she heard his coaxing voice through the receiver. "Please, Jenni, I need you tonight. Won't you come back to me? I promise you, you won't regret it."

Wanting to see Jennifer more than he'd imagined possible, Race tried offering her what he thought she wanted. She had to want something. Everyone did. "I'll give you an exclusive interview. You can get it syndicated nationwide. I'll tell you all about my new album. We can talk about that song I wrote for you so long ago. Anything you want."

Momentarily speechless with anger, Jennifer started to refuse him. Then she changed her mind. If he wanted her, he'd get her. Or at least he'd get what he deserved. How could he think that she'd trade her body for an interview? What sort of morals did the man have? Somebody had to teach this philandering egoist a lesson, and she had just been drafted for the job. Taking a calming breath, she forced herself to sound rational. "Okay, Race. Let me finish my column and then I'll run back and pick you up. Be at the back door of the hotel in forty-five minutes."

Jennifer hung up at that, letting the final decision rest with him. Suddenly a picture of what the man deserved flashed through her mind. Chuckling, she pulled a file from her desk and ran through the notes she'd made for a story she'd done last year on pornographers and prostitutes. Although she was primarily the entertainment editor, her editor occasionally allowed her to do some hard-news articles, usually a special series on one certain topic. That way she kept her foot in both camps, although she knew that someday she would have to choose between the two types of reporting or find a way to combine them.

Finding the reference, she rapidly copied an address into a small notebook. If she hurried, she could get everything set up. Forty-five minutes wasn't that long, she thought as she rushed out of the room, carefully leaving her copy at the front desk so it would make the morning edition.

Running to her car, she drove first to the instant teller at her bank and then toward a rather undesirable section of town. Quickly she pulled into the back of the parking lot of the Blue Panther Motel. From the back, the sign wasn't visible, just as she'd remembered. Steeling herself, she walked into the sleazy lobby and took out her wallet. An acned young man peered at her over a TV and asked, "You lost, lady?" in a bored tone.

"No. I want to rent a room. One of the ones around back."

"With or without a waterbed?"

"With, of course," Jennifer told the man. "I want your very best room—with mirrors; the works."

"For the night or by the hour?" the man asked her.

"The whole night. Just do it quick; I'm in a hurry." She told him, rapidly paying him in cash.

"Aren't they all?" he mumbled, giving her the register. He didn't raise an eyebrow when he saw her sign a patently false name. Unable to resist the temptation, Jennifer registered as Patti Satin—first cousin, she said to herself, to Patti Silk, Race's estranged girlfriend. When she asked the clerk to leave her undisturbed until morning, he raised a bored eyebrow and told her, "Whatever."

Five minutes later, Jennifer unlocked the room and stood for a second, staring in disbelief. The old room was done in cheap red velvet, the waterbed taking up the majority of space. There was a large TV hanging from one corner, and there were mirrors everywhere. Faded red satin hung over a series of small, high windows that looked out on the woods behind the motel. Cringing, she reached over to touch the bed and looked up to see her pale face framed by the crimson bedspread in yet another mirror, this one above the bed.

"Yuck." Without a doubt, this place was sleazy. In fact, she felt demeaned just standing in the place. Just what the man deserved, she told herself as she reached down into her purse and removed the tool kit she normally kept in her trunk for emergencies. It was lucky that she carried a good assortment of tools, having learned long ago to depend on herself. She efficiently disconnected the telephone wire and screwed the receptacle cover back on the wall to keep Race from restoring the connection. Next she took her trusty screwdriver over to deal with the doorhandle. Her mechanical skills were once again serving a useful purpose. After a few turns she was satisfied that she had sufficiently loosened the knob. She should be able to remove it entirely in a few seconds once Race was in the room. She was ready. Smiling, she carefully locked the room and walked out to her car. She hoped that after all this Race would show up. to get what he deserved—a lesson in humility.

After a brief drive, Jennifer was sitting in the alley behind the much more dignified hotel, telling herself that she'd lost her mind. The idea had seemed perfect in the midst of her anger, but now it merely seemed shoddy, selfish, even childish. She'd been around seven-year-olds too much. She was even starting to think like them. Sighing at her own frailty, she started the car. Just then she heard a loud tap on the window on the other side of her car. Startled, she looked up to see Race smiling through the glass, motioning her to unlock the door.

"Hi," she said when he got in, putting a large bag in the back. "Look, Race, I'm sorry about all this," Jennifer began as he got in and closed the door.

"Why be sorry?" Race asked, puzzled. "We're both adults. We both know what we want. Don't tell me you still haven't grown up?" Leaning back, he closed his eyes for a moment and let his face relax into its usual mask of cynicism. "We've got a deal, remember?"

"Right," Jennifer said sarcastically. "You'll give me a story, I'll give you what you want. Well, let's spell it out, Mr. Hunter. Just what is it that you expect for your exclusive story? I want it to be clear before we go anywhere together. What's the going price for your company in Nashville or Hollywood?"

As Jennifer stared at him, her eyes gleaming angrily in the semidarkness, Race realized that he'd just propositioned her. Offered to give her a story if she slept with him. Silently he swore, asking himself what was the matter with him. He knew better than that. He'd been around too many people who only took, had too many relationships that were implicitly based on barter, that he'd forgotten what a nice woman like Jenni was like.

Ever since he'd seen her slim form in the crowd at the press conference, he'd been remembering, torn between shame at the memories and the glory of them. No wonder he was hiding behind his image. He wanted her again, and he was afraid to be himself with her, knowing she'd probably reject him as he deserved to be rejected. So, fool that he was, he'd let the image take over; as he had so often before. It was so much easier to be the playboy of the country music world that everybody believed he was. The playboy that he had been until reality had caught up with him a couple of years ago, making him question his life and despair at its shallowness.

With a raised eyebrow and a look of self-derision that melted her resistance, Race looked at Jennifer and stuck out his hand. "Truce?" He offered slowly. "Can we go for coffee somewhere and catch up on old times? No strings attached."

"Why not?" Jennifer agreed, wheeling her car toward an old diner that stayed open all night. He didn't ever have to know what she'd planned. They could catch up on old times and part. Maybe they could be friends after all. "How are your parents? We lost track of them when you moved them to Florida."

"They're fine, just fine. Dad had a stroke two years ago, but he's okay now. It's amazing how they've changed since I moved them to Florida. Mom and he have both turned into avid fishermen. Got a thirty-five-foot boat and spend a lot of their time deep-sea fishing. Remember Rebecca, my youngest sister, the one who lived next to you for a year or so?" When Jennifer nodded her head, suddenly tense, Race went on, "She's an architect, married to a doctor. They've got two kids and live about thirty miles from my parents. Susie, the oldest, is in New York, still a nurse. Katherine moved to Hawaii, of all places, and is married to a landscape architect. They've got three sons."

Pausing, he softly told her, "I never told you in person how sorry I am about Mike and his son. I would have come to the funeral, but I was in Europe." Taking her hand in a friendly gesture, Race squeezed it tightly. "I still can't believe it, even after all these years. It was such a stupid, stupid waste," Race added, referring to the accident that had killed Jenni's brother and nephew several years ago. After a few seconds when they both were remembering Mike's bright presence, Race smiled and asked about Jenni's parents.

"Dad died four years ago," Jenni told him softly. "A heart attack. It was quick and painless."

"Oh, no, Jen. I'm sorry," Race exclaimed. "You sure haven't had an easy time of it, have you? First Mike and his son and then your dad. How's your mom?"

"She's fine, thank God. You know Mom, she's a survivor. It was hard, but we're both pretty well back to normal."

"Are you still living at home? You thought I was your mother when I called before?" Race asked curiously. Suddenly he realized that he hadn't asked Jennifer anything about herself. Nor had she volunteered anything. He didn't even know if she was married or not. In his foolish mind he'd assumed she would always be there, waiting for him—frozen in limbo, he supposed—even after eight years.

For a second he felt cold, but he pushed the feeling aside. After all, he rationalized, she wouldn't be here if she was attached, would she? Or would she? His years of experience in the fast lane reminded him not to trust anyone. Most other women that he'd known wouldn't have let a little thing like a husband or a lover get in the way of a big story, and he had offered her an exclusive to get her to come. As she pulled into the diner and parked, he suddenly took her hand and turned her toward him. "You never told me, Jennifer, anything about your life. Are you still alone?" he demanded, his voice gruff with suppressed emotion.

"What do you think?" Jennifer asked, genuinely curious.

"I don't want to know," he told her as he reached over to touch the back of her neck and trace the outline of her ear. "Don't tell me anything now, wait until the morning. We can work something out." His mind insisted that she was his; no matter what. He'd make her love him again. He might be years late, but he was back.

That did it. Jennifer was rigid with anger for the third time that night. She was so furious that she could barely think. If he had been any other man, she would have brushed him off and left. But this was Racine, her Racine, turned into a parody of himself. His every movement mocked her past, and fury drove her beyond rationality. So much for coffee and conversation. He deserved more. This time he would remember her, not the other way around. She leaned over and whispered into his ear, using her tongue to trace its rim. "Let's go somewhere private. I'm too old for the front seat of a Datsun."

Smiling, relieved that she'd agreed so readily, Race turned to her, his smoky gray eyes drowning in her green ones. "Whatever you say."

"I..." Jenni started to say as she headed the car toward the motel, somewhat unsure of how to bring up the topic. "I can't go home, my mother's there, so I—" Stammering, she took a deep breath and tried to continue, distracted by the large hand that Race rested casually on her thigh. "I rented a room in a hotel while I was gone." She spit it out, feeling embarrassed by her words. "I don't want to risk being seen in your hotel; it's too public." She hoped that Race wouldn't guess just how atypical her behavior was or think too deeply about what she was saying or where they were going.

He didn't. In fact, he seemed pleasantly surprised by her news. "Good thinking, babe," he told her, reaching behind the seat for the bag he'd brought. "I brought some champagne. I remember how you like it."

"Good," Jennifer said as she pulled to the back of the motel's lot. She got out of the car; clutching her purse. If this idea didn't work, she would be in for a real fight. A battle with her own desires as well as his. But he needed to know that he was not God's Gift to the women of the world and that there was one woman who might have fallen for him once but wasn't about to be used again.

With every ounce of courage she possessed, Jennifer unlocked the metal door of the motel room and held it open for Race. Knowing she couldn't trust herself if he kissed her, she slipped behind the door and whispered, "Why don't you go into the bathroom and shower? I'll get some ice, and you can open that bottle of champagne."

Race raised his eyebrows at that request but shrugged and went along with it. His Jennifer had grown up in the last eight years. She had even turned a little kinky, he thought when he saw the red room. Maybe she wasn't the same way he remembered her. He shrugged, feeling vaguely disappointed. Whatever. At least they'd have one good night. He'd never met another woman whose mere look made his blood turn molten.

"I'll hurry," Race promised as he walked into the bathroom, dropping his shirt on the floor. Turning the water on, he stepped into the shower and began to sing the song he'd written so long ago for his Jenni. This night was turning out better than he'd anticipated. Race ignored the small voice that shouted in pain and disappointment that his Jennifer was like all the others.

While Race was busy in the shower, Jenni feverishly finished her work. She tiptoed into the bathroom and took his clothing, leaving only his wallet on the dresser. Then she quietly finished removing the inner doorknob, trapping him in the room. As she left, she hung the Do Not Disturb sign on the now-drooping doorknob.

As he sudsed himself, Race let the practiced lover take over, anticipating an evening of sensual pleasure. It would be the perfect way to work off the excitement of the concert. It had been a long time since he'd done this, felt this eager for a woman. He should have returned home long ago. Jennifer had grown up and had forgiven him for their first night together so long ago. That night had been wonderful, magical and unique, he finally admitted to himself.

The song that he'd recorded recently had brought back memories of Jenni, memories of passion and innocence—and guilt. That was the one night of his life that he would have changed, if he could have. Yet, perversely, it was also the one night that had made all the others pale. He'd been right to follow his instincts and finally accept one of the many offers he'd had over the years to return to his hometown. The fact that Jenni was just as eager as he was only made his decision all the more perfect. Smiling, he stepped out of the shower and wrapped himself in a towel.

"Here I come, love," he whispered as he stepped into the empty room.

Chapter Two

Jenni tiptoed out of her quiet house after leaving a short
note on the refrigerator door in case one of the twins woke
up and found her missing before she returned. It was a little after six in the morning, and she had given up all hope
of sleep. When the first rays of dawn had peeked through
her windows, she'd sighed in regret and pulled on the thin
short-sleeved shirt and matching shorts that she wore for
jogging in the hot summer mornings.

July was an altogether unbearable month if you hadn't
been born in the South. Even if you had, you made adjust-
ments in your life-style because of the heat, which often
lingered in the nineties. Charlotte had another month or
two of heat before it became practical to run at any time
other than early morning or late evening. Slipping on her
sweatband, she pulled her hair back into a short ponytail.
Today it would be a long run.

Absently she let her eyes take in the house, its Victorian
look appealing to her. After her father's death four years

before, she and her mother had purchased this home built around a golf course in a new subdivision. Old-style charm was combined with new comfort, surrounded by a deep porch and tall trees. It made a perfect home for her children, a typical suburban setting. Even if her household did not contain the requisite average family, it worked well. She, her mother and the twins had lived here in perfect accord until yesterday.

The thought of Race set her off, and she started running down the blacktopped street. There were no sidewalks in the Charlotte suburbs, just street after street of lovely houses, all nestled in their well-tended yards. Jennifer had a route in mind, not the normal circle of several streets that composed her usual run. Today she opted to turn at another road, knowing it would take her an extra mile before she worked her way back.

Why had he come back? Jennifer wondered, but soon discarded that question as both unanswerable and not relevant. Her innate honesty soon made her face the real dilemma. Race was not the problem, her reaction to him was. Why, why, hadn't she left bad enough alone last night? Perhaps she could not have avoided the concert, considering her job on the paper, but she had only herself to blame for the rest of the evening. She should have politely left him. But she hadn't, not her.

She had lost her temper for the first time in years. As a child she'd often done stupid things like that, getting herself into untold amounts of trouble, but she'd thought she'd outgrown that sort of behavior. Ever since the twins had been born, she'd been a model of propriety. Grown-ups don't get themselves into messes, don't play pranks on their friends or enemies. She knew that and had for years repressed every stray spark of mischief that she'd felt. Until last night, when Race had managed to trigger a part of herself that she'd forcefully buried.

It was all his fault. He'd ripped past her facade; reviving memories that she'd long ago suppressed, making her feel things she'd wanted to forget. Racine was the only person in years who had shaken her control, making her react on an emotional level instead of an intellectual one.

Running up to the backyard, her body drenched with perspiration, she glanced at her watch and saw that it was not yet seven. Hopefully Rick and Rebecca would still be asleep. She'd take a quick shower before they got up and then drive them to a fast-food restaurant for breakfast before their summer camp started. That should make them feel better about her being out last night. They never liked her working at night.

As she stopped at the back door, she heard the porch swing creak and she whirled, startled to feel a strong hand clapped onto her shoulder. "What kind of kinky game were you playing last night?" Race demanded in a deep voice, standing on her porch, dressed in a pair of faded blue jeans and a rich blue cashmere sweater.

Race Hunter had spent a very long and very frustrating evening last night. He had expected a warm fantasy and had come out to find an empty room. When he'd found the phone disconnected and the doorknob missing in rapid succession, Race had known he'd been set up. There had been no way out; the metal door had been too sturdy and the fixed glass windows too thick and too small to break. After a few minutes of yelling for help, he had settled back on the bed, knowing that someone would come along in the morning to rescue him. He'd drunk some champagne and then gone to bed. At dawn the noise of a garbage truck had awakened him. He'd attracted the garbage men's attention and finally been released.

"What do you think you're doing here? *Go away!*" Jennifer demanded, trying to keep her voice quiet and only succeeding in raising it to a shrill level. "Get away from my house! How did you find me?"

"You're listed in the phone book," Race explained nastily. "And I have no intention of leaving until you give me an explanation and my clothes! Now!" he told her, his voice deepening with each word, his rage barely under control. His anger had been building all morning, and was now at an explosive point. He hadn't expected to find Jennifer living like a suburban housewife. Once the motel clerk had gotten him out of that room, he'd called one of his gofers from the tour and ordered the man to bring him some clothes. Then, on impulse, he'd demanded to be driven to Jennifer's. He would never in a million years have expected her to be living in a place like this. No single woman lived in a house this big. Not all alone with her mother.

"Go away, Race. Please go away," Jennifer pleaded, hearing only the beginning of sounds in the house.

"Are you afraid your husband will hear you? I was really surprised when my man brought me way out here. So you live in a nice house in the suburbs now? Four bedrooms, two and a half baths? All nice and respectable!" Tauntingly he asked her, "Did you tell him about the little trick you pulled on me last night, Jenni? Is this some story I will be reading about in the scandal sheets?"

"No... No... It was nothing like that, Race. Look, I'm sorry. It was just an impulse, a bad joke. If you hadn't acted like such a conceited pig, none of this would have happened. Let's call it even. I'm sorry I lost my temper, but please," Jennifer pleaded, a look of panic in her eyes, "please leave."

"Not without my clothes, lady, and a better explanation. Just what did I do to you that was so bad?" Race demanded, trying to remember exactly what he'd done last evening. "All I did was take you up on your offer," he growled.

Angrily Jennifer turned on her heel to stare into Race's gray eyes. Then with a sigh her anger was replaced with pity. Slowly she exhaled and stared at him with sincere green eyes. "I don't know if I could explain it to you. I don't know if it's even worth the effort. Just put it down to a difference in values, to a... a cultural conflict. Hollywood versus Charlotte. No big deal. Just *go away!*"

"Not without my clothes, and maybe a cup of coffee." Race announced to her, his mind clouded by her reaction. What was she babbling about values? What did culture have to do with her turning him on and then leaving him, *him*, Race Hunter, alone in an adult motel? He'd awakened that morning furious with her. In fact, he'd never been angrier at anyone in his life, and he wasn't about to leave until he understood why she'd done it to him. "Jennifer, what the hell is going on? Let me in and give me my clothes!" Race retorted, his anger growing again at the thought of what she'd done to him. "Are you afraid your husband or whoever the hell you live with will see me and wonder about last night? Did you tell him you were working? Did you ever tell him about us?" he taunted, letting his jealousy get the better of his judgment, fascinated despite his anger at the delicate color that stained her cheeks.

He cursed himself again as he acknowledged his feelings, the truth that he'd recognized last night and tried to deny. This woman was his. Hot, sweaty, mad, it didn't matter. She was his. With no makeup and her green eyes deeply shadowed and fearful...

"What are you so afraid of? Me?"

Pausing, he put one finger under her chin, raising her head until her wary eyes were staring directly into his smoldering ones. "You have every right to be afraid of me. But not for the reason you think. No, love, not for those reasons," he told her as he took his other hand and ran it down the back of her neck, then down her spine, resting it possessively around her waist. Jennifer immediately swirled out of his arms, furious at his attitude.

"Let me get this straight," she said, stalking over to lean against the rail at the edge of the wide porch. "Tell me exactly what you want and why you're here, if it's not just to get your clothes and an ounce of punishment for last night."

"I'm here for you, lady." Race announced, having just figured that out for himself. Once he'd found that old song,

Race realized, he'd been lost. At first he'd told himself it was the lure of memories that had pulled him home to Charlotte, but now he knew it was more than that. The real reason he'd come back was Jenni. He hadn't admitted it to himself before, but now he knew. He wanted her back in his life—permanently.

"Just like that?" Jennifer asked, her eyes flashing contemptuously. Sweetly she asked him, "For how long? For a day, a week? Just what do you think you're going to do with me and how, Mr. Hunter, sir?"

"Don't try to fool me, Jennifer Grange. I know you want me, too. You melted last night when I kissed you. You didn't forget that night, your first time?" Sauntering over to her, exuding sex appeal, he placed his arms on her shoulders and said, "I bet it's never been so good for you since." Or for me, love, or for me, he wanted to say, but he didn't, he couldn't. The truth stuck in his throat as he watched the color drain from her face, leaving her pale and still.

Jennifer slapped him hard and turned away from him, fighting back tears. "How could anyone have changed so much?" she whispered, as much to herself as to him. For a brief moment she remembered flashes of Racine as her older brother's friend, as the first boy who'd kissed her, as the man who'd introduced her to the sweet mystery of love.

"What has this life done to you, Racine Huntington? Whatever it is, I don't think I envy you your fame or money. Now just go. Get out of my life!"

For the first time in years, Race was fully aware of what he'd become, what the wealth and fame and women had done to him. What all the years of agents, managers, yesmen and groupies had done to his ego. And, worst of all, how hard it was for him to stop playing the role that everyone expected, and reveal the real man underneath the image.

"Jennifer," he murmured, taking a tentative step toward her, his hand turned up in appeal. "I'm sorry. I . . . I have no excuse. I never really thought you'd leave your husband. You were never like that. I plain didn't think at all. When you showed up at the concert, I just assumed... I'm so used to getting my own way...." He let his words trail off and then briskly announced, "I'll get a cab back to town and be out of your life. Don't worry about the clothes; they don't matter. They were just an excuse to see you."

Before Race could turn around he heard a door slam, and the sound of children's voices drifted to him.

"Mom, Mom, what are you doing out here? Come and make my breakfast," a soft, sweet voice said.

"Mom, I lost my tennis shoe," said another young voice. "Do you know where it is?"

"Children?" Race asked, his voice breaking. "You have children? I never thought..." he started to say as the twins appeared next to Jennifer, who was standing frozen in place.

Two small faces stared at him, dumbfounded to find a man on their porch. They were darling children, both with dark, curly hair and fine features. The boy had smoky gray eyes and the girl Jennifer's green ones. As the girl turned to her mother, looking up for reassurance, the boy stared directly into Race's eyes, gray into gray, and asked, "Who are you? And why is your hair so funny?" Without missing a beat, he turned to his mom and asked her, "What's for breakfast? Gram's still sleeping, and you told us not to wake her if you were around."

Jennifer was surprised that she'd managed to keep her voice from breaking. She sounded calm and controlled, just as she always did. The kids didn't seem to notice that she felt removed entirely from the scene. This was a puppet talking, not her. The real Jennifer watched the scene from afar, mildly curious about what was going to happen next.

"Why don't you guys get dressed fast and I'll treat you to breakfast at your favorite place?" Jennifer heard herself saying. "Your clothes are laid out on your dressers as usual. How does that sound?"

"Great, Mom," Rick shouted as he turned to run back into the house. "I'll get my soccer ball and comb my hair, too. Becca, hurry up," he yelled over his shoulder when his sister didn't stir.

The lovely child with the dark, curly hair and the fine features was still clinging to her mother's hand. "Are you all right, Momma? You look funny," Becca said, her soft voice drifting over to Race. "Who is he? Is he coming to breakfast, too?"

Before Jennifer could reply, Race walked over to the two females and bent down on his knee before the small one. "Sure, I'm coming. Will you tell me where we're going? What's your favorite place?"

After the little girl responded with the fast-food restaurant's name, she asked, "What's your name?"

"Race Hun— Just Race. What's yours, honey?" he asked slowly, mesmerized by the miniature replica of his sister's face before him.

"Rebecca Grange, sir," she replied, innocent of the shock squeezing Race's heart as he continued to crouch beside her.

In a soft voice that shook with emotions he couldn't yet identify, he asked her the last question, the most important one. "How old are you and your brother?"

Jennifer pulled her daughter to her and said, "That's enough, Becca. Go and get your hair elastics and we'll comb your hair before we go. You have to be at camp in less than an hour, so don't fool around or we won't have time for breakfast. See if you can help your brother find his shoe."

Race pinned Jennifer down with his eyes, insisting that she answer. "How old are they?" When she shook her head, he told her, "It doesn't matter if you tell me or not. I'll find out. I promise you I'll find out," he said with a quiet oath and a determination that made Jennifer bow her head in surrender.

"They're seven, Race. They turned seven three months ago." Jennifer conceded as she turned her back and walked toward the house. "Please, let me take them to breakfast. Then we'll talk. I promise you that."

"Okay, Jenni, but I'm coming to breakfast with you. With them," Race said. "How could you—" he began, but stopped when the two kids came back out onto the porch.

"Becca, go and get my purse, honey," Jennifer told her daughter as she turned around and started toward the garage, which was attached to the house by a covered walkway. "Let's get this show on the road. You don't want to be late."

Race quietly opened the front door on the passenger side and sat down, unable to do more than function. He grabbed the hat that the gofer had left for him. Without conscious thought he put it on, pulling his long hair up into it and changing his appearance radically. He was used to disguising himself like that, and he was grateful that it almost always worked. What was going on? Were these kids his? They had to be. They looked just like him. He could have been looking at a picture of himself straight from his family album when he looked at the boy.

"Jennifer," he asked abruptly, startling all of them, "what's the boy's name?" he demanded, forgetting for a second that the child was sitting only inches behind him in the Datsun station wagon.

"My name's Rick, sir," the child told him. "Rick Grange. What's yours?"

"It's Race," the man said slowly, carefully enunciating his words. "So, you and Becca are twins?"

"I'm the older one," Becca announced suddenly. "I'm five minutes older than him. And," she went on in the singsong voice of childhood rivalry, "I'm in the highest math group."

"Well, I'm in the soccer league, Becca," her brother told her. "Who cares about math?"

"Children, stop it!" Jennifer said. "We're here. You go and sit down over there and I'll bring your food in a second. Both of you want the pancakes as usual?"

Half an hour later, Jennifer sighed as the two scrambled out of the car and walked into the local recreation center. As she pulled away from the parking lot, Race turned to her and said, "We have to talk."

"Let's go back to my house. I'll fix some coffee." Jennifer agreed, driving expertly back to the subdivision where she lived.

"Why are the kids in summer camp? What is it, some fancy kind of day care?" Race suddenly asked her.

"It's a summer day camp that's sponsored by the local community recreation center. It runs for three weeks, and I enrolled the twins to give—" Jennifer stopped herself from saying any more. She didn't need to give Race any added information. There was still a small chance that he'd leave before he found out that she wasn't married and that the person she was 'giving a break to' was her own mother. "I signed the twins up because they enjoy some planned activities in the summer."

Minutes later they were sitting in Jennifer's cheerful yellow kitchen, a cup of coffee steaming in front of each of them. Finally Jennifer broke the silence. "I'll get your clothes, Race. Maybe you better call your manager or someone. They might be worried about you by now."

"No, the guy who drove me over will tell them I'm all right. They aren't surprised if I spend the night away when I'm on the road," Race said absently, not missing the grimace of distaste that passed over Jennifer's expressive face as she stood up.

"I want to apologize for last night," she finally said. "I acted in a childish manner. I always did have a quick temper," she told him with a half shrug. "Remember the time I locked you in the shed for an afternoon?"

"When I was supposed to go over to that cheerleader's house?" He gave a little laugh, "Sure I remember. I wanted to kill you then, too. Guess things haven't changed too much."

"Yes, they have, Race. Now we're grown-ups and I have a life to live. Please accept my apology and go. I hope the rest of your tour goes well."

"What about the kids?" Race asked, stopping Jennifer in her tracks.

"What about them?" Jennifer answered. "They're great and I love them to death."

"Where's their father? Why are they named Grange?" Race demanded in a sharp voice.

"I...I never married their father. They're mine, all mine. And, to answer your next question, I'm not married now, either. I live here with my mother. No one else. Do you honestly remember me so little that you could think I'd have come near you if I were married or living with someone?"

With a scornful toss of her hair, she went on. "Don't bother to answer. I know your answer already. Look," she told the stunned man sitting at the table with the cooling coffee in his hand, "I'm going to get dressed. I'll be out shortly and drive you back to the hotel. I have to get to work by 9:30. Have another cup of coffee. Here are your other clothes," she told him, grabbing a plastic bag that was sitting by the stairs and sliding it onto the table beside him. "There's a bathroom off the hall down there, first door on the left, if you need it."

Jennifer walked into her shower in a daze, mechanically preparing herself for the day's work. Never in her wildest fantasies had she imagined Race sitting in her kitchen, curious about his children. At first she had pretended that he would come back for her some day, or at least call, but that dream had died long ago. Finally, painfully, she'd grown up and put Racine Huntington into the past. He was filed in the first-love-long-forgotten department.

But one look, one kiss, and it could have been yesterday. She was still attracted to the man, to the sexual athlete of the country music world. Somehow she had to keep his real nature in the front of her mind, to constantly remind her foolish heart that although the outside was still the same—even better—the rest of the man had changed. Somehow she had to get him out of her house, out of her mind. There was no place for Race Hunter in her life.

Absently Race stood up and walked down to the downstairs, guest bathroom, wishing he had a toothbrush. It was a small room papered in a cheerful animal print that was mostly black-and-white zebras. The red tile and red accents made it look so...wholesome, that was the word. Race looked at himself in the mirror and didn't like what he saw. His long, unruly hair and beard made him look like an alien in this tidy suburban house. Rubbing the diamond in his ear, he walked back to the kitchen and forced himself to be honest.

Those were his kids. No way they couldn't be. They were just the right age and looked exactly the way he and his sister had looked many years ago. The boy had his own gray eyes, and the girl, named after his own sister, had Jennifer's green ones. His children were now seven years old and didn't know he existed. A burning-hot pain ran up and down his throat, and he fought the suspicious feeling that his eyes were misted. Briskly rubbing his lids with his fists, he forced himself to remain calm. What in the world was he going to do? What did he want to do?

Just then Jennifer walked into the room, and she took his breath away. Last night she had been dressed in a loose jumpsuit. This morning she had been sweaty in shorts. Now she was in her full glory. Dressed in a pale gray cotton suit, Jennifer was both sophisticated and coolly beautiful. Her high heels emphasized her long and lovely legs, and her small waist was accented by the belt that was wrapped around the shirt. This was a poised woman, not an angry child or a flustered housewife. This was his Jennifer all grown up.

Composing herself for the coming ordeal, Jennifer had showered and dressed carefully, purposefully calming herself down. So it had happened. Race had seen the twins and he suspected that he was their father. Nothing would happen, no real problem, she tried to tell herself. He wouldn't want them, not with his life-style and the palimony suit hanging over his head.

She would be polite and he'd go away, relieved that she didn't want anything from him. He'd go back to his life and she'd stay in hers, content, maybe even glad in a way that he'd come back. A part of her had always loved Race, but maybe now she could let go of the past and move on. Her Racine was dead, long dead.

"Are you ready to go?" she asked quietly. "Mom's still asleep, so I'll give her your regrets when I get home tonight."

"I'll give them to her myself," Race told her. "I'm coming to dinner tonight."

"You can't," Jennifer said composedly. "You have a concert in Columbia tonight."

"Well, I'll come to dinner the next night, then."

"Look, Race, what is the point? You know you'll be somewhere else. I think you move on to Florida from here. You're in the middle of your tour. I know, I read all the publicity promos that came from your manager."

"Jennifer, stop it!" Race suddenly demanded, unable to stand their polite sparring anymore. "No more chatting. Those are my kids, aren't they?"

"They're mine, Race," Jennifer told him smoothly, barely blinking an eyelash, "so don't worry about it. I'm not about to ask you for anything; to do anything, to pay anything. We're fine. Go back to your tour and forget all about us."

"Tell me that they're my kids, Jennifer," Race insisted. "Why didn't you tell me before?"

Turning, Jennifer walked over to the window to stare out into the backyard. "When was I supposed to tell you?" she asked him slowly, "How? By the time I found out I was pregnant, you were somewhere in Europe. Somewhere with some other woman. Who was it after me? I know it was after that English singer with the platinum hair. Before the French actress that you did that film with. What was I supposed to do, Mr. Superstar? Send you a note addressed to Mr. Race Hunter, Paris, France? Now that I think of it," Jennifer commented, the agony so real that it could have been yesterday instead of eight years ago, "it might have gotten there anyway. Everybody in the Western world knew where you were that year. Everyone's known where you were and who you've been sleeping with for the past eight years. All they have to do is pick up any magazine, any tabloid, and there you are. I don't suppose you kept a scrapbook, but I did; at least for the first year. Until I decided to stop hurting myself. I quit when you went past a full book. In one lousy year. Do you want to see it? I could tell you who you were dating when the twins were born or who your current 'lady' was when they were two months old. I keep it in the top of my closet and pull it out every once in a while to remind myself of what a fool I was."

"You're not a fool," Race told her, tenderness forcing his voice to turn husky. Regret rippled through him as he thought of her, barely twenty, pregnant and cutting out those clippings about him.

"I'm so, so sorry, love," he told her, walking over to place his arms around her, trying to absorb her pain. He felt as though his entire world had been turned upside down, forcing him to feel emotions he'd almost forgotten. How long had it been since he'd felt such regret, such pain over some other person? Far too long, Race realized as he reached for Jennifer's rigid body.

Pulling away from his touch, Jennifer looked at him in amazement. "You're sorry? Don't be. Not now. It's all for the best. I wouldn't trade my kids in for anything. I have a very happy life. I won't deny that it was tough in the beginning, finishing school and getting established at the paper, but I did it and now everything's fine. Don't be sorry for the past. I finally learned it can't be changed. Just understood and accepted. Something to grow from." Turning from him, Jennifer picked up her purse and put her keys into her pocket. "Let's go, it's getting late."

"Come with me, Jennifer. Bring the kids and come on tour with me. I can afford it. Don't worry about your job. I'll take care of you all," Race said impulsively. He had been right last night to trust his instincts. More right than he had ever been. This woman was his, and now he had kids, too! A real family all ready for him.

"What did you say?" Jennifer asked, cutting short his fantasies. "Let's go," she said as they got into the Datsun again. Jennifer drove quickly to the center of the town, heading toward Race's hotel.

"You'll love California," he was telling her. "We'll hire a nanny, one of the English kind, and have more kids. I've got lots of room, and if you don't like my house we'll buy another one. Maybe on the beach. You always wanted to live on the beach when we were kids."

"Come back to earth, Race," Jennifer told him, shaking his shoulder as she drove. "No one is going anywhere except back to your hotel. I told you, you don't need to feel obligated. I'm fine. The kids are fine. Go back to your life and leave us alone."

"What are you talking about, Jennifer? You're going to marry me and we're going to be a family," Race announced.

Jennifer started to laugh, slowly at first, then with more force. If there was a trace of tears behind her amusement, she wouldn't tell Race. How could anyone possibly be as arrogant as he was and live? "Race, dear," she began slowly, "listen to my words. Listen to what I'm saying. I will not marry you. You will go away and leave me and the twins alone. Period!"

"Why?"

The word echoed in the car, providing Jennifer with a score of answers, none of which she allowed herself to blurt out. He was serious, Jennifer realized, or at least as serious as he ever got anymore.

"Patti Silk, for one thing," she told him deliberately. "I don't think she would be pleased if you tried to move another woman and her kids in with the two of you. At least until you settle your palimony suit with her."

"She's nothing to me, Jennifer. She never was anything more than a...an arrangement," Race explained easily. "We wanted each other, and the publicity was good. We were both tired of temporary relationships, and we sort of slid into living together. It's over. It's been over for months."

"Tell that to Patti, Hunter."

"She knows. The suit is just publicity, honey. Patti doesn't care about me one little bit. I hurt her ego by being the one to leave, and she's trying to get me back. She thinks I love the ranch enough to come back to her. It's nothing, I tell you, absolutely nothing for you to worry about. Look, Jenni, come in with me and we'll talk some more." Jennifer turned the car into the half circle in front of the door, stopping as Race turned to her and began to speak again.

She held up her hand and told him. "Don't say another word. We are not going to do anything. Go on with your tour. Give me a call sometime or other." She caught his eye as she continued soothingly, "I promise you that you'll be glad when you've thought about this. Give yourself some time. You've been shocked and it's your ego talking. You don't want me or the kids, not really. It's just been a surprise. Once you get back to your world, you'll forget this fantasy. Don't worry, there won't be any paternity suits. We won't bother you."

"Jennifer," Race bellowed, giving the approaching doorman a look that caused him to back up, "I am not going to leave you. I'm going to marry you and be a father to my kids.''

"They're not your kids, Race Hunter. They are mine. Totally and completely mine. And I will not have you around my family with your corrupt values and loose lifestyle. Just get out of my car and leave me alone.''

"I'll get out, lady,'' Race told her as the doorman opened his door, ''but you haven't seen the last of me. I want you and I want my kids.''

"Never!'' Jennifer told him as she put the car in gear and wheeled away.

Chapter Three

Most of that day remained a total blank in Jennifer's memory. For the first time in her life she bordered on genuine hysterics, wishing that she could change the past twenty-four hours, helplessly acknowledging that she couldn't. It had happened. She had met Race again. Her secret dream had come true, but it had not been the romantic fantasy that she'd cherished in her heart from her idealistic youth.

It seemed that Race was destined to sweep into her life and out of it again in twenty-four-hour increments. Changing it forever and leaving disaster behind quite out of proportion to the amount of time he spent with her. She'd sensed a core of determination in Race's tone that frightened her. It seemed that he'd somehow lost his sense of proportion, arrogantly assuming there was nothing in the world that he couldn't have if he wanted it enough. Jennifer feared the effect that some momentary whim on Race's part could have on her children's lives.

Later that afternoon she sat in a modern lawyer's office and confessed everything to Victoria Mathewson, a woman who was not only a childhood friend but her legal adviser. When she had finished explaining the circumstances she sat back, her nails pressing into her palms. "Can he do anything to my kids, Vicki?"

"It hardly seems likely, since first he'd have to prove that they were his," Vicki reassured Jennifer. "The most that could happen if he wanted to drag this into court is that he'd get some sort of very limited visitation rights."

"Visitation rights? No way! I'd have to tell the kids that he's their father!" Jennifer protested, sitting upright in the leather chair, her pale face turning even whiter at her friend's words.

"You mean they don't know?" Victoria prodded. "Jenni, I'm afraid you've kept silent for too many years. That luxury simply is no longer possible. You know I'm your friend, but as your lawyer I have to have the complete truth in order to help."

"I never told them much about their father, only that I'd loved him and he hadn't been able to stay with us. I didn't lie, but I wasn't about to tell them," Jenni said in a sardonic voice, "that they're the product of a one-night stand. There's no delicate way to say that."

"You loved him, Jenni," Vicki countered strongly. "It may not have meant much to Race, but it was never casual to you." She looked Jennifer straight in the eye and went on. "I've known you since high school, and it was no secret that you worshiped that man, way before he started to get famous."

"You were still so innocent at twenty," Vicki said, and Jennifer could hear the empathy in her friend's voice. "You were still living at home with your parents and seldom dating. Of course you know your pregnancy surprised everyone—including me." Vicki smiled gently. "You know I never pried too deeply—I could see how embarrassed and hurt you were whenever the subject was raised. Why didn't you ever tell me Race was the father of Becca and Rick?"

"I never told anyone. I think Mom must suspect. Rick is the spitting image of Racine as a child, but we've never mentioned it. I wanted to forget all about Race. I felt so dumb the next day when I realized what I'd done." Sighing, Jenni confessed, "It was as much my fault as his—more, probably, if you want me to be honest. He was in town to close his folks' house and stopped over. Mom and Dad were in Raleigh, and I was alone. I fell into his lap like a—like any other groupie. He didn't know I'd loved him for years, and he was so upset when he found out I was a virgin...."

"Oh, Jenni," her friend exclaimed sympathetically. "Life isn't always fair, is it? Giving us what we want most in the world."

"Not always. But it seems to balance out in the long run. I have never once regretted the children. They have added so much to my life. I only wish it didn't have to all circle back on me now."

"It'll be all right," Victoria told her, touching her comfortingly on the shoulder. "He probably was only talking. He has his hands full with that mess in Hollywood. You most likely won't see him again for another eight years."

After her talk with Vicki Jennifer crossed her fingers and went on with her life, forcing the tendril of fear back into the corner of her mind. Day by day, week by week, Jennifer relaxed as time passed and she didn't hear from Race. Finally September came and the twins started second grade. Jenni worked hard reviewing the fall movies and writing a series of articles on area day care centers.

The only thing that had changed was her social life. For the past year she had been sporadically dating Jeff Wenset, the twins' pediatrician. Suddenly he was pushing her to deepen their relationship; and he was speaking of a future together. Before Race had returned, Jennifer might have consented. Now she was oddly unsettled by Jeff's demands.

Until she'd seen Race again, she'd successfully convinced herself that the magic of that night had been a dream, that she'd manufactured that profound ecstasy out of her imagination to rationalize her own wanton behavior. She'd been sure that passion was overrated and that she could be content with mild pleasure and a peaceful serenity.

Now her assumptions had been shattered. Jennifer had to admit that she had not exaggerated her remembered response to Race and that she was capable of much more than the luke-warm responses that Jeff elicited from her. While part of her longed to surrender to Jeff's safe, undemanding life, something was holding her back. She had promised Jeff an answer soon, hoping that her common sense would return and that she'd stop thinking of Jeff as if he were a part of her past instead of her present.

One morning a large moving truck and several workmen pulled up to the house next door to Jennifer's. There had been no word that the Harrisons were moving, no sign in front of their house, nothing at all. The house was emptied in six hours.

Margo, Jenni's mother had soon discovered that the Harrisons had received a huge and unexpected cash offer for the house on the condition that they move out immediately. By the end of the day they were gone and delivery trucks from the best store in town had pulled up to refurnish the house. Margo was clearly beside herself with curiosity as she relayed the events to Jenni on the phone that afternoon.

"Wait, I think I see our new neighbor," her mother told Jennifer, who was holding her breath.

"Who is it, Mom?" Jennifer demanded intently.

"A really handsome man," Margo told her, standing on tiptoe and peering out the side window. "He looks about fifty, maybe more, with gray hair and a nice posture."

"Mom, listen to me," Jennifer insisted. "Do me a favor. Keep a close look out for Race."

"For who?"

"Racine Huntington, Race Hunter, our old next-door neighbor." When her mother murmured that she remembered, Jennifer went on. "I'll explain everything later, but do me a favor. Please pick up the kids after school. Can you pack them a bag and spend the night with Aunt Alice? I'll call to arrange it." When her mother began to question her, Jenni cut her off. "I'll be home in no time. And I'll tell you everything." After thanking her mother, Jenni hung up.

It was Race. She knew it for sure. His tour had ended last week, and he must have decided to come here next. Who else could afford to buy someone out and then get a complete new set of furniture? She refused to believe otherwise, even if her mother saw an older man out directing things. Race would always have someone else doing things for him. It had to be him.

Quickly she finished the piece she was working on, giving the restaurant a slightly better review than she had planned. She was already done with the movie review. Thank goodness she routinely worked several days ahead of her deadlines and had some flexibility in her schedule. Saving her column in the computer, she printed a copy for her editor and scrambled out into the parking lot.

Jennifer was pleased that she'd arrived home at two, knowing she'd have half an hour with her mother before school was out. Straightening her shoulders, Jenni walked in, prepared to tell her mother all about Race and her suspicions of the new neighbors.

"Mom," she shouted as soon as she walked in the back door, "where are you?"

"In the living room, Jennifer," her mother's well-modulated voice replied. "Come and see. Our new neighbor has come for a visit," Jennifer heard just as she walked around the corner.

"Racine, is that you?" Jennifer asked, looking at a vastly different man than the one she'd seen on stage two months ago. His long hair was gone, and he was clean-shaven. He was clad in a pair of old blue jeans and a simple short-sleeved polo shirt. He was dressed like every other man who lived in the neighborhood. He looked absolutely wonderful. He looked like her old love.

While she was assessing his changed appearance, Race caressed her with his eyes. Her magnificent golden-red hair was shining-clean, and he nearly stepped closer, wanting to smell its fragrance. Her green eyes were wary and her expression closed, but Race still found her beautiful. His eyes finally moved down, over her generous breasts to her narrow waist and then her slender legs. Somehow she seemed more fragile than she'd appeared this summer, and Race wondered if she'd lost weight.

"What are you doing here with my mother?" she managed to ask, telling herself to stay cool.

"I'm your new neighbor, Jenni, and I came over to say hi," Race told her reaching out his hand toward hers and smiling the thousand-volt smile that never failed to bring out a response in anyone lucky enough to receive it. "You can't imagine how pleased I was to find your mother living here with you and the twins. Doesn't she feed you enough?"

"Feed me enough? What are you talking about? And why are you surprised she's here? You knew she was here," she told him, forcing herself to remain impassive while deliberately ignoring the hand that he offered. "What are you doing here in Charlotte? Why did you buy out the Harrisons? You live in Hollywood."

"I have a house there," Race drawled, pulling his hand back and tipping his head slightly toward her. She was making herself very clear, disapproval of him and his presence written all over her unsmiling face. He could see she didn't want him taking care of her—at least not yet. It didn't matter, though. He was every bit as determined as she was, determined about what he wanted and when he wanted it. Obviously they were going to have to get over the preliminaries and her cursory objections. "And now I have a house here. I own several houses. They're good investments."

"Sure, Race. Buying the house next to mine at double the market price is a good investment. Don't patronize me. I know why you're here and I'm not buying any of it. Go back where you belong." Turning, she looked into her mother's troubled blue eyes and said, "Mom, can I speak to you in the kitchen for a minute?"

Nodding her acceptance, Margo, a slim woman with prematurely white hair and a sweet face, got up. "You," Jenni told Race as he started to join them, "stay put. I want to talk to you later. *Alone*."

As the kitchen door swung shut behind them, Margo put her arms around Jenni's shoulders and spoke softly. "You don't need to worry, honey. I've guessed Race was the twins' father since the beginning. You didn't want to talk about it, honey, but I always understood. So did your dad, God rest his soul. I know you and the twins saw him this summer, but you never said anything."

"Mom," Jenni said slowly, "I should have told you, but I didn't want you to worry. I hoped it would all go away. He thinks he wants the twins, and he's only here because I told him no." She sighed. "I can take care of myself, but Rick and Becca can't."

"Don't worry. I don't think he'd ever want to hurt the children. I don't believe Racine has changed that much. He may lead a fast life, but he was never mean as a boy. You'll be able to talk some sense into him. After all, it must have been a shock for him, as well."

"Poor man," Jenni commented dryly, regaining her normal poise. "I never expected this! I figured maybe he'd call or come visit, not buy the house next door. What sort of jerk would do that?" Then she answered her own question. "Obviously a rich one who's used to getting his own way. Well, I guess it's going to be my turn to teach him that money can't buy everything."

"I'm sure you will," Margo told Jenni. "I'll go and get the twins now. I already put their suitcases in the car. I'll talk to you tonight, Jenni. I know that you can handle it." With a quick kiss, she left to pick up the twins.

Slowly Jennifer walked back into the living room, determinedly clamping down her own riotous emotions. This was no time to show any sort of weakness at all. Race would take advantage of anything he could.

Before she spoke, Jenni allowed herself to stare for a moment at the man who stood gazing out her back window. He looked incredibly handsome with his black wavy hair cut in a traditional look, the silky strands just touching the back of his collar. His build was still the same, long, lean legs and slim waist. His shoulders were broad and muscular, and Jenni acknowledged that he looked better at thirty-two than he had at twenty-four. Too much better for her peace of mind or her blood pressure.

Clearing her throat to get his attention, Jennifer stood up straight and looked him in the eye. "What are you doing back here in Charlotte?" Jenni demanded, trying to keep their communication as to-the-point as possible.

"I came back for you and the twins." Race announced deliberately. He walked directly to her. Taking her hand in his, he forced her to look at him. "I've come back to marry you, Jenni," he told her softly. "I told you I would be back last July."

Race was totally unprepared for the pained grimace on Jenni's face or the look of disbelief that flickered through her eyes. A look of patience finally settled over her face, and she allowed him one slightly bitter smile. "Come on, Hunter. Give me a break. You can't be serious. We haven't seen each other for more than half an hour in eight years; and you waltz back here expecting to marry me? This is not some fairy tale, and you most definitely are not my prince. You're about seven and a half years too late."

Now that Jennifer wasn't concerned about the children walking into the house, she relaxed a bit, realizing this situation would have been almost humorous if the twins had not been involved. Now that she didn't want him near her, he'd decided to come back. Not when she'd needed him or when she'd have given her soul to hear him call her name, but now.

She had all night to get rid of Race and convince him that he really didn't want to stay in town or in her life. He was offering her marriage? Race Hunter get married? She'd sooner believe that he was going to take up the accordion and play polka music during his next concert.

After the shock of their first encounter, Jenni was feeling more confident. His sudden appearance had been a surprising jolt, but she was over the worst of it. Once she got her bearings, Jenni realized that Race no longer had any power over her. She was in her home, in her town. Her only objective was to convince Race to leave as quickly as possible.

Walking toward the kitchen, she surprised Race with a suggestion that they have some coffee. "Look, we're two rational adults," she began as she poured the water and measured the coffee into the coffee machine. "We can talk about this situation, and then you can go back where you belong."

"I belong with you," he said calmly, "and with my kids."

"Are you listening to me at all?" Jenni repeated, as though she were talking to a stubborn child. "You cannot come back here and act as if nothing has happened. Those are not *your* children, they're *mine*." With a malice that she didn't like to admit she was capable of, Jenni added, "Why don't you go and track down some of your other children? You must have several floating around somewhere whose mothers would welcome the famous Race Hunter with open arms. If children are all you want, I'm sure that—"

"Jenni, stop it," Race demanded, breaking into her harangue in a hard, angry voice. "I won't say that I've been celibate—"

Jenni interrupted him, her voice as hard and angry as his had been. "Don Juan would be rolling in his grave if he knew about you. Don't you ever tell me that I don't know about you and your women," Jennifer lashed out. "Everybody in the Western world knows about your love life."

"That's enough," Race snapped. "I know I've been around, but nowhere as much as you think. Those ridiculous magazines have me sleeping with every girl I've ever met, even with some I've never met. Most of my reputation is just hype, publicity. One picture, one dance with any lady, and it's in the papers. No one could have done half of what I've been accused of doing, even if they tried. My schedule is too busy for that. And when I did find the time, I've always taken precautions, for my own sake as well as for birth control. I am not the womanizer that you read about in the papers. I do not have scads of kids all over the country—I only have two, here in Charlotte. I've changed, Jenni. Give me a chance. I've come back to you."

"You can't come back to what you never had," Jennifer explained once more. "We had one night together, eight years ago. It was a mistake—we were both wrong. It was as much my fault as yours, so just forget it. You don't owe me anything."

"Yes, I do, Jennifer Grange. I've been thinking about that night ever since I found that song a few months ago, and I've decided that we were both stupid."

Jennifer told him, "You got that right. So, let it go."

"No, let me finish," Race insisted, tenderly resting his hand on her shoulder. "I knew that you loved me, I just didn't want to admit it and accept the responsibility. I tried to make myself think that you were only experimenting with sex."

"You were the one who was experimenting, Race," Jenni whispered. "You were the one who never came back."

Sighing, Race admitted, "I was too young to appreciate you, honey. I wanted to believe you weren't any readier to settle down than I was. Otherwise I'd have had to change my whole life and admit that I was in trouble, that I cared about you, too." When Jennifer looked away, Race's voice deepened, and he turned her toward him. "At least admit that I didn't plan on seducing you, that it just happened."

Jennifer looked up into Race's face, her eyes pained with remembrance, and then shook her head, slowly focusing once again on the present. "It really doesn't matter what happened eight years ago. The bottom line is that we made love and you left. That was a long time ago, and we've both grown up . At least I have. You don't know me at all, and I don't like the man you've become."

"No," Race said, unused to hearing such harsh rejection. "I won't believe that! You gave yourself to me eight years ago, and now I'm back to take what's mine." Race had not intended to come on so strong, but he'd spent the last months dreaming of Jennifer, planning ways to get her back into his life. Now that he was here, all he could think of was primitive possession. He realized now that Jenni had been totally in love with him, and he refused to admit that she no longer cared. She'd responded to his kiss last July, and he knew that somewhere beneath her controlled facade she still wanted him.

Losing her temper again, Jenni stood up and faced Race, fire in her emerald eyes. "Listen to me. I have a whole life here, Race. I haven't been waiting in some sort of limbo for you to decide to return. You can't recapture what you never had. It was a mistake, made long ago. I don't need or want you in my life. I'm nearly engaged to another man, for Pete's sake."

Race stalked over to her, filled with a gut-ripping jealousy that he'd never felt before. He put his hands on her shoulders and forced her to look at him. "Tell me, Jenni, that your boyfriend makes you feel this,'' he demanded bringing his lips down to hers.

His lips were smooth and cool, touching the sides of her mouth and slowly pressing more and more firmly on hers. His tongue flicked quickly along Jenni's bottom lip and traced the line of her top one, teasingly gentle. When she tried to pull away, he insinuated his tongue between her throbbing lips and she opened to him with a sound that was half protest, half surrender. Fires burned as he tasted her sweetness, explored the honeyed warmth of her mouth and plundered its soft recesses with his thrusting tongue. Expertly he sought her response, teasing her with small nips, retreating and then returning, until Jenni could resist no more and melted into his arms.

Race pulled back, taking her head in his hands, looking at the passion glazing her eyes as he murmured, ''See what passion really is.'' Then he brought his lips back to hers, his tongue finding its way back into her mouth as though he had every right. ''Admit that we belong together.''

Elbowing him in the chest, Jenni wrenched herself from Race's embrace and whirled away from him. ''That's it! Get out!'' she demanded, letting all her desire explode into anger. ''I've tried to be reasonable, but you keep using all your little tricks. Just stop playing games. I willingly admit that you have great technique, you might be one of the world's greatest kissers, maybe even one of the world's best lovers. The trouble here is that I am not interested in playing any games with you, sexual or otherwise. I will not tolerate your treating me like some mindless body, some woman who can be swayed by her raging hormones. If you touch me one more time, Hunter, I swear that you'll live to regret it.''

''If I don't touch you again I'll live to regret it,'' Race told her gently. ''And so will you.''

''You're good at what you do. You should be with all the practice you've had. I'll even admit that you possess a terrible attraction for me. But I do not want you. I will never allow myself to surrender to mindless physical needs, to some sexual trickery that you've mastered."

"Jenni," Race said with some difficulty, "I'm sorry. I never thought you were mindless. I just wanted to let you know how I felt."

"Frankly, I don't care how you feel. You don't seem the least bit interested in how I feel. You're a stranger to me, Mr. Hunter, and I'd like you to quit playing around with my memories and leave me alone. I am happy. I have a wonderful man who loves me and the twins. I do not want you involved in my life at all. How can I be any clearer?"

Angrier than he could remember ever having been, Race stalked into the living room, his legs stiff, his normally smooth movements feeling awkward. He forced himself to look out the window and think before he spoke. She was wrong, all wrong. She belonged to him, and that kiss had just proved it. But it also proved a lot of other things, and Race was smart enough to finally realize that she was not going to fall in with his plans without a great deal of effort on his part. There was even the possibility that she would never want him again.

Right now, with her golden-red hair mussed and her green eyes glowing like embers, he wanted Jenni more than he'd wanted any other woman in his life. But wanting wasn't enough, and she was no hanger-on, no insecure actress who would lie to him in order to get what she wanted. Vaguely Race realized that his behavior was uncalled-for and that his ego had become vastly inflated. Hollywood and millions of dollars had made him into just what Jennifer thought he was, a selfish, arrogant manipulator.

Suddenly, incredibly, megastar Race Hunter was ashamed. Of himself, of his life-style, and most of all of his behavior toward the woman who was glaring at him across the living room. If he forced himself to look at the situation from Jenni's point of view, he could see that she had a right to be angry. He would have to convince her that he was sincere. Then she'd come back to him. At least he hoped that she would.

"Jenni, love," Race said softly as he turned to face her, "I'm sorry. I know you have a life of your own and that it's been eight years. I don't expect you to welcome me back with open arms. It'll take you some time to get used to me again, to the idea of living in Hollywood. That's all right," he went on, beginning to feel his familiar confidence again. "I can wait."

"Race," Jennifer said softly, "you really have a problem with ego. Thank you for your forebearance, but I beg to decline your great honor. It will freeze in hell before I come to you. You can wait forever, as long as it's not in my house. Go back to all the yes-men, all the willing women, and leave me alone."

"Jenni," Race said, inspiration coming to him, "let me get to know my kids. Do Becca and Rick know that I'm their father?"

Blanching, Jennifer turned to him again, this time daring to walk within inches of his masculine body. "*No!* They don't know who you are and they never will."

"Why not?" Race asked. "I'm sure they want to know their father. They must ask about me now and again."

"All they know is that he's gone. Jeff will be their father if I marry, no one else. Certainly no man with a past like yours." Taking a deep breath, Jenni argued convincingly, "Look, you're only using them right now. If you'd been concerned about the twins you wouldn't be bringing them up as a last resort, one more ploy in the battle. Please, try to be rational about this whole mess. Think about what you really want. This is not a game."

"You can't keep me away from them. I have rights, too," Race exclaimed, hearing only the first part of the argument. "And just who is this wonderful man that you keep talking about? What is he to you exactly?"

"He's the twins' pediatrician. We've been dating for almost a year. He's asked me to marry him," Jennifer stated, not wanting to tell Race anything about her real feelings for Jeff. Or to admit the fact that she had been uncertain about marrying him since the night Race had kissed her. As much as she liked and respected Jeff, something was missing from their relationship. There was no grand passion between them. But now, with Race in her living room, she held on to Jeff as if he were a shield.

"By the way," Race said, looking at his gold watch, unaware of the turmoil that Jenni was feeling, "where are they?"

"Mother took them for the night so we could work this out privately. They are not going to get hurt by you, too," Jenni stated firmly. "I will not have them around someone like you. They aren't going to absorb any of your arrogant, selfish attitude. Rick and Becca know the values of work and love, honesty and sharing. Nothing at all like your values."

"Just what do you mean by that?" he demanded through clenched teeth. This was the first time in five years, that he'd been outright refused anything or been dismissed as a mere nuisance. Those were his kids. *His!*

"I will see my kids, Jennifer Grange," Race insisted, furious that his own children didn't know he existed and hurt that Jennifer refused to even acknowledge his claim on them. "Even if their mother thinks I'm no good. I deserve that much. My lawyer will be in touch," he stated as he walked out the door, slamming it hard enough to rattle the adjacent windows.

"What a stupid mess!" Jennifer cursed vehemently as she dialed Victoria's office. When her friend answered the phone, Jennifer took a deep breath and told her, "I think I have a bit of a problem."

Chapter Four

"What in the world?" Jennifer mumbled when a loud banging noise forced her reluctantly awake the next morning. Groggily she peered at the clock beside her bed and realized that it was nearly eight o'clock.

"Good grief! We're late again! Get up!" she shouted as she jumped out of bed. School started in fifteen minutes, and the kids weren't even out of their beds yet. Yelling her children's names again, she dashed madly down the hall toward the twins' bedrooms, convinced that she had overslept once again.

She jerked open Rick's bedroom door and saw the empty bed, then rubbed her eyes, remembering that the children were at Aunt Alice's. Race had moved in next door. The noise continued downstairs, and Jenni belatedly realized that someone was ringing the doorbell and knocking briskly on her back door.

She returned to her room and grabbed the old blue corduroy robe that hung on the back of her closet door. While slipping it on she wondered who was making such a racket. Race did not strike her as a morning person.

She ran a hand through her tumbled hair and decided that she couldn't look a great deal worse and that she really didn't care. Jennifer had slept very badly last night, tossing and turning until she'd dropped into a troubled sleep around four in the morning. Now her eyes were slightly puffy and dark rings showed under them. Her hair was tangled and snarled, badly in need of a comb.

The banging noise didn't stop as she walked down the hall and into the kitchen. She opened the back door slowly, leaving the chain on and peering through the crack. "Who's there?" she asked, seeing only a huge bundle of roses and the top of a man's gray head.

A clipped British voice answered her. "I'm your other next-door neighbor. Robert Jameson. I've brought you some flowers and an invitation."

Jennifer slowly opened the door and backed into the room. She pulled her robe tightly around her waist as she allowed the man entry.

"I'm pleased to meet you, Miss Grange," the older man continued. "Mr. Hunter has spoken of you often."

"I just bet he has," muttered Jennifer under her breath. "He was just pining away for me for the last eight years." Out loud she asked, "Who are you? Race's butler or something?"

"Correct, madam. I'm his butler, his houseman . . . his keeper, you might say," the distinguished man told her with a twinkle in his eyes. Jennifer allowed herself to really inspect the man and noted that although his voice was British and therefore quite distinguished-sounding, the rest of him appeared rather Americanized. He was wearing a pair of soft leather moccasins, expensive tailored black slacks and a blue cashmere sweater against the early-morning chill. His face wasn't exactly homely or exactly handsome. He looked rather average with his pale eyes, rounded face and slightly oversize nose. He was somewhere around his mid-fifties, Jennifer guessed, noting that he kept himself in excellent condition for a man of his age.

"I've been with Race for several years," Jameson explained. "I'm responsible for handling all of the details of his everyday living situations."

"So," Jennifer said, pulling back from the man cautiously, "what are you doing here in Charlotte?"

"The same as always, taking care of Race. I'm doing the shopping, cleaning, cooking here myself. Usually we stay in larger establishments and I supervise a staff to keep the house running."

"How dull for you," Jennifer interjected, "being stuck in such a tiny house in such an out-of-the-way location. If I were you I'd try to talk your boss into going back to his normal life. He'll never be content here."

"I don't know, miss," Jameson said with a hidden smile. "He's been very restless the last couple of years. Perhaps this is just what he needs."

"Thank you for the flowers," she said politely, dismissing the man. She'd hoped for an ally in her attempt to drag Race back to the fast life, but it didn't look as though this man were going to be of any assistance.

"I'd like to tender an apology with them," the older man said tactfully. "I'll find myself a vase," he told her as he walked into her country kitchen. The large room was divided into two separate areas. The kitchen, with its various appliances and its long center counter, was bordered by a friendly family room, complete with fireplace. Three easy chairs and a sofa were grouped around a small coffee table, allowing the person in the kitchen to remain in contact with the rest of the family.

When Jennifer noted the man's subtle inspection of her home, she decided to try again. "Not quite what you're used to, Mr. Jameson?"

"No, it's much homier," Jameson commented truthfully.

"It must have been a lot of trouble, moving here like this," Jennifer added, taking a different tack. "Where are you going next? Race must be scheduled for another tour or a movie."

"Not that I know of. As far as I know, we're here permanently."

"That's impossible," Jennifer exclaimed. "He must have commitments."

"I'm not sure, ma'am, but he started rearranging things two months ago, just after he visited here in July, I believe," Jameson told her. After setting the red roses, now neatly arranged in a cut-crystal vase, on the coffee table in front of the couch in the combination kitchen-den area, he turned to the woman staring at him. "Mr. Hunter would like to invite you for brunch at his house. He sent me to show that he had no ulterior motives," he added.

"Today?" Jennifer asked, absently enjoying Jameson's interesting British accent and the tactful way he answered questions.

As she was about to refuse the invitation, she remembered Victoria's advice from yesterday's phone call. If Race wanted to talk, she'd talk. She wanted things settled before the kids got home. "Okay. I'll be there," she agreed. "What time do you want me to come?"

"Would ten-thirty be all right with you, ma'am?"

"Fine. I'll call my office and be over," she told the older man as she checked the large mantel clock that ticked over the fireplace, "in two hours."

Jennifer walked back upstairs, planning her schedule. First she'd call her mother and then the paper. She could afford to take the morning off if she went to the late movie that night.

After talking briefly with her mother, who returned home just moments after Jameson left, Jennifer took a long, leisurely shower and dressed carefully, deciding on her favorite beige suit. She brushed her hair back from her face, anchoring it with two tortoiseshell combs that lost themselves in her glorious hair. A minimum of makeup and she was ready. If only, Jennifer thought, it were as easy to control her feelings as it was her outside appearance. She looked cool and collected, but she was anything but that inside.

As she rang Race's doorbell, Jennifer commanded herself for the twelfth time, "Keep your temper. Be cool. Remember that the twins are depending on you to keep them safe." Before she could formulate any other warnings, the door opened and Race stood staring at her.

His hair was uncombed and it was obvious that he had not been up and waiting for her to arrive. His blue jeans were riding low on his lean hips, and he was still tucking in a rough cotton shirt. The top half of the shirt was unbuttoned, and thick black hair on his chest contrasted sharply with the powder blue of the shirt. A genuine smile lighted his face as he rubbed his hand across his lightly stubbled chin. For a moment he looked so like her old love that she thought her heart would stop. But, too soon, he straightened up and reached out to touch her and Jenni remembered that this was Race Hunter in front of her, not Racine Huntington. That he was wearing a two-hundred-dollar shirt, not a twenty-dollar one.

"Hey, love, you're early," he said, his gaze moving leisurely down her body and up again. The playboy country singer was apparent in his blatant stare as he contemplated her. "You look fabulous."

"I'm on time," she retorted coolly, stepping around him as she entered the house. She let her eyes evaluate his body as he had hers. He was still slim, but he was now muscled rather than thin. His face was the real barometer of change, she noted objectively. "It's hard to believe that you've changed so little, Race. I always suspected you owed your looks to makeup."

"Makeup?" Race asked, his right eyebrow raised.

"Yes. I thought you'd be more used-looking, if you know what I mean. But you don't look much older, not really."

"Thanks a lot," Race replied, feeling somewhat peeved. "I'm only thirty-two, Jen," he told her, "not fifty."

"I keep forgetting, Race," Jennifer said, wondering how to get the conversation back to a more impersonal subject. "I'm sorry. It's none of my business, anyway. What did you want to talk to me about?" she asked, turning to look around the room. "The flowers were lovely."

Her eyes rapidly ran over the room, noting the differences between the former neighbors' room and the one that now appeared before her. The quiet colonial room that she was used to was gone. In its place was a modern room full of expensive furniture, all in muted shades. The butter-soft leather sofa and matching chairs were a neutral gray that just happened to match Race's eyes. Modern art was framed on the walls, and the only other splashes of color were a few coffee-table books placed strategically on the matching chrome-and-glass end tables. It was attractive but totally impersonal.

Anyone could have lived in that room, and no one did. Jennifer found herself hoping that all of Race's homes didn't look like this, surprised that she cared that he lived such an empty life. What did she expect? A person with several homes, always on the road, would have no real home of his own. Maybe the ranch where he lived with Patti Silk was different. Part of her hoped so, for Race's sake.

"The house looks nice," she commented neutrally.

At her noncommittal words, Race followed her gaze and for a moment saw his house through her eyes and compared its sterile perfection with her home. He'd felt strangely relaxed in the warmth that she and the twins lived in. It had been a long time since he'd seen a house that didn't come with maid service. He'd actually enjoyed the slightly worn furniture, the batters and scrapes. He'd even enjoyed the sock that he'd seen hiding under one of the couches and the jumble of coats and shoes beside the back door. There had been crumpled magazines and open books scattered throughout the room, all sure signs of a busy, well-lived-in home.

"It's all new," Race found himself telling her. "Jameson picked it out for me. I haven't had a chance to settle in yet," he explained, trying to convince himself as well as her. For an instant he realized that all his homes looked like this one, exactly like this one. Maybe the colors and shades were different. Maybe the English home had a Victorian antique look, but they were all alike—beautiful, perfect and sterile. No one lived in any of his houses long enough to turn them into homes. Perhaps he'd tell Jameson to have the maids quit picking things up so promptly.

"Of course," Jennifer murmured. "You are too busy to do anything like that yourself. He has lovely taste." Prowling, she walked over to the couch and looked down at the title of the art book lying there. It was an expensive compendium of Georgia O'Keeffe's pictures. For a second she almost gave in to the impulse to pick it up. She'd noted the book when it had first been published, but it had been too expensive for her to buy. She wondered briefly if he knew that Georgia O'Keeffe was one of her all-time favorite painters.

Rather, did Jameson know? Or was it all coincidence? *Jennifer, you are getting paranoid!* she told herself, purposefully letting her gaze drift from the book back toward Race. He was standing there staring at her with a strange expression on his face. An almost honest expression, she told herself as she broke the silence.

"So. Jameson said that you wanted to talk to me?"

"Right," Race said, suddenly galvanized into action. "Come in and have some food. I need a cup of coffee."

"Thank you," Jennifer told him. "That would be nice."

Politely she allowed herself to be guided into the dining room and then out onto the screened porch that overlooked part of the golf course. It was blissfully empty at this hour, and she sat down on a comfortable padded rattan chair and waited for Race to speak.

"Jennifer," he began as Jameson brought them coffee and started to assemble a luscious brunch before them. "I'm sorry about last night. I don't want to take this matter into the courts if I can help it. But I do want to see Rick and Rebecca. You can't deny that they're mine."

Jennifer chewed her lip. She'd known that this was coming, but she was still totally unwilling to deal with it. "I don't want to go to court, either," she answered slowly. "But I honestly don't see where you could fit into the twins' life. I don't even know, if push came to shove, that you could prove that they *are* your children. Your name is not on the birth certificate. And for all you know, I might have slept with somebody else the next night."

"Well, pretty Jenni," Race said crudely, "I remember enough of that night to know that you'd slept with no one before me."

Turning a dull red, Jennifer twisted away from him to regain her composure before she lashed out at him. "That's more than I could say for you, Race," she said bitterly as she whipped back around to face him.

Standing up, Race stood towering before her as she sat in the brown chair. Leaning down before her, the tall singer put a finger under her chin and forced her to look into his blazing gray eyes. "I told you last night, Jennifer Grange, I was a stupid fool eight years ago. I threw away something precious. I'm not stupid anymore. I'm not a boy anymore. Those are my kids. We belong together, all of us."

Pulling away, Jennifer clenched her jaw to keep herself from snapping back. Exhaling slowly, she looked into his stormy eyes and replied coolly, "We went over this last night. It was a long time ago. I've grown up, and I wish I could say the same for you."

Composing her face, she told him firmly, "We need to talk about the children and what you intend to do about them. If you hadn't threatened me, I wouldn't be sitting here right now. My lawyer tells me that she thinks there is virtually no chance that you would get any satisfaction if you try to prove the children's paternity in court. Since that's the case, why don't you pack up and get out? I see no reason to upset the twins."

"You've talked to your lawyer about this?" Race asked, somehow surprised. He hadn't done that, just threatened to. The last thing he really wanted was a court battle and all the publicity that would go along with it. Before Jenni could reply, the phone rang and they both heard Jameson answer it.

While Race excused himself to take the call, Jenni sat back and sipped her coffee. Her conversation with Victoria had not been very reassuring. Vicki had been as shocked as she had to find that Race had moved in next door to her.

"What do you suggest?" Jennifer had asked her friend last night. "He said he was going to call his lawyer." Cursing fluently, Jenni had thrown out some of the possible solutions that she'd thought of. "Could I get a restraining order or something?"

"The best thing you can do is to avoid the courts at this point. He has no case, but you don't want the kids to get involved in any publicity, do you? Why don't you give the man a little rope and let him hang himself."

"What do you mean?" Jennifer had queried.

"Didn't you tell me that you thought he was only kidding himself and that he'd tire of the kids as soon as he had a real dose of them?"

"Yeah, I'll bet this is just some quick momentary quirk of his. A midlife crisis or something. No man like him really wants kids. Not real kids." Taking a slow breath, Jenni had gone on, speculating out loud. "I can't imagine him living in a minor-league town like this for more than a week or two without terminal boredom setting in. This is a great place to live, but it's not exactly L.A. or Paris."

"Then I think your best bet is to try to make peace with him and let him see the children a bit. If this gets into the courts, it'll be an all-round mess." When Jennifer hadn't replied right away, Vicki had gone on to reassure her. "Now don't get too upset about this. At the very worst it's a matter of visiting rights, no more. And you might think of what this might mean to the kids financially. They do," Victoria had said, though Jennifer had started to interrupt her, "have a legal right to some of their father's money. The man is loaded."

"You know me better than that," Jennifer had begun, indignation in her voice. "I don't ever want anything from him. My kids do not need him or any of his money. What kind of friend are you, Vicki?"

"A realistic one, Jennifer. As your friend, I sympathize with how you feel and I agree with you. But as your lawyer I feel obligated to point out those things. Those twins of yours have a very rich father who is not denying them. Whether you like to think about it or not, there might be a time when you need him to help with the bills. I'm not suggesting that you compromise yourself in any way. Merely that you think about all the various possibilities before you do or say anything that drives him into the courts."

"You're right," Jenni had said as she'd ended her call to her lawyer. "I'll take it slowly and try to wait him out. Besides," she'd added flippantly just before hanging up, "if I ever want to get rid of him, think of the scoop I'd have with the paper. All I have to do is print his address and he's history."

Victoria had had the last word when she'd reminded Jennifer, "Publicity like that will undoubtedly get Race out of Charlotte. It would also most likely expose his reason for being here in the first place."

Startled out of her memory by a sound, Jenni looked up and realized Race was back from his call. He repeated his previous question, asking if she'd talked to her lawyer.

"Of course I did," Jennifer told him dryly. "Several times. Do you honestly think that I'd be in the same room with you unless I was concerned for my children?"

"Jen," Race protested softly. It was then that he realized that Jenni was not playing a game, that she was dead serious. She was not playing hard to get, she actually did not want him near her or her children. In a chastened voice, he explained, "I—I only wanted to be with you and the kids. I thought you'd be happy to see me."

"Blast you, Race," Jennifer told him, covering her eyes with her hands as she responded to the apparent sincerity in his voice and eyes. How could the man look so ridiculously honest? He must have a picture of himself somewhere that showed the results of his life-style, à la Dorian Gray. He actually looked vulnerable and caring, almost like a real person. "Can't you let this drop? Leave us alone? I swear that I don't want anything from you. Not one penny."

"Jen," Race admonished her, "money had nothing to do with this, and you know it."

When Race looked at her that way, the sincerity and pain shining in his eyes, she melted for a moment. She believed him again. Jennifer barely stopped herself from replying in kind, wanting to soothe him and promise him anything he wanted. Darn him. It was so unfair that he could nearly always cut through her defenses as if they were nonexistent. Why could this one man, this dark-haired devil, come to her with the voice of an angel and tempt her to believe him? Especially when she knew that they weren't even talking the same language.

Reaching over, Jennifer took a sip of the cooling coffee and decided to try again. *Keep it all matter-of-fact,* she ordered herself. *Try to get out of here in one piece. Rick and Becca are depending on you.*

"I don't give a rip about the money," Race was telling her. "I know you don't want my money. For goodness' sake, I'm not stupid. If you'd wanted money you would have contacted me long ago. I want you and my kids.''

"Why? Answer that," Jennifer said, turning to lose herself momentarily in his mysterious gray eyes. "Please think of the consequences of what you're doing for once in your life. Rick and Becca are real, breathing people, sensitive children, not some sort of possessions. They have feelings, Race, that could be damaged so easily. You only want them as symbols of something. You say *my* children like you say *my* car. You can't own people, Race. And that includes the twins and me. I won't let you hurt them.''

"I'd never hurt them," Race protested instantly, pain again visible in his eyes. He didn't want to own the children, only to be their father. He wasn't so sure about Jennifer. A masculine part of him did want to own her, to keep her away from every other man. He'd have to think about that later, but for now perhaps he'd better not tell her that he wanted to claim her again.

"Good, Race. Keep that in mind while you're trying to change their lives. There are many kinds of hurting. I know you'd never hurt them physically, but you could hurt them emotionally so easily. They are happy, well-adjusted kids. Regular kids. Like you and Mike and I were when we were growing up. They deserve as normal a childhood as we had," Jennifer told him, trying to be as logical and compelling as she could. Somehow she had to convince him to leave before he brought any further discord into their lives.

"What do you think would happen to them if, all of a sudden, superstar Race Hunter claimed that they were his children and we got into a legal battle over them? Your affair with Patti Silk would be old news compared to this. The newspapers would go wild. Your fans would mob the place. Your illegitimate children would be on the cover of every national scandal sheet. Think about Rick and Rebecca, Race, before you threaten me with legal action. Those two innocent children would be torn to shreds by the publicity.''

"You're right, Jennifer," Race admitted after a few seconds of consideration. How could he have ignored such a basic fact? Anything that he did was news. He'd known that when he'd bought the house under an assumed name. Why else had he cut his long hair and shaved his beard off before moving in? "I thought it could all be handled quietly. Maybe in family court."

"No way, Huntington...Hunter," Jennifer told him. "Any legal action with your name on it would be bound to leak out. In fact, I'm surprised that you've managed to be here for an entire day with no publicity. Where does everyone think you are? What name are you going by?"

"I told them all that I was going to the Virgin Islands for a vacation and that I'd be in touch. I'm using Jameson's name."

"For how long?" Jennifer demanded.

A few months," Race admitted, knowing full well what he intended to do but not mentioning it to Jennifer. His lawyer knew right where he was, as did his agent. Both of them were expecting him back in a short period. Race had allowed himself two months to work his way back into Jennifer's confidence, charm the kids and marry her. Then he'd return to Hollywood.

Now he realized that he'd been a bit optimistic. As he looked at Jennifer, sitting there so proud and vulnerable, he realized that there was a chance that she would never come back into his life. She really didn't want him, didn't want Race Hunter. It was no game. She was sincere in telling him to walk out of her life. Unfortunately, every minute that he spent with her confirmed his original gut feeling. This was his love, the woman who matched him in every way, the mother of his children, his woman.

"Okay," he hedged, still stunned by the nature of his thoughts. "What can we do to compromise? I agree that I don't want to have any publicity. But you must agree that I can get to know my children. They must ask about me!"

When Jennifer looked at him, truly puzzled, Race lost a little of his calm exterior. "What have you told them about me? About their father? They must wonder who their father is."

"They do," Jennifer said in a flat voice, remembering all the agonizing hours she'd spent wondering about that very topic, the days she'd cradled her bulging stomach when she'd been pregnant and the hours she'd cried while holding them when they'd been babies.

"I've told them the truth, at least a part of it. That I loved their father very much but that our relationship didn't work out. I've hinted that there was a quick marriage and a quick divorce, but I've never outright lied to them about it. It's enough for now, especially with the number of divorced kids in the schools. I'll tell them about you when they're older—a whole lot older—and can handle the facts."

When she saw him ready to speak, she stopped him with a sharp comment. "You don't want me to tell them how they really were conceived, do you? Hey, kids, you're accidents, the product of a one-night stand? Want your son and daughter to hear that?" she asked Race, daring him to answer back, her face open and vulnerable. "Want me to let them see what a sterling example of good morals their mother is? Do you want me to tell them that sexual impulses are Okay? Sleep around as much as you want, regardless of the consequences. Do you want your kids to live like you do?"

"It wasn't like that," he told her, staggered by the reality of what she'd felt and what she'd gone through. For some reason, even after he'd seen the kids and realized that he was a father, the true nitty-gritty of Jennifer's past hadn't gotten through to him. He'd realized that she'd been hurt and felt bad, but this bitter, raw pain was more than he'd expected. For once he was facing real pain, not some glitzed-up, sanitized version of it. The shards of guilt and bitterness in her voice tore through him like knives.

Jenni stood up and went on, "It was exactly like that. Or it wouldn't be eight years since I'd last seen you. You never even called or dropped me a postcard. I was one more notch on your belt. A small one at that." Setting down her coffee cup to keep the china from clattering in her trembling hands, she walked to the window and gazed out at her own house, wanting to run back to it more than she could say. "If only I hadn't gone to that stupid concert," she whispered to herself.

"I'm not sorry that you came, Jennifer," Race replied from behind her, his voice sweet and soft. "You were never that to me, though. I've never forgotten you. Never. Why do you think I came back? Recorded that song?"

Jerking back, Jennifer realized that she must have voiced her thoughts aloud, and she drew herself more tightly under control. She had to get herself in order. She could not give him one tiny piece of her, or he'd try for more. More and more, until she was lost again. Then, when he left once again for his life, she'd be devastated.

"Well," she managed to say in a moment, her voice deliberately brisk. She refused to respond to that last bit of garbage. Sure he remembered her. Sure he'd come looking for her—after eight years. What kind of fool did he think she was? Luckily, anger gave her strength, and she forced herself back to the present problem. All she cared about was getting her children out of this mess without hurting them any more than was necessary. "Let's not cry over spilled milk. What's done is done. You have your life and I have mine." *Lord, Jennifer,* she lectured herself silently, *you sound like a book of platitudes gone wild. Get a grip on yourself and talk like a regular person.*

She turned to find him right behind her, a look of tender regret on his face. For a second she paused, but then she moved rapidly away. Turning, she rested on a chair arm and retreated behind her most official facade.

"For the last time, Race. Please leave me and the kids alone."

Placing his fists on his hips, Race looked into her turbulent eyes and almost granted her request. Part of him wanted to make her pain go away, even if it meant that he would be hurt. But he couldn't. She knew that he wanted her and the kids. She had to give him a chance to prove that he could have a place in her life. Damn her. He was Race Hunter, one of the most eligible bachelors in the entire Western world. Hadn't some newsmagazine said so only last year? Sooner or later she'd realize what a great catch he was and she'd be grateful that he'd stayed around for her. "No," he finally said, "I can't."

Sighing deeply, Jennifer settled back and began bargaining, for herself and for her children. "Can we both at least agree that we'll keep this out of the courts? You must realize what the publicity would do to Rick and Becca if it got out that you were suing for paternal rights."

"So you do admit that they're mine," Race snapped, wanting at least that much satisfaction from her.

"No. I will admit nothing. Even if this does end up in court, I will swear that you are not their father," she told him in a cold voice. "I will do anything to protect my kids."

"Except marry me."

"That would not be protecting them. That would be throwing them into a den of iniquity," she snapped, almost, but not quite, losing her temper. "Look, this is getting us nowhere. I won't admit anything. Now or ever. For all I know you have tape recorders taping this whole thing."

"I can't believe you think that of me," Race said. Then he stopped for a moment as he realized that she did expect that of him. She expected him to hurt her again, after all these years. Shame, an emotion that he'd forgotten until he'd returned to Charlotte, once again ran through him.

He should have told those French movie people to forget it all those years ago. If he hadn't been offered the lead in that stupid movie, he would have come back to see Jenni. He had intended to after he returned from Paris, but he'd never gotten around to it. Somehow he'd make it all up to her and his kids.

As she stood looking at him, her arms crossed over her breasts in the classic defensive pose, he decided to start over. No more threats. "I promise not to take you to court," he said, gratified at the sudden sharp sigh of relief that came from Jennifer, "if you will let me get to know the kids."

"How?" Jennifer burst out. "I will not tell them that you are their father."

"Fair enough," Race agreed. "At least for now. Can we compromise for a while? Let me enter your life as their neighbor. I could tell them that we were old childhood friends and I moved in here by accident. I'm willing—" he cringed inwardly "—to be their Uncle Race for a while. At least let me get to know my own children."

Knowing what that concession must have cost a proud man like Race, Jennifer weakened. It was one possible way out. The kids wouldn't be too damaged if they made friends with Race and then he moved away. A small voice warned her to be careful, but her common sense overrode it. The sooner Race got a dose of the kids, the sooner he'd tire of this little game and go back to his glamorous life in Hollywood.

"Okay, but only under my conditions," Jennifer said. "I want them to be supervised at all times by either me or my mother. They cannot come over here without an adult with them. And," she added, quite seriously, "I promise you that you will never see them again if you tell them anything or if you try to take them away from me. I'll charge you with kidnapping so fast that you'll...you'll know it," she finished, unable to find the cliché that she had felt waiting when she'd started the sentence.

"Kidnapping?" Race said, blanching slightly. "You think so little of me that you think I'd steal my own children?"

Recognizing his genuine distaste, Jennifer softened a little. "My Racine Huntington would never do anything like that, but he's been dead for eight years. I can't take any chances, that's all. The children are my entire life, Race," she told him by way of apology.

"You have a deal, Jennifer. I'll get to know them, but only with you or your mother present. What time do you want me for dinner tonight, then?"

"Dinner?" Jennifer asked. "What do you mean?"

"Well, I think I should be formally introduced to my kids, don't you? When do we eat?"

"U-usually about six-thirty," she stammered. What had she done now? She was going to protect the kids, but who was going to protect her? Her thoughts and feelings swirling, she walked out the door, pausing at the screen. "Fine. I'll see you tonight," she said. "I hope you like turkey casserole."

"Anything. I'll like anything you have," Race promised. Somehow things had gotten out of hand for a moment, but they were back on track now. He would start his campaign tonight.

"Jameson," he shouted as he watched the slender curve of Jenni's back as she walked toward her own house. "Get the car. We're going shopping."

Chapter Five

Becca, for the last time, will you pick up those dolls and take them up to your room!" Jennifer scolded her daughter. "It's nearly six-thirty, and our guest is going to be here any minute."

"Oh, Mom. I'll do it in a minute," the older of the Grange twins replied, turning to flash her mother a charming smile while quietly sneaking another pillow from the couch to add to the pile that she'd already borrowed. "Barbie is climbing mountains right now, and she can't stop until she gets to the top," she explained seriously.

"Becca, obey your mother," her grandmother added, walking up behind Jennifer with Rick at her side. "Can I do anything more to help before I leave?" Looking her daughter directly in the eye, she offered again, "Are you absolutely sure you don't want me to cancel this evening and stay?"

Although she was tempted, Jennifer refused. She straightened up and gazed into her mother's worried eyes with a cheerful look on her face. "No. Everything's under control. The casserole is in the oven and dinner's ready. There's no reason for you to miss your bridge night. You look forward to dinner and cards with your friends every week. Besides," she added convincingly in a low voice, "I don't want the kids to think this is anything special."

"All right, honey," Margo agreed. She was a great believer in facing trouble head-on, Jennifer knew. Since Race had moved in next door, they had both realized that he was not going to disappear. Trying to treat Race as a friend of the family was not a perfect plan, but it was better than the alternatives. As long as Race agreed to act the role of an interested next-door neighbor, he had to be allowed to visit the twins.

While Margo went to get her purse, Jennifer looked down at her two kids and hoped that they would remember their manners at dinner. Unfortunately, they were both tired, hungry and not in the mood for company. Perhaps it was for the best. This was the reality of parenting. Maybe Race would lose his illusions about parenthood more quickly if he saw them at their worst. Let him get a taste of the real twins tonight, not those cute kids he had had breakfast with two months ago.

"See you later, Grandma," Rick shouted as Margo took her coat out of the closet. Margo walked over to brush a kiss on his cheek, then Becca's. "Be good, loves," she whispered.

A few moments later, when the back doorbell rang, Becca took one look at Jenni and scooped up her dolls, running up the back stairs. Jennifer took a deep breath, smoothed her hair one last time and answered the door. The calm greeting that she had rehearsed was forgotten when she saw Race standing in her doorway burdened with two huge boxes. Before she could ask him what he'd brought, Rick came up beside her.

"Wow. What have you got there?" his clear young voice asked curiously.

"Yes. Just what *do* you have there?" Jennifer demanded as Race pushed his way into the room. She stood back to let him in, mentally bracing herself as she caught sight of him. He was wearing a pair of tight-fitting navy jeans and an ivory cashmere sweater that looked as though it had been custom-designed for his slim torso. If Race had not been able to sing, he could have had an equally successful career as a model. With his hair slightly tousled and his gray eyes shining with emotion, he was almost irresistible.

It was absolutely unfair that any one man should be so appealing. Mentally she ordered herself to get a grip on her raging hormones. To think of Patti Silk. To think of the sexuality that he automatically projected. It was all pretty packaging. All right, gorgeous packaging. As much as she wanted to fight it, he was the handsomest man she'd ever met. Always had been, and probably always would be. If only the inside matched the outside. "What's this?" Jennifer demanded again as Rebecca walked down to join them, immediately drawn to the brightly wrapped packages.

With a flashing smile, Race hunkered down on his heels. "Hi, kids. Remember me?" he asked. "I'm your new—"

Jennifer interrupted quickly, finishing for Race as he straightened. "Kids," she announced matter-of-factly, "say hi to Mr. Jameson, our new next-door neighbor and an old friend of mine."

Becca gazed shyly up at the tall stranger, hiding slightly behind her mother while Rick moved up and stuck out his small hand, his gray eyes shining with bright eagerness. "Are you all by yourself?" he asked in his high voice. "Do you have any kids?"

"No," Race answered huskily, giving Jenni a poignant glance.

"I think that Rick was hoping that another boy his age was going to move in next door." Turning to her son, she explained, "Mr. Jameson has a lady friend in California, but she's not here now." Ignoring the fierce scowl on Race's face, she went on, "He's staying with his father for the time being, another Mr. Jameson. In fact, since there are two Mr. Jamesons, why don't you call Race here Uncle Race? He was a good friend of my brother Mike when we lived in the old house."

"Oh," Becca said, moving to stand next to her brother, curiosity getting the better of her shyness now that the man had a name. "What's in here, Mr. Uncle Race?" she asked, pointing at the packages that sat on the chair near their visitor.

"A present for you and your brother," Race announced, feeling more assured by the minute. This was a snap. The kids seemed to like him already. "Go ahead and open it," he told the two as they rushed to the boxes and began ripping off the paper.

"Race," Jennifer whispered sternly, "why did you do this?"

The kids squealed with excitement as they uncovered the boxes and read the labels.

After a few minutes of chaos, during which Jennifer had to hunt up several batteries, both children were holding the latest computerized toys in their hands. They were each outfitted with laser guns, helmets and belts that were coordinated so that they could shoot at each other and have the number of hits recorded on each other's belts. And, the box proclaimed, the guns would interact with a particular cartoon on TV.

As the first squeal of noise beeped its way into Jennifer's ears, she swirled to Race and told him sarcastically, "Great going. Really great." Resigned, she tolerated the next several minutes, feeling each and every computerized beep and buzzer. She had to admit that the kids were having a great time and that the toys were quite clever—except for the terrible noise level. Smiling, she watched Race for a moment while he watched his kids. His face was twisted into an amazed grin, and he almost shuddered every time

one of the rascals raced around him to hide and shoot off
another bolt at each other. Jennifer gave them five minutes to explore their new toys and then called a forced truce.

She had to shout to be heard above the din. "Okay, kids,
put those away. Dinner's ready."

"Aw, Mom," Rick protested, "let us play a little longer.
These guns are really awesome!"

"Absolutely not. From now on you can only use them
either in the playroom over the garage or outdoors."

"Mom," Rebecca protested angrily, "what about the
cartoon program? You have to let us bring them in for that!
You have to!" the little girl insisted dramatically.

"We'll see, Rebecca," Jennifer said firmly. "Right now
you put them back in the boxes and wash your hands for
dinner."

"Wait," Rick demanded, coming in from the other
room. "Don't you remember Uncle Race said that they
worked with the television? I wanna see if they do. Turn it
on," he demanded as he raced over to the remote control
and flipped on his favorite cable channel. Cartoons came
blaring out of the receiver, and Rick and Becca excitedly
blasted their guns at the screen. Nothing happened, so they
tried again while the decibel level rose to something approaching that of a jet plane.

Jennifer restored order, and both children started to
complain. After flipping off the television she calmly
walked over to the overexcited kids and put her hands over
their guns. "One more beep and they're gone. Sorry, folks,
but that's it for now. These guns go away for the night.
We'll look at the instructions later and see if they work with
television. Most of the time, no matter what, they are going
to have to be played with outdoors. They are too loud for
the house."

As both children started to protest again she stuck her
fingers in her mouth and whistled. The twins immediately
shut up, because they knew that their mother only did that
when she was really angry. "No more. First you two thank

your uncle Race for the gifts. Then you go and wash your hands. Dinner is ready, unless you prefer to spend the rest of the night in bed."

Protesting slightly, they both walked off to the bathroom after thanking Race for his gift.

Leaving Race to fend for himself, Jennifer moved back toward the stove and silently took the casserole out of the oven. She put the vegetables into the microwave oven for the last four minutes and took the milk out of the refrigerator. "Do you want milk or ice water?" she inquired as she set out colorful glasses decorated with cartoon characters. "I have a red wine if you'd prefer, but I warn you it's not expensive."

"Wine," Race said, uttering his first word in more than five minutes. This was sheer bedlam, he thought as he walked over to the table and saw the setting for four. How could two small children make so much noise? "Those boxes should have had a warning label on them. I had no idea that they would be so loud," he finally admitted to Jennifer. "I've played the real game in the arcades and the guns aren't anywhere near that loud. My concerts aren't even this loud! Or as hectic."

"You've got to promise me no more presents without permission," Jennifer told him firmly. "I could have told you that those guns were loud. A friend of mine bought something very similar to those last Christmas. Luckily she put the batteries in them and tested them before she gave them to her kids. She took them back before they ever found out and warned all the rest of us. Consider this lesson one and two in parenting. Number one is to check to see if the toy is acceptable to you before you give it." When Race looked at her, she went on, trying to remain stern but unable to hold back a smile. "Lesson two: always check for and bring batteries."

Jennifer was finding it hard to maintain any emotional balance this evening. While she was unable to deny a certain level of self-satisfied smugness because the meeting was

not going the way Race wanted, she was also a bit ashamed
of her children's unbridled behavior.

Tonight was turning out to be a real lesson in how ob-
noxious small children could be. Not only were they both
hungry and tired, they were also overexcited because of the
new toys. From past experience, Jenni knew that they were
also clueing in to her own extreme tension and reflecting it
in their nervous play. Maybe it was the curse of all single
parents, but her kids always seemed really in tune with her
emotions. With the huge waves of anxiety and anger she
was projecting tonight, it was no wonder the kids were
picking it up and acting more out of control than usual.
Well, Race wanted to be a father, let him find out what real
kids were like. After all, he was the cause of all this unease
in the first place.

"Kids," Jennifer yelled down the hall. "Put those guns
back in the boxes," she insisted when she heard the faint
beep of electronic noise from upstairs. Immediately she
shouted, "I heard that. Surrender those guns and get your
behinds down here to eat. Now!"

There was one rebellious beep, then the sound of trudg-
ing feet. The microwave added its own beep as the kids
came down and Jenni waved them over to the table. During dinner Race made several attempts to get to know the
twins, but they soon decided that they were not interested
in answering what they saw as dumb questions.

The evening went from bad to worse when, somehow,
they picked up on the subtle behavior that told them that
Race was interested in their mother, as well as in them.
Once they discovered that Race was not giving them total
attention, they perversely wanted his attention back. Suddenly they would not shut up even long enough to eat. They
vied with each other for Race's attention and succeeded in
making the dinner table another madhouse. Good manners vanished until Jenni threatened them with no dessert.

Rick refused to eat his broccoli until the very end and
then complained that it was too cold. Becca managed to

spill her milk, almost getting Race's lap. Finally the food was gone, and Jennifer stood up to begin clearing the table. The twins were kicking the table legs when Race mentioned that he'd known their mother as a child. They perked up and gave him their undivided attention.

"Wow! You really knew Mom when she was a kid?" Becca asked. "Long, long ago?"

"Did you know our daddy, too?" Rick asked, more bluntly.

"No more questions," Jennifer interrupted quickly. "Can I interest any of you in some dessert? There are brownies and I've got vanilla or fudge ripple ice cream."

By the time the dishes were cleaned up and both children had bowls of fudge ripple ice cream in front of them, the question was forgotten. The rest of the evening passed in a blur. Race insisted that he wanted coffee and parked himself in front of the television with the children while Jennifer went to put some on to perk. When it was time for the kids to go to bed, they both protested vehemently.

"Look, Race," Jennifer finally told him bluntly, "both of these kids are tired and overexcited. They need baths and to choose their clothes for school tomorrow. I'm going to put them to bed. It's time for you to go home."

"Ah, Mom," Rick protested in the whiny voice that he used when he was tired. "Uncle Race was going to tell me about the time he threw a football to the Dolphins. He actually knows their quarterback," he told his mother, hero worship beginning to show on his face.

"I'm glad for him, honey, but you'll have to hear about it another time. Now off to bed. Say good-night and thank you to Mr. Jameson," Jennifer ordered, her no-nonsense voice telling the kids that they had pushed their luck as far as possible. Pushing the twins up the stairs in front of her, she said, "Lock the door behind you, Race," and left him sitting in her den.

Forty-five minutes later she walked down the stairs, drying her hands on the towels that she carried with her, feeling the tiredness of another day seep deeply into her. The first few minutes after the children went to sleep were some of the sweetest of every evening. She knew she had an hour or so of absolutely free time before she had to do anything.

"Race," she exclaimed as she pushed open the door and saw him sitting right where she'd left him with a grim look on his face. "Why are you still here?"

Looking at Jennifer as she walked into the room, Race stifled an impulse to pull her into his arms and shake her, or kiss her, or both. She looked as tired as he felt, Race realized. Her blue jeans had a milk spill down one leg, and her bright green T-shirt, with its large white emblem proclaiming Just Say No, was damp and wrinkled. Her hair was not neatly combed, and all her makeup had long since vanished. The more he thought about it, the more he wanted to kiss her.

"I wanted to talk," Race told her softly. "Those kids are quite a handful. I had no idea. Are they always like this?"

"Pretty much, although usually they aren't so wired. They normally don't get hundred-dollar gifts before dinner and have a guest who's so busy asking them questions that he doesn't have time to eat," she observed wryly. "I'm sure the casserole wasn't up to your usual standards, but you could have tried."

"Jennifer, stop it. The food was fine. It wasn't that. It's the kids. What did you tell them about me?" he asked, anger coming back as he remembered the evening. "Why don't they like me?"

"What?" Jennifer asked in disbelief, her voice rising. "You think that I told them to be nasty to you? Are you kidding? What did you expect? I admit that my kids aren't perfect, but then they are real kids. I didn't make them put on their restaurant manners, but you never told me that you expected little robots. This is real life. Real kids. They don't know you from Adam, and I thought that they were very patient with all your dumb questions. Not that many second-graders are at all interested in talking about world affairs. Or telling you what subject that they like best. Exactly what did you expect?''

When Race looked at her, his gray eyes honestly confused, Jennifer sighed. ''I know, you wanted television kids. Perfect, cute and clever. Kids whose little arguments are always fast and funny. No spilled milk, no whiny, tired complaints. Sorry, Race. I'd love kids like that, too, but as far as I know they don't exist. If you think about it, those television kids are cute because they are only on for half an hour a week. They never sass back or whine. Think back to our childhood,'' she suggested. ''You were no angel. I can't count the number of nights that your parents sent you to bed without your supper and you climbed down the drainpipe and came over to our house for some dinner. Remember?''

Feeling suddenly older than him, she added, ''Why don't you just plain relax? You don't have to impress Rick and Becca or buy their affection. There isn't even any law that says you have to like them. You can go home anytime you please.''

''I wasn't trying to buy them,'' Race interjected before Jennifer could go on. ''I just wanted to give them something from me.''

Sighing, Jennifer wondered how she was going to deal with this Race. A father who honestly, it seemed, wanted to get to know his kids. Biting her lip, she reminded herself about his lies, the fabulous ability that he had to sound sincere and mean absolutely nothing by it. Why he wasn't acting in more movies, she didn't know.

Patiently she told him for the third time, ''We have a deal, remember. You can get to know them and be their friend, but no more.'' She waited until he looked up at her before she went on, deliberately keeping his eye as she told him, ''I don't want them hurt. No more presents unless there is a reason. No more name-dropping. How long do you think you're going to be able to keep your presence here quiet if you keep telling the kids about all the famous people you know? Rick is impressed that you know someone on the Dolphins team, and I guarantee he'll tell every boy at school tomorrow. It's going to get around if you do too much of it. Then you're going to have two choices. Either you'll have to introduce Rick and his gang to some of these famous people or the kids are going to think you're lying to them.''

''Lying?'' Race asked, realizing that Jennifer was right. Most people didn't know many famous quarterbacks, or at least not more than one or two of them. He was trying too hard to impress them, his beautiful, mouthy kids. ''I was trying to make conversation,'' he admitted. ''I guess I'm not very good at it. I wanted them to like me.''

Her honesty was pulled forth by his vulnerability. Although a part of Jennifer told her to shut up and let him struggle with his own children, she couldn't. She found that his need was too great and her heart was too involved.

''Nobody has a lock on any one way to deal with kids. The only reason I can talk to them is that I've worked my way up. You start with the first 'Mama,' and the rest just comes naturally. You're trying too hard. Kids are the most honest beings in this world. They don't lie unless they've been taught to, and my kids are probably more honest than most. I've tried to bring them up so that they're in touch with their emotions and so they aren't going to behave in some particular way just because someone tells them to. There's a fine line between squashing children and indulging them. I think I'm a bit too far on the lenient side, but it's hard to be absolutely certain. Sometimes you plain don't know if you're right or not. Being a parent turned out to be a lot harder than I ever expected.''

Race looked at Jennifer's serious face and had to smile tenderly at her. For the first time she was talking to him as though she were admitting that the twins were his. Not that he had even the faintest doubt about their biological parentage. Finally he'd made some progress in his quest to prove that he could be a real father and her real husband. For the first time since he'd seen Jennifer at that press conference last summer, he was encouraged. She trusted him enough to be honest about her own self-doubts as a mother. "You seem to be doing a good job of it."

"Sometimes I don't know," she admitted with a sigh. "If Mom hadn't been with me, I don't know what I would have done. I coped all right with baby-sitters and friends when I was in school, but it wasn't easy. Since Dad died and we combined our households, it's been a lot easier for me and much better for the twins."

Deliberately he asked another question, trying to draw Jennifer from the past to the present. He could not change the past, or even much of the present, but he had high hopes for their future. He knew that Jennifer was still attracted to him, at least physically, and he'd start working on that. That and her innate goodness of heart. "What did I do wrong?"

"Not a lot, really. You're just in too much of a hurry. There's no instant love, except in the movies. Never with children. They have to learn to trust you, to come to you, rather than the other way around. You can't buy their affection. There aren't enough toys in the world."

"Nor enough money to buy your affection, my Jennifer," Race whispered, forcibly restraining himself as he looked at the woman sitting next to him. Things were going too well. He didn't want to grab her and scare her off. Slowly, he told himself, slowly, as the blood burned in his veins.

He turned to look at Jennifer. "Becca is beautiful, Jenni," he said quietly. "She looks so much like my sister Rebecca it gives me a little shock every time I see her."

"Yes," Jennifer admitted, "I can see the resemblance myself. More so every year. I ran across some old pictures last year, and the likeness is amazing."

"I can't wait until my mother sees her," Race mentioned. "She's going to die when she sees the twins."

"Race," Jennifer reminded him sharply, "you can't tell anyone. You promised. I won't have the kids hurt."

"Well, think about it. It's not fair keeping them from their grandparents." Race was unashamedly using every trick he could think of, and he noted that this plea had an impact on Jennifer. If all else failed, he'd invite his parents up to meet the twins. At least that would be one more claim that she could not deny.

To Jennifer's relief, Race dropped the uncomfortable subject and asked for more coffee. Although she felt that Race had forfeited all rights to the twins by his own behavior and life-style, she had always felt badly about denying both the twins and the Huntingtons their family relationship. Silently she wished that things were not so complicated.

"What's with the T-shirt?" Race asked idly as she dropped a spoonful of sugar into his black coffee.

"Oh," Jennifer looked down, laughing at her more-than-appropriate choice of clothing. "It's an antidrug club that they sponsor in school. The Just Say No Club. They're trying to use peer pressure to give kids permission to say no to drugs and sex instead of yes. We had a club meeting this afternoon, and I left it on."

That was the truth, Jennifer told herself, not wanting to think of the motives that had led her to keep the shirt on after she'd gotten home. She could have changed. Both of the children had, although that was because they'd both spilled chocolate syrup down their fronts at the ice-cream party they'd attended. Maybe she'd figured the bright green color would be ugly enough to discourage Race. Or that she'd be adult enough to do what the shirt suggested—Just Say No.

As she sat next to Race on the sofa, she made the mistake of gazing up into his warm gray eyes. How was it, she wondered, that those eyes could look so different? They could be as cold as ice or as hot as glowing embers. Right now they were sparkling in appreciation of her. Her common sense protested as Race reached up to trace the line of her cheek with his finger.

"Thank you, Jennifer," he whispered as he leaned over to brush a light kiss across her freckled nose.

"For what?" Jenni asked, lost in the blaze of his eyes and the feel of fire that his finger ignited on her soft skin.

"For having my children," Race told her. "You could have had an abortion."

"A what?" Jennifer said, sitting back abruptly. Blast the man, he'd done it again. He'd lulled her into wanting him and then proceeded to insult her again. "An abortion? It's time for you to leave, Race," she told him, rising to her feet. When would she learn never to trust herself around Race? For her he was like chocolate for a diabetic. Rich but dangerous.

"Go?"

"Yes. Get up and walk out of my house."

"What's the matter now?" Race protested. "What did I do to make you angry?"

"Nothing. Nothing," Jennifer said, relieved that she'd overreacted without him noticing. Now that she'd moved a few feet away from his potent spell, she realized that he hadn't really insulted her. He probably thought that he'd given her a compliment. It was such a different world that he lived in, a world where abortions were commonplace and physical perfection counted for more than human values. Not for her, Jennifer realized. Suddenly, to her horror, she found herself talking to Race, sharing feelings that she'd never revealed to another.

"I thought about it, Race," she slowly admitted. "For a while, before I told my parents. But I couldn't do it. I just couldn't." Tears welled up in Jennifer's eyes as she recalled the exact day when she'd finally faced the fact that she was pregnant. And all alone. The day she'd known in her heart that her baby, conceived in love, was a part of her that she could never harm.

Thank goodness her family had understood and stood by her through it all. She would never have made it without her parents or the loving support of her brother Mike and his wife. Stephanie had given birth only nine months earlier than Jenni, and she had helped Jenni through her pregnancy more than anyone else. Jenni had been very fortunate in having four wonderful people behind her, supporting her in her decision.

Race stood, touched by her tears, and hesitantly pulled her into his arms. "I'm sorry. So sorry," he told her, his heart aching. How he wished he had spared her all the pain, how he wished he'd been more responsible. But then, if he had, this moment wouldn't have happened, and his two children wouldn't exist. Suddenly his heart seemed to swell and he found himself choked up. Tightening his grip on Jenni's slight form, he buried his face in her fragrant red-gold hair. Finally it hit him, emotionally and intellectually. He was a father. Those two black-haired scamps upstairs were his children. His. Part of him and Jennifer.

Helplessly he drew Jennifer to him and kissed her. Tenderness guided his hands as they soothed the tension in her shoulders. His mouth brushed her brows, closing each eye with a feather-light touch. Sipping from her mouth, he worshiped first the top lip with his tongue, then the bottom, sighing as her mouth slowly opened for him. With care he began to explore the sweetness that she offered so freely to him.

Tenderness turned fierce as desire instantly roared through them. Fire flashed as his tongue caressed hers, calling forth a response, demanding a flame to meet his own and a surrender to meet his need. His hands moved to caress her waiting breasts. Their hard tips beckoned him through both her T-shirt and her thin bra, and he expertly moved his hand down the back of her spine, pulling the shirt up with his hand. In one practiced move her bra was unfastened and her breast captured by his waiting hand. "Jennifer," he whispered against her neck as he strung fiery kisses down her collarbone and dipped to touch her throbbing breast with the tip of his tongue.

Suddenly the electronic beep of one of Race's phaser guns drifted down the stairway. Jennifer was instantly jolted back to reality, a reality that included Race holding her bare breast in his hand with his mouth sucking gently on its tip. "Let go of me," she demanded, pulling away from him, jerking the shirt down to cover herself. "You promised to leave me alone," she sputtered, frightened by her own uncontrollable response to his merest touch.

Her breasts still heaving, she looked at him with fire in her eyes. "Get out!" she ordered in a low voice, anger and humiliation making her voice deep and vibrant. Pointing her finger toward the door, she said, "I can't believe you did that. The kids might come down at any moment." Forcing herself to calm down, she tried to sound firm. "Promise me you won't try that again. Don't treat me like all your other women. You already proved your magic with me once. If I give in to you again, I'll never forgive myself. Don't you see that?"

"Jennifer, love..." Race began. He could see that she was really upset. Dimly he realized that if he, as experienced as he was, could be shocked senseless by their explosive reaction to each other, she must be doubly so. Softly he tried to explain their remarkable response. "Don't you understand?"

When she didn't respond, Race went to her and told her, "The problem is not that I've got the most wonderful technique in the world."

"It is, too," she snapped. "It has to be that. You've got it down to a science."

"No, Jenni," Race said quietly, talking to himself as much as to her. Awe tinged his voice as he figured out the real answer. "It's that we both react to each other like that. You think it's technique, but it's not. Take my word for it. I've been kissed by some of the world's most practiced women, and nothing has ever hit me like this. It's like everything vanished except you. It's something more than technique, something much, much more.''

"No," Jennifer said, looking at Race with suspicious eyes. His entire face radiated honesty and desire. With his open hand he reached for her, taking one of the silken strands of her hair in his finger and twirling it absently.

"It's magic, love. When we touch...I can't resist you one bit more than you can resist me. We belong together. This magic is stronger than all the years. All the others. You are mine, and I am yours."

"No, no," Jennifer told him, shaking her head. "Just shut up. I don't want to hear one more word. Go away. Keep your line and your wonderful lies for somebody else. We don't belong together. You belong in the Guinness Book of World Records for...for...the most pathological lover, and I belong in it for being the—''

Race interrupted her, trying not to laugh. "The most pathological lover?" His hurt was tempered by the realization that she would not be reacting so vehemently if she were not feeling the same attraction. "Where did you come up with that?"

"I just made it up. It's a perfect description of you. You lie every time you touch me, or any other woman. Every time you open your mouth and start telling your pretty stories." Walking over to the door, she opened it silently and gazed at him with a pained expression in her eyes. "Go home, Race. I won't deny your seeing the children, but you must promise no more passes."

"I'll leave for now, but you know that you can't trust a pathological lover, so I won't bother making promises you know I won't keep," he told her as he touched her cheek on the way out the door, frustrated when he saw her stiffen at his touch. He was nonetheless determined to prove his sincerity. "I will promise I won't rush you. I'm going to prove to you that we belong together, Miss Grange. For more than one night. For the rest of our lives."

"We do *not* belong together," Jennifer vowed as she watched him walk across the yard, wishing she could convince herself. She would be fine if she could figure out a way to stop melting every time he touched her and to stop wanting to believe his lies.

Chapter Six

With a great deal of diligence and a touch of luck, Jennifer managed to avoid spending any time alone with Race for most of the next week. When he took the kids to a movie she had to see a feature that was playing at the next cinema, and she arranged to come home separately. When they played miniature golf she had to review a new restaurant with her editor. She had a deadline to meet when Race invited Rick and Becca over to his house to learn to play pool, and Margo accompanied them in her place. Somehow Jennifer's schedule seemed to conflict with whatever plans Race made with the children, and that made it possible for her to keep her distance from him.

Race realized what was happening after a couple of days, but he was stymied. He had to find a way to get close to Jennifer. One afternoon, as Margo was sitting with him on the side porch of her home drinking iced tea and watching the twins play on the swing set in the back yard, he asked her advice.

Though Margo certainly understood Jenni's fears, the older woman was less prejudiced against her old next-door neighbor than was her daughter. Because Racine and her late son had been the best of friends all through high school, Margo had known Race in a way Jenni hadn't. Margo could see Race's appeal, the intense sensual pull that he exuded without even thinking. No woman alive could be totally unaware of his appeal. Her poor daughter had never had a chance all those years ago.

Initially Margo had thought it was an act, a practiced act, but after a few days in his company she had begun to wonder. As she'd watched him patiently throwing a football with his kids a few minutes earlier, she'd finally realized that he was naturally sensuous. A man who had sexual charisma in overwhelming doses. The fact that he was a talented singer made it inevitable that his popularity would soar and that his ego would soar not far behind it.

"Race," Margo asked him, "do you try to be so attractive to the opposite sex?"

"No," he answered finally. He knew what she was asking. Heaven knew he'd been asked the same question over and over in his career. She wanted to know what drew women to him, and he really didn't know how to answer her. She was his lady's mother, in some ways more of a mother to him than his own mother. It was Margo to whom he had confided his hopes and dreams, Margo who had bought him his first guitar. She deserved the truth, as much of it as he knew. "I don't know what it is. I started to notice in high school, and after. Women think I'm coming on to them even when I'm not. And when I really am, they just . . ."

"They just surrender," Margo finished for him.

"Yeah. Sometimes," Race mumbled, feeling uncomfortable. "Usually." It was like talking about his sex life, his overactive sex life, with his own mother. He knew he'd been like a child with his hand in the cookie jar the first few years of his career, but that was over now. He hadn't touched a woman since that July day when he'd kissed Jenni. No one would do but her. Not that she would ever believe that.

Reaching over, Margo patted his arm and looked him in the eye. "I wasn't trying to make you uncomfortable. I've known for a long time that you are the twins' father."

A glow came over Race's face when Margo said that. And at that moment, Margo succumbed to her instincts. Race really did love those children. He deserved a place in their lives. What he felt about her daughter was another story.

"Do you know that you're the first one who really admits that they're mine?" he asked her in a soft voice. "Jennifer keeps pretending that they're not." Quietly he turned to her and said, "I'm not blaming her. She's afraid that I'll try to take them, or hurt her. I won't."

"I think I finally believe you, Racine." Margo said, unconsciously using his old name as a sign of her growing trust. "But she's been through a lot. She's scared."

With a bittersweet trace of regret in his husky voice, he said slowly, "I know. I really don't blame her. I haven't exactly done right by her or my kids."

Patting his shoulder, Margo told him, "What matters is the future. You can't change the past."

Turning, Race stared into the older woman's sympathetic blue eyes and asked an honest question. "Do you think I should stay and fight for her?"

"If you're absolutely sure that you won't change your mind and that you want her once and for all. You'll have to love her with all your heart, and that means marriage and fidelity to Jenni. If you can't promise her that, just be her friend, the father of your children, and leave her alone. You've hurt her enough. Think it over before you start something that you can't stop. Now I'm going in to start dinner. Are you going to stay, or has Jameson concocted another feast?"

"He's making hamburgers for us all, if that's all right."
Race replied. "By the way, he asked me if you had any
special gentleman friends. Do you?"

Blushing prettily, Margo said, "No. You may tell him
that I'm not keeping company with anyone," before she
went into the house.

Forcing her mind off the older man next door, Margo
considered the situation between Racine and her daughter
for a moment. He seemed sincere, but there was still an
element of doubt in her mind. Even if—and with Race this
was a huge if—Race stayed true to Jennifer, he was a rich
and famous man who would make many demands on and
changes in their lives. All she knew for sure was that Racine deserved to know his own children.

For a few moments that evening, Race caught up with
Jennifer. She was leaving to see a movie with her friend
Victoria when Race walked up to the door and waited there
for her to come out.

As always, Jennifer was formal and polite. She introduced Race to Vicki, noting that she was her lawyer, and
then left. Race didn't interfere. He took her hand in his,
looked deeply into her eyes and softly told her to have a
lovely evening.

Victoria tried to encourage her but could offer no new
advice. "Now that I've met him," she said sympathetically, "I have some idea of your problem. That man is
drop-dead gorgeous. I don't know how you resist him,
especially with him living next door and constantly after
you. I know he's a louse, but you have to admit that he's
got something."

"You got that right!" Jennifer had agreed glumly. "I
wish he'd take his something and move away. Where he
isn't disturbing my sleep."

"No comment," Vicki said, then after a moment she
added, "I know you don't want to hear it, Jenni, but I'm
beginning to wonder if Race might not be as black a character as we've painted him. I almost wonder if he might be

just what you need to shake your life up a bit." She cut short Jenni's attempt to interrupt. "You know I don't want to see you hurt, but in the last several years you've become so well-ordered and conservative that even I sometimes wonder what happened to the carefree tomboy I grew up with."

As if Victoria's interference wasn't enough, her own mother chose that evening to have a mother-daughter talk with her. "Honey, you can't avoid him forever."

"Mom," Jennifer protested. "Not you, too. Victoria's been after me to confront Race, but I don't want to. I'm trying to wait him out. Sooner or later he'll get bored with the kids and leave."

"I don't know," her mother said carefully. "I've spent a lot of time with him this past two weeks, and I think he plans on being a permanent part of their life. Yours, too, if you'll let him."

Jenni turned to her mother, her face vulnerable. "How can I trust him again?" Her eyes focused on the far wall as she admitted the truth. "I still want him, Mom. After all these years, after all the pain, he kisses me once and I turn into mush, like some dumb teenager. I don't want to repeat the same mistake. I won't let him hurt me again."

"Daughter, I wish I knew what to tell you." Sighing deeply, Margo reached out to stroke her hair as she had when Jennifer had been a small child. "My only advice is to listen to your heart. Maybe he really has changed. If you don't give him a chance, you'll never know. Giving love never makes you a fool, only a human." With a warm hug and a kiss on the cheek, Margo left her daughter, saying "I'll be here no matter what you decide."

Jennifer spent one more long, restless night, thinking of Race and her mother's advice. She hadn't been alone with Race since the night he'd kissed her and she'd discovered that her reactions to him hadn't changed over the years. She wondered if she was wrong to ignore him. Did she dare believe that Race had changed or that there was some place in her life for him? More importantly, was there any place in his glamorous life for her or the kids?

Finally she got out the old album that she'd filled with articles about Race and looked at all the pictures of him with beautiful women. He had been so very young, Jennifer realized when she saw his face, full of an almost innocent awe as he gazed at the various women he was dating. Maybe, she thought as she put the book away and lay down for a few hours of sleep, he's grown up. Perhaps they both could put the past behind them and give the future a chance.

Saturday morning dawned beautiful and clear. It was the beginning of October, but today could have been May, warm and lovely. Becca and Rick came barreling into Jennifer's bedroom at nine o'clock and landed on either side of her on the bed.

"Mom," Becca demanded sweetly, "wake up."

"Mom," Rick chimed in, "get up. We're supposed to go to Carowinds today. It's the last day of the season and we need to buy our new tickets for next year." Shaking her, her son added the kicker. "You promised! Last month when we were there you promised that we'd get season tickets for next year. You said it'd be cheaper. Please."

"Pul-eeze, Mommy," Becca added, dragging out every syllable as she snuggled up to her mother's side and threw her arms around her neck.

"Okay, okay," Jennifer said, emerging from the covers with a lunge. "You rascals remember everything." With an arm around each of them, Jennifer captured them and drew their warm, pajama-clad bodies toward hers. For a second she allowed herself the luxury of holding them tightly and kissed each of their silky black heads before she released them. "Out, you scamps. Go get ready. I'll get dressed and we'll leave in a half hour. Both of you put on your tennis shoes. No sandals."

Smiling, Jennifer crawled out of bed. Smoothing down the old T-shirt that she slept in, she caught a glimpse of herself in the mirror and grimaced. Dark circles were visible beneath her eyes. She needed more sleep, plain and simple.

The smell of coffee drifted up to Jennifer as she dressed, pulling on her most comfortable outfit. Soon she was dressed in light green chambray slacks with a matching jacket and a green-and-white striped blouse. Grabbing one of her large canvas purses, Jenni walked out of the bedroom, ready for a fun day with her kids. She always enjoyed Carowinds, and with the season tickets they'd be able to go more often for barely more than the price of two admissions each.

"Ready to go?" Jennifer asked as she rounded the corner. "Who was the angel who made the coffee?" she asked before she focused her eyes on a large, masculine form wearing a red polo shirt and jeans and perched on a stool at her kitchen counter.

"Race. What are you doing here?"

"You may call me angel," he said teasingly, determined to keep it all very light. "I made you some coffee," he told her, offering her a cup as a peace offering, fixed just the way she liked it. "Your little rug rats invited me to Carowinds with them." With a smile that echoed the children's enthusiasm, he asked, "Do you mind if I come?"

Rick and Becca jumped up and down, shouting, "Mommy, Mommy, please let Uncle Race go. He'll love it."

Looking at all three pairs of eyes pleading with her, Jennifer surrendered. What harm could a few hours at an amusement park do? It wasn't as if they'd be alone, was it? she asked herself cautiously. "All right. Off we go."

"Do you mind driving?" Race asked Jennifer as they stepped out of the house. "It's been so long, I don't recognize half of the roads here anymore. This area has grown phenomenally since I left." Slipping on his aviator sunglasses and another wide-brimmed hat, Race quietly helped the twins get into the back seat and reminded them to buckle their seat belts before Jennifer could. Just in time she bit back a comment that he seemed to be taking his fathering duties very seriously.

This outing might be more difficult than she'd initially thought. It was obvious that Race had developed a real rapport with the twins during the last few days, and Jenni didn't know if that pleased her or not. She had been so sure that he'd be gone by now. But he hadn't left. He was still here and giving every indication that he was enjoying the kids.

Putting on her own sunglasses against the bright Carolina sun, Jenni thoughtfully pulled out of her driveway and headed for the South Carolina border. She occasionally glanced at Race, but he seemed content to have her drive, making only occasional comments about the changes that he noticed in the town since he'd been there last. Within an hour the car was parked and the kids were jumping up and down in eagerness.

"Remember the rule," Jenni told the twins. "You don't run off. If anybody gets lost, you go to one of the workers and tell them you're meeting your mom at the end of the main street. Now, let me put sunscreen on your faces and we'll be ready."

As she rubbed the white lotion onto Rick's nose, Race moved up close behind her. When she finished, he murmured, "I need some too, Mom," and stood there until she forced herself to rub some lotion over his nose and upper cheeks. His skin was warm and smooth, soft and wonderful. Jennifer had an unexpected urge to sample its texture with her lips.

Race insisted on paying for all their tickets, and for a moment Jennifer started to protest. But the the sight of the twins' enthusiastic faces forced her to swallow her pride. After all, he could afford it. Soon the four of them walked into the park and were standing on the main street. The kids had a wonderful time with the black brick line that ran down the middle of the road. One side was North Carolina. The other was South Carolina. It was not too often that you could stand with one foot in two states.

"The real question is," Race told Jennifer solemnly as he pulled up her sunglasses and looked directly into her eyes, "exactly where are you when you are right on the line?"

"That's for you to tell me," she whispered back, knowing he was talking about their relationship and the fine line of distrust that Jennifer would not allow herself to cross.

"Later," Race promised, bending down to let her see the desire blazing behind his sunglasses. "Later we'll cross that line together."

Suddenly Becca and Rick returned from walking up and down the narrow brick line and the day began in earnest. Holding hands, they started to the right and rode all the rides that didn't seem too grown-up for the kids.

It was one of those absolutely perfect Southern days. The temperature hovered around seventy-five, there was a slight breeze and the air was soft. The park was not terribly crowded and the lines were short.

Following the twins' example, Jennifer let herself go. She and Becca chased Race and Rick on the old-fashioned cars, almost catching up with them. They had so much fun that they got in line again and rode once more. This time Becca and Jennifer were in the lead, and they enjoyed winning the race.

The antique carousel was fantastic. Getting off and then on again, they rode the painstakingly refurbished merry-go-round several times. Becca and Rick were delighted with their freewheeling mother. For a change she was totally carefree, almost giddy. Finally they got off for the last time, mildly dizzy, and set off looking for lunch.

An hour later, Race found himself standing next to Jennifer as they watched their offspring burying themselves in a pool of large Ping-Pong-type balls. Although they were almost too old for Smurf Island, the twins wanted to do their favorite things there, and that involved the ball jump, as well as the Bamm Bamm Boat float and the Scooby Doo roller coaster.

Suddenly Jenni turned to Race and asked him a question that had been preying on her mind since he'd moved in. No one was near them, and they could talk in total privacy.

"What do you do with yourself during the day, Race? When the kids are at school?"

"Lots of different things. I've been writing quite a bit lately. Stuff for a new album. And I told you that I'm doing the music for a film, a sort of updated cowboy movie. Also, I've been—" Pausing, Race turned away.

"You've been what?" Jenni prompted, intrigued by the look on his face.

"Trying to write a script. About a friend of mine who... Never mind." Race was quiet for a moment, looking at his children and their exuberant joy. He didn't want to tell Jennifer about his past, about the tragedy that had made him reevaluate his life and find himself wanting. Not now, in this place of fun and childhood innocence.

"That sounds like a lot of work," Jenni finally said when Race remained silent. "It must be fascinating to do a movie score. This is your first one, isn't it?"

"Yeah, though I've had a few of my songs used before in different movie soundtracks. Hey, it's no big deal. Why don't you come over sometime and I'll show you some of the rough cuts they've sent me and explain how I go about working the music into the story." Enthusiastically Race continued, "I'm just getting the hang of it. Maybe you'd have some ideas I could use. It should be right up your alley as a film critic."

"I doubt that I would be of much help," Jenni said, suddenly feeling rather presumptuous. Race was scoring a major movie, and she was a rather new movie reviewer from a medium-size Southern town. "I'd be a little bit out of my league. Don't they need you back in L.A.?"

"No. It doesn't matter to them as long as I do the work. I use the phone a lot and good old overnight-delivery mail." Without a pause, he gripped her arm and looked directly into her eyes. "What was that crack about being out of your league supposed to mean?"

"Just what it sounded like. You are a superstar, Race, and I'm a small-time movie reviewer struggling to keep things afloat. Never mind that, what did you mean when you said that they didn't care where you work? Do they know where you are? And why?" Jenni asked, suddenly panicked by the thought of anyone from his life intruding on hers.

"No. All the details are handled through my agent. Don't worry. No one knows where I am except my agent and my lawyer. I call everyone else, not vice versa. I promised that to you and the kids. Remember?"

"I remember. I just hope that you do," Jennifer told him as he went to help the twins put their shoes back on. As they walked toward the next section of Carowinds, Race reached down and grabbed Jenni's hand. "Don't think about it all. I'm just a man today. An ordinary father having a wonderful afternoon with his lady and his kids. Have fun!" he implored her as he ran over and bought her and the twins huge helium-filled Mylar balloons shaped like cartoon characters' faces.

Laughing as Race tied the silver balloon around her wrist, Jenni let it all go. Feeling as light as one of the balloons, she grabbed Race's hand, and they raced up behind the twins. Before they left the park, Race insisted on buying them all matching T-shirts with the Carowinds logo as a souvenir of their wonderful day.

The sun was setting as Jenni and Race drove slowly back to the house. The kids sat in the back seat, clutching their bags of T-shirts and cotton candy, their balloons in their faces, so tired that they barely stirred. Neither of them objected when Jenni told them they had to go straight to bed when they got home.

"I'm glad we decided to eat dinner back there," Race said, looking back at his exhausted kids. "I'm not sure that they're going to make it back to the house awake."

"It's a toss-up, all right. I can't remember ever having a day like this. I don't know when I've walked that much. Or ate that much junk food. I swear we tried everything that they made. It's nothing short of amazing that the twins haven't gotten sick. And my feet are about ready to fall off."

"Mine, too. You know, Jenni," Race said, sitting sideways on the seat and letting his arm reach across to capture a strand of her silky hair in his hands, "this has been one of the best days in my life."

"Mine, too," Jennifer agreed without thinking.

"It feels right, doesn't it?" Race questioned gently. "The four of us being together. A family like we should be."

Pulling into the driveway, Jennifer looked into his soft gray eyes and feared she was lost. "Oh, Race. Don't do this to me. It will never work."

"Yes, it will. Don't worry, I'm not rushing you this time. Never again," he promised as he quietly opened the back door and reached in to guide his sleepy son into the house. Jennifer helped Becca get out the other side and caught her balloon just as it headed out the car door.

With the sleepy, grouchy children in tow, they managed to get into the house and up the stairs without any major accidents. Both kids were nearly out on their feet, and they complained loudly when they were forced to brush their teeth.

"You can't go to sleep with that cotton candy on your teeth," Jennifer explained firmly when Becca whined that she was too tired. Finally both kids had brushed their teeth and gone to the bathroom and were clad in their night clothing. Race smiled tenderly at Rick as he tucked his son into bed and brushed the sleepy boy's head with a kiss.

"Night, Uncle Race," his son said, reaching up with trusting arms to give the tall man a hug. "Thank you for the balloons."

Jennifer bumped into Race as she exited Becca's room and blinked at the expression on the strong man's face. A part of her heart melted as she saw him standing there, trying not to cry, touched by something that had obviously gone on as he'd put Rick to bed.

As she touched his hand softly he turned to gather her in his arms. "Jenni, I've missed so much," he rasped, burying his head in her soft hair.

"Come and have some coffee," Jennifer suggested diffidently, "and I'll show you my picture albums, if you'd like."

Race whistled slowly as Jennifer came down the stairs a few minutes later with eight or nine photo albums. "Didn't want to take any chances on forgetting anything?" he joked as he helped her set the books down on the coffee table.

Sipping coffee and nibbling on some homemade cookies, Race and Jennifer spent the next hour looking at a pictorial record of their children. From their first day in the hospital to their last Fourth of July, Jennifer had faithfully taken pictures of each and every major event in her children's lives. She showed Race shots of everything from their first steps to their first day in school.

Laughingly she shared many of the warm, silly stories that can appeal only to a parent, and was surprised to find Race listening intently to her every word. Finally she leaned back, tired not only from the day but from the journey of memories that the pictures had triggered.

"You've done a remarkable job," Race told her. "It must have been horrible when Mike and his son died. Then to lose your father only two years after that. I'm sorry that I didn't make it to the funerals."

"It's all right, Race. There wasn't anything you could have done to help. The twins were too young to realize when Mike and Mike, Jr., died. They do remember Grandpa a little bit. You didn't know about—" Cutting herself off, Jennifer sighed and leaned back on the couch, closing her eyes. "I was going to be nasty, but you don't really deserve it. I think I understand for the first time that you've missed as much, if not more, than I have. I may not have had the glamour and excitement, but I've had something as precious, something real and lasting." Finally Jennifer began to release the anger and resentment she'd felt at having been left alone with the children while Race had been off having fun. With a start, Jenni realized that she was the one who'd been living a full life, not Race.

"That you have," Race agreed, reaching over to enfold her in his arms. "Thank you for sharing your memories with me. It means a great deal to me, love."

Enjoying the warmth and comfort for a second, Jennifer rested her head on Race's broad chest. He felt so good to her, their embrace felt so right. She wished with all her heart that this could be real and that she could spend the rest of her life knowing that Race was her safe haven and other half. Shocked, she pulled back and looked at him with dazed eyes. She refused to feel that way again, especially with Race.

Jennifer moved to pull away but was captured instead by strong hands. Slowly Race lowered his mouth to hers. He gently fitted their mouths together and coaxed a response from her. Sighing, Jenni adjusted her arms around his neck and pulled him closer. After a long, tender and somehow reassuring kiss, Race reluctantly moved away from her and pulled her to her feet. "I'll see you tomorrow," he promised as he let himself out.

Jennifer walked up to bed confused, grateful and, absurdly, disappointed. After the day and night they'd spent together, she felt closer to Race than at any other time since he'd burst into her life. She wondered again if she could successfully shut him out of her life.

Twice the next day Race started to call Jennifer but didn't. He thought she might need a little time to try to absorb all the feelings from yesterday. He certainly did. He'd been unbearably touched by the visual record of his children's history and found it hard to accept that those years were lost to him forever. He wanted to have shared all that with Jennifer.

Finally he could wait no more. After dinner was over he crossed the lawns, carrying a new croquet set, and knocked on Jennifer's door. He had been very careful not to give the children any more presents, but he didn't think a croquet set, especially if he kept it at his house, was out of line. Not now that they were so close to being a family.

Margo answered the door and smiled warmly at him. She had come home last night from a date with Jameson about an hour after Race had left, and she'd smiled at the albums that were still open on the coffee table. Things were definitely going well if Jenni was relaxed enough to show Racine the albums, Margo decided.

"Great idea. I haven't played croquet in years. Remember the set Mike had? We played so much the balls were almost chipped bare," Margo told him as she spied the wooden mallets and balls. "The kids are out back. I'm sure they'd love to help you set up the course." Shyly Margo asked, "Is Jameson going to play, too?"

"Sure. The more the merrier. There are six mallets and balls per set. Just right."

"We'll only need five tonight," Margo said delicately. "Jennifer has a previous commitment." When Race started to comment, Margo continued quickly, "She promised to attend a civic dinner with Jeff Wenset, the twins' doctor, two months ago. She can't break the date. Don't ask her to."

"A date?" Race repeated in a deep voice. "She's going out with another man?"

"That's what I said," Margo told him, secretly amused at the genuine surprise on his face. "She does have a life here. A very full one. You are not the only man who no-

ticed her, Racine Huntington. She had quite an active social life before you came back."

"I know," Race said. "I thought she'd stopped dating,
I guess, now that I'm back. She hasn't been out in three
weeks now."

Jennifer, walking up behind her mother and hearing
Race's comment, told him, "It's none of your business who
I date or how often."

"You look wonderful," Race said coldly, barely holding his jealousy in check as he gazed at her from head to
toe. She was the most dressed-up he'd ever seen her, and he
realized that she would have fit in perfectly at any Hollywood cocktail party. Her delicate white leather high-heeled
shoes matched the navy-and-white scarf that fell gracefully over the white-and-blue dotted georgette blouson
dress. Her golden-red hair was pulled back into a twist at
the back of her head, emphasizing her cheekbones and the
green glory of her sparkling eyes. Makeup covered her
freckles, and she looked subdued and sophisticated.

"Thanks," she told him, almost backing away from the
glittering intensity of his gray eyes.

After Jeff had called to remind her of their date she had
taken extra care to look lovely, and she knew by the look on
Race's face that she'd succeeded. Before she had a chance
to say anything more, Jeff's car appeared and she crossed
in front of Race to greet him before he got out of the car.
Waving, she smiled at Race and the kids and gracefully
climbed into Jeff's silver BMW.

"Who was that?" Jeff demanded as he backed the car
out of the driveway and headed downtown. "Is he the reason that you've been too busy for me lately?"

"My next-door neighbor," Jennifer told him truthfully,
upset more by the stormy jealousy that Jeff had correctly
read in the tall man's dark face than by Jeff's own cool
voice.

"What's he doing over at your house?" Jeff asked angrily. "Exactly who is he?"

"It's hard to explain," Jennifer began, realizing that she spoke the truth. She wasn't able to stick a label on Race. Last week she could have told Jeff that Race was a troublemaker, someone she didn't like one bit. Tonight she found she couldn't say that. Somewhere along the line her feelings had changed. But now wasn't the time to think of that, she realized as she glanced at Jeff's face. Deliberately she murmured some neutral answer to his question and deftly steered the conversation into safer but more boring channels.

Knowing that Jennifer shared his taste for light comedy, Jeff mentioned a play that was opening in Charlotte the following month. "I'll pick us up some tickets," he announced casually.

As they pulled up to the hotel where the banquet was being held, Jennifer found herself hedging. "Let me get back to you about the dates." While Jeff walked around to help her out of the car, Jennifer realized that she had nearly refused him outright. Something did not feel right tonight. She wasn't enjoying Jeff's quiet humor or feeling any rapport with him at all. In fact, being with him seemed all wrong.

Jennifer roused herself enough that she enjoyed the evening. She sat and chatted normally, drawing on her background in entertainment to keep the conversation going. She and Jeff sat at a table with six other professionals from the area, and the conversation flowed evenly. Jeff looked at her strangely a couple of times but didn't say anything as they drove quietly back from town.

"Do you want to come back to my place for a drink?" Jeff asked, placing a gentle hand on Jenni's shoulder. As they pulled up to a stoplight, he leaned over and softly kissed her neck. "You've been far away tonight. Come back to me."

As Jennifer felt his lips on her shoulder, she stopped fighting reality. She could deny the truth no longer. She felt only friendship for Jeff. She had never really loved him as a woman should love a man. The passion that burst into flame with Race's touch convinced her of that. Jeff's touch was merely pleasant, never exciting.

Suddenly the future was a giant question mark, one that blazed with passion. She knew that Race wanted her back in his bed, and she wondered if he would succeed or if her common sense would protect her from him. The only thing Jennifer knew for certain was that she was going to have to break it off with Jeff. she owed it to him and to herself.

"Jeff," Jennifer began, moving away from his gentle touch, "I'd like a drink. Could we stop somewhere quiet?"

Several minutes later as Jeff guided her into the intimate bar, Jenni felt confident that she was going to do the right thing. But she also sadly realized that what she really wanted was the impossible, a man who combined the sweet, caring nature of Jeff and the wild, passionate chemistry that Race ignited in her veins.

As soon as they had their drinks in front of them, Jenni took both of Jeff's hands into hers and looked into his eyes. She didn't want to hurt him. She regretted her feelings, but she knew they wouldn't change.

"I'm sorry. I wish that I could say this a better way, or tell you what you want to hear, but I'm afraid it's over between us. I can't give you what you want," Jennifer told him, her eyes swimming with tears. She liked Jeff so much and had tried so hard to fall in love with him. "I can't give you what you need. I realized it this evening, and I care too much for you to drag this out any longer. I wish things were different."

"Please, don't say that," Jeff protested. "We could go back to the way we were before. I won't push you for more. You'll grow to love me. I can wait."

"No, Jeff," she said, touching his face gently. "It's better this way. I know that you'll always be my dear friend, but never anything more. You deserve more in a woman, and you'll never find it waiting around for me."

Although Jeff tried to change Jenni's mind, he soon realized that she was adamant. They left then without having touched their drinks. Jeff drove Jenni home slowly, unwilling to say goodbye to her. "I'm still the twins' doctor," he noted. "And I'll always be your friend. If you should change your mind..." he whispered.

"I wish I could, Jeff, but I can't. It wouldn't be fair to either of us." Leaning over, she gave him a gentle farewell kiss and got out of his car. "Thank you, Jeff," she whispered as she watched him drive off.

Race stepped from the shadows and grabbed her arm. "Just what are you thanking him for?"

"Being a gentleman," she told him. There was no way she would admit that she'd told Jeff goodbye forever. She was much too vulnerable to Race already.

"Why? Because he brought you home so late? Because he kisses so well?"

"It's none of your business. Now, if you'll excuse me," Jennifer said, looking up at Race and stepping around him, "I'm tired. It's been a long night."

Grabbing her arm, Race pulled her to him, his nostrils flaring when he caught a faint whiff of the other man's cologne. Without thinking, he lowered his mouth to hers. He ground his lips on hers, almost brutally, trying to erase the other man's touch and taste. "You belong to me," he rasped as he moved from her lips to her neck. He pulled her firmly into his body to emphasize the electric response they generated whenever he held her in his arms.

Jennifer raised her head defiantly. "I belong to no one."

Chapter Seven

Jennifer pushed herself free of Race's embrace. "It's none of your business who I sleep with, or when. You have no rights at all."

"The hell I don't," Race shouted at her. "You hadn't slept with this fellow before I got here, and unless you did tonight, you never will," he vowed, pulling her back into his arms.

"What did you say?" Jennifer demanded furiously. She ceased her struggling and stood stock-still.

Race reluctantly released her when he felt her icy response and backed up a bit. "I don't remember," he said, realizing that he'd really blown it this time. He could handle passionate anger—that he understood. But this frozen implacability was something else.

"You said I hadn't slept with Jeff," Jennifer reminded him icily. "Just how do you know that? No one knows that, not even my mother or Vicki. They never asked."

"Ahh...I just guessed," Race offered with a crooked smile.

"Try again," Jennifer stated, her arms now propped on her hips, her eyes blazing. "Everybody assumes that I do sleep with him. Everyone but you. And you are the last person in the world to assume a man and woman wouldn't be sleeping together."

"All right," Race conceded. "Come and sit down on the porch and we'll talk. I want you to promise to hear me out. That's all."

As he watched, Jennifer sat down and hugged her arms around herself. Looking Race in the eye, she agreed to his request.

"When I first met you, last July, I told you that I'd be back. I also told Jameson, then my lawyer and Manny, my agent, that I was going to come here as soon as the tour was over. I started Jameson looking for this house and had Manny set the movie score contract for me."

"So?" Jennifer said. She understood all that. She had known that his sudden appearance must have taken some planning, as well as a lot of money.

"Manny and my lawyer were surprised about all this. Upset that I'd told them I'd found my kids." *And my woman,* he added silently. "You've heard about the other lawsuit I'm involved in?"

When Jennifer nodded her head, Race went on, now wanting to get it all out in a rush. "They hired a private investigator. I didn't know about it until very recently. In fact, I only found out about it last week. I had nothing to do with it. Honest," Race vowed as he watched Jennifer turn white and then red.

"They had me investigated? Private detectives? Someone followed me around, talked to my friends? How could you?" Jennifer spit out, almost stunned by the news. She was more furious than she could remember ever having been, and totally humiliated, as well. She felt like punching someone or something—preferably Race. "I feel like someone was peeping in my shower."

"Jenni, I know. I ordered it stopped as soon as I found out. I'm sorry. They only did it to protect me." Patting her shoulder, he wished he'd been able to keep his mouth shut. If he'd been a bit more careful, she would never have found out. In a way, though, he was glad. This was the last of the secrets standing between them. He was beginning to hope that if they could work through this they could have a relationship.

"Blast you, Race. It makes me feel creepy, knowing that someone knows everything about me. That my entire life history is written on a neat little sheet of paper somewhere." Without thinking, Jenni was confiding her feelings to Race, somehow confident that he would accept them. Never mind that he was the cause of all the pain in the first place, her brain pointed out logically, even as her body longed to be held safe within his strong arms.

Forcing herself to think, Jennifer looked at him and asked, "If your agent and your lawyer had it done, how do you know what it said? It sounds like you read the whole thing."

Sighing, he turned to look beyond the porch into the deep shadows as he admitted, "I did." When he heard her sharp intake of breath and felt her shrink under his hand, he released her and tried to explain. "I should have torn it up, but I couldn't. I had to know about your life. What happened to you. Can you forgive me? I know I shouldn't have looked, but I simply couldn't resist."

"So you thought I might be another Patti Silk in your life?"

"No. I never thought that. But my lawyer and agent did. They were not convinced you weren't some old friend who wanted to take advantage of my coming to town. They suspected you set this whole thing up, from a 'staged meeting' to the 'convenient children.'" When Jennifer edged to the end of the porch swing, Race put out his hand to detain her. "I never thought that for one instant, Jenni. I have never doubted you, never. Please believe that, at least. I only wanted to know about your life, that's all."

"What did you think I was lying about? You'd seen the house, and the kids and my mother. Did you think I had a rich lover tucked away in the broom closet? You can't honestly believe that *I* wanted something from *you*?"

"Dammit, Jenni. You know I didn't think that. If you want to know the bloody truth, I'll tell you. I wanted to know how you managed to get enough money to buy this cozy house. How serious you were about this Jeff fellow."

Jennifer sat for a moment, considering the circumstances and what Race had said. She had told him that she was deeply involved with Jeff and this house had been considerably more expensive than their old one. Race had no way of knowing that her dad's life-insurance policy had given her and her mother the financial freedom they both now had. It was the last way she'd ever have wanted to receive money, and she seldom spoke of it.

Before she had a chance to reply to him, Race spoke again, "It's hard to believe anyone after living in Hollywood for so long," he explained. "I was sure that there was a logical explanation, but when I found that report I couldn't rip it up without reading it. It was simply too tempting."

"I don't know what to say," Jennifer said honestly. "Did they find out everything about me? My past? How did they know about my relationship with Jeff?"

"I think the investigator talked to Jeff's partner, who apparently has a big mouth. Aside from that, they didn't get too much. I told you, Jen. I stopped it as soon as I saw the preliminary report. I'm sorry it happened. As far as I know, they did not dig very deeply into your past. They weren't on the job that long." Unable to resist, he asked, "What's in your past that you don't want me to know?"

"Ten thousand lovers," Jennifer hissed at him, incensed that he would dare wonder about her past love life, considering his own, "the same number as you!"

"It's none of my business, is it?" Race asked her, hurting to think that she'd been with some other man but knowing that he had no right, no right at all, to question her. "Love, I'm sorry," he said again. "And it wasn't that many lovers."

"So am I," Jennifer said, feeling numb again after the momentary shaft of anger. She didn't know if she was mad, or glad, or even if she really cared. "Look, I'm going to bed. It's been a long night and I'm so tired that I'm not seeing straight. I'll talk to you tomorrow. If you're still here."

"Oh, I'll be here, Jennifer. I'll be here," Race promised, trying to judge her reaction and failing dismally.

Jennifer stood at her window and watched Race walk home in the dark. The streetlight illuminated his slim body as he moved gracefully across the green lawn. If only she could be as angry as she knew she should be. It was an insult, an invasion of privacy, yet she was just annoyed, rather than furious.

After pouring herself a generous glass of brandy, she rested her elbows on the counter in the dark. She wondered what the report had said about her. It must have been really interesting reading, her life story. If you could get excited by the PTA and car pools.

Had the detective rummaged through her garbage, interviewed her friends? It was strange that she had never heard anything about it. Aside from the indignity of it all, why wasn't she more upset? She should be screaming mad. She should feel something. After all, it had been an event-filled day. She'd told her year-long boyfriend to get lost and had come home to find that her ex-lover's staff had sicced a detective on her.

What was wrong with her? Something must have short-circuited. All she felt were waves of regret. Fool that she was, she had actually believed Race when he'd sworn that he wasn't responsible. It bothered her that she'd so easily accepted Race's explanation. *He* bothered her, on every level. The worst part of the whole mess, she finally admitted, was that she wanted nothing more than to lose herself in the passion that he'd reignited on that first day back in July. Jennifer quickly finished her brandy and ordered herself to bed. In the morning she'd surely be thinking much more rationally.

Race walked back to his house, deep in thought. It wasn't easy for him to deal with someone else's emotional needs. Sadly Race realized that he was simply not used to considering people's feelings. For too many years, life had been too fast and too easy for him. Everyone always praised every move he made. How was he ever to realize when he'd hurt someone's feelings or made them mad? No one ever told him. Everyone catered to him, wanting to stay close to the fame and money and excitement so desperately that nothing else mattered.

Now everything mattered, and Race realized that he was finally growing up. He needed to think things through before he confronted Jennifer again. His agent had been pestering him to meet with the producers of the movie he was scoring. Walking straight to the back of the house, he knocked on Jameson's door and told the drowsy man to arrange for a flight in the morning. He was going back to Hollywood for a couple of days to tie up all his loose ends, so that he could return to Jennifer totally free to love her as she deserved to be loved.

A large flat envelope rested in the space between the screen door and wooden one the next morning when the twins woke up. Becca lifted it up curiously and turned it over in her hands before Jennifer noticed the package her daughter held.

"It's for you, Mom," the little girl told her mother, shoving it toward Jennifer as she balanced the car keys, two lunch boxes and Rick's social studies poster. "Put it on the table," Jen directed, "and let's go. School starts in twenty minutes."

As soon as she returned, Jennifer walked over to the envelope and cautiously read her name, which was printed on it in large block letters. Armed with a pair of scissors, she cut the heavy packing tape and found a manila folder and a small tape recorder. A note on the folder ordered her to listen to the tape recorder before she opened the file.

Sitting down, she fumbled with the device for a second and finally got it going. Race's voice filled the room, and Jenni found her nails digging into the palms of her hands. Good grief, she thought before she began to listen, he's leaving because I was mad last night. Gone again, for another eight years, she thought as tears threatened to gather in her eyes, the pressure aching for release. "I will not cry over him anymore," she said out loud as she rubbed her hands over her eyes and willed the tears away with pure anger. She was glad he'd left. Wasn't she?

Race's firm voice came from the small tape recorder. "Jennifer, this is not what you think. I'm going back to L.A. to finish some long-overdue business. I will be back in a few days. Don't worry that I'll do anything about the kids. Or change my mind about us."

"I taped this because I couldn't find the right words to write, except maybe in a song. If you're wondering about the package, it's for you. It's the report from the investigator. After our talk last night, I spent a long time thinking. About you and me and lots of things. I decided that seeing the whole report would be much less unsettling than wondering about it. I know you need some time to think." After a long pause Race continued. "I have to settle some things in my life, too, before I come back to you."

What was she supposed to think now? All she knew was that he was gone once again, and that part of her wanted him to stay away and part of her wanted him back with a need that was frightening in its intensity. It reminded her all too well of the long days she'd spent waiting by the phone for him to call and haunting the mailbox for a note saying that their night had meant something to him. Now he had done it to her again.

Yet the soft, foolish side of her believed he would be back. He was different this time. He could be trusted—the man who'd had her investigated and was trying to take her children, the man who was already back to the glamour of Hollywood. "Right, Jen. He'll be back," she said mockingly to herself. "That's the ticket."

Jenni pushed the rewind button and slowly walked over to pour herself a cup of coffee. Life would go on. It would all be for the best. She had managed once, and she would do it again. She put the folder flat on the table and opened the cover. A typewritten page stared back at her. Its title read Subject: Jennifer Grange, unmarried, age 28.

She read the three page report carefully and then closed the folder. It felt strange reading about your own life as though it were a work of fiction. The report was more superficial than she'd expected. Mostly it skimmed the events of her life and quoted a few of her friends, who generally described her as a nice, if somewhat conservative, person. The financial report was more complete, listing not only the insurance settlement but her current salary. Her credit rating was excellent, and her job was secure.

Thankfully there was no mention of her personal history or of any other men except Jeff Wenset. A short paragraph noted that it was rumored that Jennifer had been married briefly and divorced, although there were no records of the union. The date and place of the twins' birth were noted, along with the fact that they both used her maiden name. That was it.

Margo walked down at nine and asked her daughter what she was doing still dressed in her drive-the-twins-to-school clothes. Waving a hand for her mother to join her, Jennifer turned on the tape recorder and played Race's message for her. Then she pushed the folder over to the older woman without comment and went to get dressed. Margo gave her daughter a warm hug as she left for work that morning and told her encouragingly, "He'll come back, Jennifer."

"Maybe," Jenni answered. "But I don't know if I want him to or not. My life was fine before he showed up. I'll be fine again if he stays away."

As Margo watched her youngest child drive off, she spoke aloud. "It would be fine but empty, my daughter."

Five days later the doorbell rang about eight o'clock in the evening and Rick rushed to get it. He was dressed in his pajamas, fresh from the bath, and ready as always for any interruption of the routine that he and Becca followed every night before bed. A giant box was resting on the back porch, and Rick screamed for help before he opened the screen door.

Jenni came down, her sleeves rolled up and her hair damp from helping Becca bathe. Curiously she joined Rick on the porch, looking at the large box and then quickly across the lawn at Race's house. The lights were on for the first time in days, and Jenni knew that he was back. "Race, are you there?" she called in a loud voice. When no one answered, she told the kids that they could open the box, which had their names on the outside.

Instantly four busy little hands pulled the cardboard box open. The children were stunned speechless by its contents. "Wow! Look at these! Fantastic!" they squealed delightedly as they pulled furry bear costumes for them both from the box. There was a female for Becca and a male for Rick, complete with the clothing used in a popular science-fiction movie.

As the children went crazy trying to put them on, Jennifer gritted her teeth. Although she doubted that the twins realized it, she could tell at a glance that these were professional costumes. Perhaps even originals. They were way, way too fancy for a Halloween in Charlotte, and probably much too warm.

As the children ran into the house to show their grandmother their costumes, Race stepped from the shadows. "It looks like they like the costumes," he said as his eyes drank in her disheveled appearance. His five days in Hollywood had taught him even more about what he wanted from life. He wanted this. Reality. A woman who didn't smell of expensive perfumes. A woman who didn't smile every minute, showing off her capped teeth, or hold her face poised to show off her best angles. He wanted Jenni, forever.

As he walked up the steps, Jenni watched him, her green eyes dark and mysterious. Instead of stopping, he walked straight to her and captured her in his embrace. "Lord, woman, I missed you," he murmured before his mouth claimed hers. Expertly he captured her mouth, running his tongue along the tops of her teeth, urging her to taste him as he was sampling her. Magic, Jenni thought as she surrendered to his kiss, feeling the fires build within her every second his lips caressed hers. He pulled her to him, letting her know of his need, firing a similar one of her own.

"Mom, Mom! Look at this!" a small, furry space creature shouted at her, and Jennifer turned in Race's arms. With total ease as if he'd been doing it for years, Race held her there, casually leaning against him. Becca thrust a perfect replica of the costume she was wearing into her mom's hands, and Jennifer realized that Becca's costume came with a matching miniature doll of its own.

"It's darling, Becca. In fact, I can't believe that your Uncle Race brought you these costumes. It's still two weeks from Halloween, and we haven't decided what you wanted to be."

"Oh, Mom, don't be silly! I'm going to be a lady space bear. Wait till Sally and Melissa get a load of this. Wow! This is the best costume in the whole entire world," Becca announced, rushing behind her mother to give Race a big hug. "Thank you, Uncle Race. Thank you!"

Rick came back a few seconds later and was equally excited and grateful. He held a realistic-looking slingshot that

Jenni immediately confiscated, much to Rick's dismay. Before either Race or her son could say a word, she told them, "No more weapons, pretend or otherwise," in a tone of voice that brooked no argument from either of them. Undeterred, the children scampered off to look at themselves in the bathroom mirror again.

"Okay," Jenni said after a few minutes of unrestricted admiration of the costumes. "Up to bed. Tomorrow's a school day, and you are now half an hour late getting to bed. Thank your Uncle Race and move it. Take these up to your rooms and jump into bed. I'll be up in a couple of minutes to tuck you in."

"Oh, Mom," they both groaned. "Do we have to? Can't we stay up just a little longer?" they wheedled. "Pleeease."

Margo walked into the kitchen as Jennifer refused for a third time to give them any more extensions, and volunteered to supervise the kids' bedtime. With a wink she suggested that they might need a bit of help getting the costumes off.

Jennifer muttered to Race as they left, "A little bit of help? Grandma is going to have to blast them off with dynamite." With a disgusted look on her face, she turned to Race and asked him, "Why did you do that?"

"Bring the costumes?" Race asked in genuine puzzlement. "Halloween's coming," he told her, as if that explained everything.

"Right. Those costumes look suspiciously like the real thing," Jenni commented, hands on her hips.

"Well," Race admitted, "the guy who's producing the film that I'm scoring knows somebody in the studio costume department, and I did happen to mention that I had two small friends. He didn't have any use for them. Look," he told her in an exasperated voice, "he had hundreds of them just rotting away. I didn't pay anything for them. They were free."

"Great," Jenni told him. "It isn't the price, it's the costumes themselves. They're way too fancy for a Halloween here. How am I going to explain where I bought them? How are the kids going to deal with all the jealousy that's bound to erupt when their friends get a load of those costumes? I'm going to have to say I ordered them from some speciality shop and..." Sighing, Jennifer told him, "It was a nice idea, but next time, ask. We are plain people, not Hollywood, here. Can't you ever understand that? You can't just walk off for five days, then come back with a fancy present and act as if nothing happened."

Turning, Jennifer started to walk up the stairs. Race caught her shoulder and asked, "Aren't you wondering what I did when I was gone? Where I was? Who I was with?"

"I assume you were back home, at the ranch with Patti," Jennifer snapped. "I have no right to know what you were doing or with whom. If I were interested, I'd wait for the next edition of a supermarket magazine and read all about it with the rest of the world."

"You have every right, Jennifer Grange, even if you won't admit it yet. For your information, I spent four days with the movie producer going over the music. And the other with my lawyers, setting up a trust fund for the kids and settling some old business. I slept in a damned hotel." His face turned hard as he thought of the old business.

"What!" Jennifer exclaimed. "You did what?"

Starting, Race realized that she was talking about the kids, nothing else. "There's nothing you can do about it, Jennifer," he informed her. "It's done. Rick and Becca each have a half-million-dollar trust fund now. You can decide how and when to tell them about them, but there's nothing you can do. When they're twenty-one, they'll each find out whether you want them to or not. Until then, my lawyers will be in touch. You can deal with the interest any way you see fit. Spend it, save it. Burn it! I don't care. They're my kids and they're provided for. Now, any more comments before I leave? Have I done anything else wrong? Want to start on the list now or wait till later?" After a pause, Race stepped onto the porch. "I'll be going now. I'm tired. Believe it or not, I was working eighteen hours a day so that I could hurry home to you. That should give you a good laugh."

As he started walking back across the lawn, Jennifer called out, "Whatever I'm doing, Race, it's not laughing."

For a moment Race considered turning back and confronting her, but his common sense told him to let it go for tonight. He couldn't tell if she was angry because he'd brought the costumes, because he'd been gone or because he'd come back, or whether she was upset about that report. It couldn't be the report, he decided, it wasn't that big a deal. It was a lot less personal than the constant magazine articles that ran about his life.

His life. It was a rotten mess right now. At this particular moment, he wasn't sure he was good enough for Jennifer and his kids. Patti had found out that he was back in town almost immediately and would not leave him alone. She'd refused to believe that he hadn't come back to her and had ignored everything he'd said. Finally Race had agreed to see her, in order to end their relationship once and for all.

They met one evening in the lounge of Race's recording studio. For a few seconds Race simply stared at Patti. Thinking that Race was admiring her beauty, Patti obligingly stood still, posing in her skintight black jumpsuit for her lover. She tilted her head toward the right, knowing that her profile was best from that angle, and carefully placed the long red nails of one hand on her hip, emphasizing her slim waist. Letting one tear fall from her mascaraed eyes, Patti waited for nearly a minute before she moved up to Race. Putting her hand up to his chest, she nestled against his chest and sighed, "Honey, I've missed you so much."

"Race?" she said when he didn't respond, moving away from him so that he could observe her cleavage as she pulled the zipper down a few inches and let her lush breasts nearly spill out of the black leather. "Let's go back to the ranch and heat up the Jacuzzi."

"Patti," Race said slowly, "I'm sorry, but it's been over for us since last summer. I've met someone else, and I'm going to get married."

"Married? You—" Patti caught herself, and stood still for a moment, trying to decide what to do next. Slowly she began to cry, tears running down her perfect face in a slow stream, her blue eyes shimmering in the light. "How can you marry someone else after what we've shared?" she asked in a soft, quavering voice. "You know that I love you."

As her perfume wafted toward him, Race tried to feel something for her, for the woman he'd lived with for so many months, but he couldn't. He recalled their days together and the nonstop activity they'd shared. Whenever they hadn't been working they'd been busy doing something—riding, swimming, playing tennis, attending nearly nightly parties, rarely talking about anything but their activities or the business. Despite everything, they were still strangers in every real sense of the word.

Race knew Patti was only acting, that she'd never cared for him at all, only for the country star and the money. He recognized all too well the crafty look that passed over her face before she began crying. That was the look she wore when planning strategies to get her way. Maybe he did know her a little, after all.

Again Race repeated himself, and again Patti insisted that they would never be through with each other. Finally Race lost his temper, told Patti that they were done and stalked out of the room. Race later wondered how she had managed to fool him for so long. Everything about Patti was artificial, her glamorous look, her tears, even her feelings.

Unable to sleep that night, he drank several Scotches, knowing that it was stupid even as he did it. He missed Jennifer so much that he actually ached. Alcohol never solved any problems, he knew, but that night he needed something to help him sleep. Nightmares plagued him through the night, and he was relieved when the phone rang the next morning with his wake-up call. Relieved until he turned over to see Patti lying beside him in his bed. As he opened his mouth to ask her what she was doing in his bed, Patti sat up, letting the sheets uncover her delightfully naked body. Yawning, she struck a pose for him, one hand in her hair, while she asked, "Wasn't last night wonderful?"

"Last night?" he asked, his mind a total blank. He'd drunk too much and then fallen asleep. He had no memory of Patti or of anything else. Horrified, he questioned her but found no satisfaction. Patti swore that she'd bribed the bellboy to let her in and that Race had been glad to see her. They'd made love twice, and Patti was ready to take him back.

Furious, Race told her that she had made the whole thing up and insisted that she leave. After a long, painful scene, Patti left, still swearing that she loved him and that they'd made fantastic love the night before. In no uncertain terms, Race told her to leave him alone. If they had made love, he had not wanted it, did not remember it. He did not want her.

After Patti left, Race got up and took a long shower, trying to wash the smell of her perfume from his body and the scene from his mind. If only he knew what had happened. He hoped that he had not made love to the woman, but if he had, it really didn't matter. He certainly had not meant to.

After he calmed down he called his lawyer, Edward Kurray, and ordered him to do anything he had to to get Patti out of his life. He told Edward in a quiet voice to give her the ranch and to make it very clear to her that Race never wanted to see or hear from her again.

Race hurriedly finished his business the next day and rushed back to Charlotte, drawn to sanity and love. What he needed was time to think about a way to incorporate that last incident with Patti into his life and the new start that he wanted with Jenni. He could never tell Jenni about it. He'd never felt so used in his entire life, nor as angry. Ironically, he saw it as a fit ending to his years as a swinging country singer.

"Uncle Race," a small voice shouted the next afternoon as Race sat on his porch reading a novel, "do you have a black cape I can use? Becca and I are in the school Halloween play and I need a black cape. I'm going to be Dracula!" Rick announced proudly, pulling his top lip up and making growling sounds.

"I'm going to be a fairy princess." Becca added, coming up behind her brother. "I need to get a crown. Mom says that I can't have a real one, that they cost too much. I'm going to have to make one out of tinfoil. Yuck," the small girl said, clearly hoping to con Race into buying a crown for her.

"Becca? Rick?" Mrs. Grange called, walking slowly over to Race's house.

"They're here," Race shouted back. "They came over to see if I had a crown or a black cape that I could lend them. It seems that they're both in the Halloween play."

"Oh?" their grandmother said in a wry voice. "This is the first time that I've heard about any play."

"It's all on a paper in my book bag, Gran," Rick told her. "I need a cape to be a good Dracula and Becca needs a crown." In a teasing voice, the little con man told her, "You know what great costumes Uncle Race has," his father's charm oozing out of his little pores. "I didn't want you and Mom to worry about how to get them."

"All right, young man," Margo said, pointing her finger back toward their house. "You and your sister head back to our house and we'll discuss this. I want you both to apologize to Mr. Jameson and promise me that you won't ever ask him for anything without permission."

"Grandma," Rick said, protesting the unnecessary restriction, "Uncle Race doesn't mind. Do you?" he asked his father, gray eyes shining innocently up into identical ones.

"No problem. I don't mind, Rick. In fact, I enjoy seeing you and Becca whenever you come over here. I'll be glad to buy you a tiara, honey," he told Becca, reaching down to touch her soft hair for a moment. "You will make a lovely princess."

"Race," Margo said sharply. "I'll take the kids home now, and you might want to talk this over with Jenni later."

"Sure. Look, I've got a great idea. Why don't I take you all shopping when Jennifer gets home. I can buy the kids everything that they need for the play. Where should we go?"

"K-Mart, Uncle Race. They have everything," Rick and Becca both said.

"You do your homework, and we'll go after supper," Race promised them, ignoring Margo's frown. "Come on over when you're ready."

These were his kids, and they needed costumes for their play. What was Margo frowning about, anyway, he wondered in disgust. He wasn't planning to buy his daughter a real tiara, only one made of glass. Picking up his guitar, Race settled back and began strumming softly.

While he waited, Race started playing some of his old music, but with a change. The songs of raunch and partying were now turned into slower, minor-key ballads. Race seemed to be mocking his life. The rollicking tunes that had brought him fame and fortune during his wildest years now sounded like songs of regret for a foolish past—laments for his lost youth and for the false values that he'd embraced for far too long.

Jennifer walked up to Race's home angry, but stopped to listen to his strangely moving voice. Her fury rapidly turned into another, stronger emotion. She'd come to yell at him for promising the moon to her children and ended up hearing a personal confession that tore at her heart. The bittersweet songs made her feel his pain over lost love and lost chances, reminding Jenni of her own lost hopes. Finally Race sang the song that he'd written for her long years ago, with such longing and feeling in his voice that she could not deny that he wanted her, deeply and with all his heart.

She stood listening quietly while she tried to control her own heart. Whatever had happened to Race back in Hollywood had not changed his basic desire. It was clear from that song that he wanted a chance.

What she feared above all else was that she and the twins would not be enough, that the novelty would wear off and the lure of the glittery life would call him back. She doubted that a man with his experience could ever be content with one woman. Particularly one who was so inexperienced that it was laughable. No, she thought as she walked over to him. Whatever she thought about Race, it didn't make her laugh.

"Race," she said, walking up so that he noticed her. "I need to talk to you about the kids." Seeing the emotion shimmer in his gray eyes, she turned to watch the golfers on the course through the screen and slowly told him, "I heard your singing. The old songs sound different when you do them like that. Almost like they were new."

"Maybe they are, Jen. I know I don't look at anything quite the same way anymore. You and the kids have made a huge difference in my life. Maybe I'm finally growing up," he told her seriously.

"Oh, Race. I wish I could believe you," Jenni told him, regret shining in her eyes. "But every time we take a step farther, we take two backward. You can't keep buying things for the twins. I don't want them to think of you as just a person who buys things for them. Sure, they're going to like you, but is that what you really want? To buy their affection?"

"If that's the only way I can get it, then yes. Money means nothing to me, Jen. If I can make them happy, then I will. The only way they'll ever learn to love me like a father is for me to be a father. As long as I'm Uncle Race," he told her, arrogance peeking out from his gray eyes, "I'll buy them whatever I want."

He hadn't meant to sound so abrupt, but Jennifer had interrupted him when he was in a vulnerable mood. Pity had shown in her eyes, and Race had reacted. No one was ever going to pity him.

"Not without my permission," Jennifer snapped, wondering why Race was suddenly so defensive.

"Well, then, may I please have permission to take them to some store and buy them the props that they need for their Halloween play?" Suddenly Race realized that he was reacting out of pride, and he toned it down. "Hey, I didn't mean to get you mad at me. I guess you sort of made me feel like I didn't count."

"I didn't mean to. You do count, but please, Race, no more presents unless Margo or I give the go-ahead before you tell the kids." Reaching out, Jenni touched his shoulder and told him, "The twins like you just fine without any presents." Pausing, she went on, "Since you did promise them, why don't we go shopping?"

Feeling better than he'd felt since he'd gotten back, Race changed his mood rapidly. The songs helped him put his past in perspective, as his music always did, and now Jenni was willing to spend some time with him. *Soon, so soon, I'll have my family with me and we can go back to Hollywood together. On second thought, maybe we should live in London for a year or so, until this last mess with Patti dies down,* Race thought.

"I'm ready," he announced, checking his wallet. "Where are the kids?"

"Waiting on our porch for the outcome of this argument," Jennifer told him dryly. "I think they'll be ready to go in about fifteen seconds. Are you sure you want to chance K-Mart? So far you've been lucky that no one's recognized you, but it is a very well-lighted store."

"Hey, no problem," Race told her, pulling out a pair of plain horn-rimmed glasses and sticking a battered old baseball cap over his hair. "Don't I look pretty average to you?"

"As long as you can wipe that silly grin off your face, we've got a chance," Jennifer told him with an unwilling grin. "If you're ready, so am I. How long has it been since you've been in a discount store with a kid?"

"About ten or twelve years. Have they changed much?" Race asked in a puzzled voice.

"Neither kids nor the stores have changed much at all," she told him dryly. "But I doubt if your memory serves you correctly."

Thirty minutes later, Race looked at her and agreed. He was not ready for the crowd or for the shining fluorescent lights that made everything look so bright and available. It was a shock for someone who'd last shopped in Beverly Hills. Taking the cart that Jenni shoved in front of him, he pushed it after the twins, finding it difficult to keep his head from turning around like a tourist's. "They have everything," he told Jenni in a loud whisper.

"Almost everything," Jenni told him, trying hard not to laugh. "Right now the kids are most interested in the costumes," she pointed out as Race walked up behind his children. He browsed over the bottles of hair coloring, the tubes of face paint, everything from fake blood to glow-in-the-dark makeup. Finally he told the twins to get whatever they wanted, adding that Jennifer had the power of veto over their purchases.

Luckily, Rick found a great black cape that was not only long but could double for a rain poncho on a wet night. Becca spotted a crown made with glitter and sequins that she said was absolutely perfect. After putting those things in the cart, the children begged to be allowed to go to the toy department. Jenni told them that they could go a little way down the aisle that they were on now, but that they had to stay within her sight.

"While we're here, why don't you buy your candy?" Jennifer suggested, keeping one eye on her offspring. When he gave her a puzzled look, she explained, "You know, for trick or treat."

"Jameson does that," Race started to say, but decided it would be fun to see what Jennifer had in mind. They walked over to the candy counter, and soon Race had several bags piled in his cart and was rapidly going out of control. "Lord, woman. How have I lived for so long without gummy frogs and chocolate caramels? I swear it's been twenty years since I ate my last chocolate-covered raisin. Remember the Capital Movie House and all those matinees your father used to take all us neighborhood kids to?"

While Race seemed totally relaxed and at ease, Jennifer found herself glancing carefully around to see if anybody had noticed him. Although a few women stared at him, she dismissed them. Anyone with good taste would stare at Race, even if they didn't know exactly who he was. He was *that* good-looking, even in old jeans and a baseball cap.

Right now, much to her amusement, the superstar of the country-and-western world was going crazy in the candy department. He'd moved from the bagged Halloween candies into the regular selection and had added a box of candied almonds, a bag of cherry licorice whips and a bag of those puffy orange marshmallow peanuts that defy description and was closing in on the potato chip section when Jennifer felt obliged to say something.

"Isn't this about enough for one night?"

"Did you see this stuff? I haven't had any of this since I left home years ago. What is this stuff?" he asked her eagerly, holding up a box of caramel-covered popcorn and peanuts. "I've never heard of this before." As he read the box, he picked it up, and several others, too. "Jameson never buys anything for me but health food stuff, even on the road. I haven't had junk food like this in years! This is great. Don't you love all this stuff?'' Race asked, his face alight with boyish enthusiasm.

Laughing, Jennifer reached over to touch his cheek and heard herself say, "How could I not love a man who can go crazy over caramel popcorn?''

"What?'' Race asked, his eyes lighting up like neon signs. "Did I hear you right?''

"No... No.'' Jennifer flushed deeply and tried to take back what she'd blurted out by accident. "I said that I'd be crazy to love... that I'm crazy about caramel popcorn, too.''

Ducking her head, she pushed the cart away from Race, swearing under her breath at herself. She cursed her own stupidity in loving Race again and her total insanity in realizing it in the middle of a busy store. But most of all she swore at her own incredibly big mouth for letting him know. Just what was she going to do now? That klutzy performance was not going to fool a man like Race.

Not looking behind her, she rushed off to gather the children up with her. Quickly she ordered them to put back the toys they were looking at and get ready to leave. "Do either of you need anything for school while we're here?''

When they both shook their heads no, she curtly ordered them to follow her. The twins looked at each other, wondering at the sharp tone of her voice, and prudently decided that this was not the time to ask for anything else. With her back stiff and her eyes bright, Jennifer walked back to Race, who was patiently waiting for them, casually holding two six-packs of root beer in his hand.

"I heard that,'' Race whispered into her ear as she walked by and he put the soda into the cart. "We'll talk later.''

Although Jennifer refused to answer him, she could feel his hot gaze on her the entire time they stood at the check-out counter and in the car on the way home. She couldn't believe she'd said anything that crazy. She didn't want to believe that she was foolish enough to love him again—if, in fact, she'd ever really stopped.

Chapter Eight

An hour later Jennifer sat at her own kitchen table, clutching a cup of cold coffee as though it were a life preserver. The twins were halfheartedly wiping the remains of root beer floats off their faces, trying to stay awake to enjoy the unexpected treats. Margo patted her daughter on the shoulder and volunteered to put the children to bed, if she and Race wanted to take a little drive together.

"Mom" Jenni replied with a strained smile, "quit already. I'll go up and put the kids to bed." Looking directly at Race for the first time in an hour, she added, "I'll get a sweater while I'm upstairs. I could use a little fresh air."

"Fine," Race agreed. He turned to the twins and softly stroked the tops of their heads briefly. "Be sure that you come over to show me your costumes when they're ready," he told them as they walked upstairs.

"By the way, thanks," Jennifer managed to say calmly, "for the costumes and everything." As she walked up the stairs, she wondered what would happen next. She couldn't very well pretend to be indifferent to Race after her admission in the store.

All too soon, Jennifer was walking down the dimly lighted road with Race at her side. Her clenched hands were tucked in her pockets, and she was fighting the urge to burst into a full run and escape her fate, escape her feelings, escape Race. As they walked along, he finally broke the silence and asked in a slightly amused voice, "Are you going to talk to me or just walk all night?"

"Walk," Jenni told him. "In fact, I'll jog, if you don't mind."

Putting his hand on her arm, his voice husky, he told her, "I do mind. Ever since I got back here you've been running from me. Isn't it time you stopped?"

"I can't," Jenni told him, her pace picking up and her hair streaming behind her in a red-gold halo. As they walked past one of the infrequent streetlights, Race saw the apprehension in her eyes and sighed.

"Why not?" he demanded. "I'm not such a terrible fellow. I'm not bad to look at. I'm kind to animals. I love our children, and I love you, Jennifer Grange. Why can't you accept that?" he asked her tenderly, pulling her to a stop at the edge of the golf course. Taking her arm, he pulled her off the road and over to a bench that was sheltered by the trees.

"You aren't such a bad fellow." Jenni told him in a ragged voice. "If you were almost anyone else in the world, I'd be throwing myself into your arms right now," she admitted, hearing the hiss of Race's breath and feeling his hand tighten on her arm. "But you *aren't* just another man. You're Race Hunter, superstar. Superlover extraordinaire. I can't let myself love you again. I can't!" Unshed tears glimmering in her eyes, she turned to him, anguish all over her face, "I . . . Please, Race. Let it go. Isn't it enough that you know that you made me love you again? Can't that satisfy your ego this time? You don't need one more woman. You've got Patti waiting for you. I'll let you see the kids. I'll even tell them the truth," she offered, "if you'll leave me alone. Can't you just go away? I was fine until you got back."

Pulling her gently into his arms, Race felt a protective urge to shield his woman from the entire world. "Please don't feel like this. Don't be afraid of me." Stroking her cheek gently with one large hand, he murmured to her as she leaned against his chest. "You know that I love you. I'd never hurt you again. Forget about Patti. She means nothing to me. It's you that I love, only you. I promise. Please don't cry."

"Race," Jennifer begged before his lips descended, "please let me go. You don't need me."

"That's where you're wrong," he said as he spotted the backs of their houses across the golf course. Bending down, he picked her up and determinedly began walking toward his house. When she started to struggle, Race stopped moving and looked deeply into her eyes. The full moon shone down on them as they stood in the middle of the wide green expanse. "I can't let you go, Jenni," he whispered. "You are my life. You already love me. I'll teach you to trust me again. I swear I'll never hurt you."

Jennifer listened to the sincerity in Race's voice and felt his arms tense around her as he began walking again. She was lost, and she knew it. She could not resist him today any more than she had eight years ago. Destiny had decreed that his was the touch to set her body aflame. She no longer fought the sensation; but only wondered why it had to be. Why did she respond only to him? Why not another man, one who would care for her always?

She had no doubt that Race loved her now. At this very moment. As deeply as he was capable of loving. But she also had no faith that he would stay. Sooner or later another woman, another Patti Silk, another experience, would come along and she and the twins would fade into the background. She would learn to cope with it when the time came.

Jennifer tightened her arms around his neck and let herself enjoy the experience of being carried in Race's strong arms. Perhaps it wasn't wise, perhaps she'd regret it later, but tonight she was his.

"Race," she murmured against his neck, "I'm not ready for this."

"Yes, my love," Race replied huskily, pausing to kiss her again. "You are."

Seconds later Jenni struggled to speak again, knowing that she could not afford to lose her head. "I mean I'm not protected," she whispered in a small voice. "I can't take any more chances . . ."

Race took in a harsh, painful breath and promised her that he would take care of it. "Our next child, Jenni, my love, will be conceived after we're married, not before."

Jenni sighed her acceptance, believing that he would protect her, not believing that they'd every marry, fighting her desire to believe that they would.

Race strode purposefully across the lawn to his house and onto the porch. As they approached the lighted back door, he paused for a second and noted gratefully that Jameson's car was still gone. As they approached the light, Race looked down to see calm acceptance on Jenni's face and an almost resigned look in her eyes.

What in the world could he do, he wondered briefly as he pushed the door open and headed up the stairs toward his bedroom. He knew that she loved him, but also that she didn't trust him, not for the long run. He didn't blame her. He paused briefly on the steps, but then walked forward. He didn't want her this way, but he feared that if he let her go now, without claiming her body once again, she'd manage to lock up her feelings and deny his claim on her.

Suddenly black rage built up within him, rage at her and at himself. Dammit, he loved this woman and she loved him. He would prove to her that they belonged together in the most basic way that he knew. Eight years ago he'd been an impetuous lover, taking her tenderly but with no technique. Tonight he'd use all the knowledge he'd gained since then to make her his woman. Once and for all. By the morning, she might still have her doubts, but she'd never refuse him again.

Race let her down and quietly led her into his bedroom, closing the door behind him. With a tender brush of his lips across her brow, he settled her on the lightly undulating waterbed. When she began to protest, he hushed her with a gentle touch, his tongue rapidly feathering over her open lips. Slowly he eased down to sit beside her, his gaze burning into her own. The windows were open, letting the moonlight enter the room to cast a silvery glow on its contents, adding a slight touch of unreality.

"I love you," Race whispered as he reached down to trace her collarbone with his long finger. "Let me love you," he urged as he followed his finger with his tongue, setting her on fire. Moaning, Jennifer moved her head to one side to allow him access to her neck. It had been too long, Jennifer realized dreamily as she felt Race's fingers lightly trace her body, barely touching her breasts, her waist, the curve of her thigh. His finger felt as though it were burning through her clothing, and she needed that heat.

Sweetly, softly, her body relaxed and she murmured her surrender into the night. Let Race show her all the fire that would burn her very soul. If he was the only teacher, at least the lessons would be worth the pain.

Race rejoiced at Jenni's surrender and vowed that she would not regret this night. Not now, and not ever. As she moved beneath his roving hands, he clamped his desires under fierce control, determined to take her slowly and carefully.

"I'll never hurt you, my Jennifer," Race vowed as he slipped her clothing from her body. With ease he unbuttoned and unzipped and gently pulled her clothing from her until she lay open to his inspection, wearing only a pair of brief panties. His fingers had been light and teasing as he undressed her, never actually touching. He'd leaned down to blow on her hardened nipples when he'd reached around her to unhook her bra, but he'd done little more than tempt them before he'd moved away. His finger lightly brushed her hip and then her thigh. The only time she'd felt the touch of his lips had been when he'd taken off her shoes and he'd taken a moment to kiss the back of her heel. "You are so beautiful," he told her as she watched his gaze travel up her body, feeling its hot stare as an almost physical sensation. For the first time in years, Jennifer gloried in her sensuality, proud that her body pleased him. She arched slightly toward him, wanting more. "My lovely," he murmured as he reached down to run his tongue around her navel, noting the clenching of her muscles and wanting nothing more than to bury himself in her. Not yet, he ordered himself as he raised his head to watch her green eyes darken even further. Finally he leaned over and gave her the first full kiss of the night.

As his lips claimed hers, Jenni reached up and wrapped her arms around his neck. She melted as his mouth caressed hers, tempting and teaching. Passion flowed as she pulled him closer, her hands trying to work between their bodies to remove his soft cashmere sweater. She wanted to feel his flesh, to press her breasts against his warmth. Feverishly her fingers pulled at his body, and she murmured her need to touch him.

Race pulled away briefly, and she heard the rustle of his clothing dropping to the floor alongside hers. When he turned away for a moment to prepare himself for her, Jenni smiled in relief. He had remembered the protection, and she could trust him, at least for tonight. She gasped as he returned to the bed and slid his length against her. His body was hot, burning, melting her own, and she nearly jumped as though shocked when she felt the strength of his arousal.

Race took a deep breath and reminded himself of his promise. To take it slowly and show her all the pleasures that were possible. The moment that she'd touched his skin, he'd felt a flare of passion that had stunned him. Never before had he felt such an urge, such an intense need to lose himself in a woman, to wipe out the entire world and to be hers alone.

For the very first time in his life, Race was learning what it meant to make love with a woman. It was vastly different and vastly better than "having sex." This night was even different from his first night with Jennifer. That night had been wondrous. This night was so much more. His feelings now were so much more complex, and the magic that they were sharing was nothing short of miraculous. Suddenly he realized a truth that had eluded him since he'd first seen Jennifer so many long months ago. She had fully as much power to hurt him as he did her. Momentarily he pulled back, uncomfortable with that possibility.

Groaning, he pushed all thought to the back of his mind and let his feelings come forward. He deliberately forced himself to pull away from her body and ran his tongue down her throat, kissing and nibbling a line of liquid flame that led directly to one hard-tipped breast and then the other. With exquisite tenderness, he used his lips to trace a line around each breast, leaving a trail of fire behind him. Jennifer stirred and moved, trying to hurry him along, putting her hands in his hair to guide him to her aching breasts. Finally he surrendered to her need and took one nipple fully into his mouth. Sucking and nipping, he devoured her, causing an arc of instant passion to shoot through her like a bolt of lightning.

Jennifer felt herself melting and dissolving in his strong embrace, while her hands threaded into his thick black hair to urge him closer. She moaned as he released one throbbing peak and moved to the other, giving it equally tantalizing attention.

When Jennifer thought she could take no more, he released her breasts, replacing his mouth with his hands. As his thumbs deftly stroked her diamond-hard nipples, he moved his head down and gave her navel a deep, sweet kiss.

Abandoning her breasts for a brief second, he reached down and removed her last item of clothing, stripping the thin satin from her legs with a slow, sensuous motion.

Before she could recover, he reached up to trace the outline of her lips with one hand and spread her thighs with the other. His head had dipped down, and he was kissing her intimately. When she opened her mouth, whether in shock or in protest of his invasion, Race gently insinuated one of his fingers into her mouth, softly mimicking the movement of it with his tongue.

Jennifer reached a pitch of passion that she'd never realized was possible. Seconds later, he tenderly moved to gather her in his arms, holding her tightly to him. As he held her, she began to return to reality. As soon as her glazed eyes began to clear and she looked directly at him, chagrin and embarrassment beginning to show in her eyes, Race moved rapidly and with one rapid stroke entered her body.

When she grimaced from a momentary twinge, Race smiled to himself in joy. He did not know how many other lovers she'd had, but from the tight, hot, sweet pressure of her body, he knew that there had not been many, and not for a very, very long time. Race was simply too experienced with women not to know this.

"I love you, Jennifer Grange," he told her as he saw a faint touch of apprehension enter her eyes. "Only you. Only this," he told her as he began to touch her again and started slow strokes within her. "This is real. This is love," he told her as he brought them both to the utmost peak of pleasure. As his hand reached between their bodies and touched her, setting off a series of exquisite contractions that led to a higher place than she'd imagined possible. Even as he followed her, Race remembered his love and told her, as ecstasy shook her beyond reason, "I love you, Jennifer. Only you."

While they floated back down to reality, Jennifer felt his warm weight pressing her back into the slightly rocking mattress. She didn't want to move. Didn't want reality to come back. For a few precious minutes she'd felt complete, one with the entire universe and full of such incredible joy that she feared she'd die from its intensity. As she lay, feeling his warmth still tightly sheltered within her body, she knew that she'd never felt anything remotely like this before, and she was profoundly grateful to Race. Whatever happened between them, whenever he left her, she now had this incredible memory to sustain her for the rest of her life. At least now she knew what true ecstasy was.

Their first experience together had been a prelude to this one. It had been wonderful, too, but light and insubstantial, like cotton candy, sweet but not satisfying. Today Race had not only shown her that peak of ecstasy, but he had taken her on a journey to the farthest limits of joy.

As Race watched her dreamy smile he felt himself growing hard again, and he wondered at her power over him. He'd never experienced such a high before, never been half as satisfied before, and now, mere minutes later, he was wanting her again. "Are you a witch, Jennifer, my love?" he asked her as he moved experimentally within her and watched the pleasure break over her face. "I want you again," he rasped as his lips descended.

Passion flared more brightly between them. This time tenderness was absent. Race claimed her in a frenzy, driving them both farther and higher as passion and a desperate need to possess raced through them both, leaving them gasping and unbelieving in the fiery aftermath.

This time, Race eased from her body and settled her head on his shoulder. He pulled the silken coverlet that had been dislodged during their loving over them both as their heated bodies began to cool.

Not knowing what to say, Jennifer let herself drift into a half sleep. As she dozed contentedly, she was as aware of Race's muscular length beside her as she was of her own body. Like Scarlett O'Hara, she thought dreamily, she'd face the facts in the morning. Even Rhett couldn't have pleased Scarlett as thoroughly.

After several minutes of reliving the experience in her mind, she sighed and let reality begin to creep back. All right, she wasn't as patient as Scarlett. But then, Scarlett didn't have twins and her mother waiting next door. All she had to do was to get up and go back to her own house. It would never do for the twins to know that she hadn't slept in her own bed. She'd wait until Race fell asleep and then she'd leave. Whatever happened, she didn't want to mar tonight with any more words, with false promises, with pretense. She wanted this memory to be perfect.

In minutes she felt Race relax and loosen his hold on her. Quietly she eased her way off the bed, a trick she'd learned when the twins had been younger and she'd often sat with them until they'd slept. Gathering up her clothing, she pulled them on just inside the bedroom in case she ran into Jameson on the way out. She moved into the hall barefoot and padded toward the stairs.

Race had been aware of her leaving his bed but had decided not to interfere. As he watched her from the side window making her way back to her own house, he replayed the evening and the loving that had surprised him as much as it had her.

From her responses, he knew without a doubt that he'd taken her places she'd never reached before, and the masculine part of him was proud. But it also scared him, because she'd done the same to him. *Him*. Race Hunter, lover extraordinaire, had just found out, to his own great surprise, that he'd never really made love before in his entire life. He'd been with many women but had never, never experienced anything close to this universe-shaking feeling that Jennifer created within him, not even the very first time he'd made love with her, all those long years ago.

For the first time ever he'd forgotten technique, forgotten everything and only felt, only loved. Now what was he going to do? It was ironic in a way, he told himself as he poured himself a large Scotch and wandered back up to his room. He'd decided to brand her with his loving, and it'd turned out the other way. He was hers for life, if only she'd have him.

Jennifer awoke the next morning feeling more relaxed than she'd felt in years, easing her way out of sleep, filled with a delicious lassitude that had seeped into her very bones. Then she remembered why she felt so wonderful and was instantly wide, wide awake. With a quick glance at the clock, she decided that she had time for a brief half-hour run if the kids would cooperate and stay asleep.

After a quick, hard run, Jennifer reentered the house and headed for the shower, determined to forget Race for the day. While she ran, flashes of their loving kept coming to mind. A vision of his dark head against her breast. The memory of the feel of his hand running down her long legs. Needs so recently awakened resurfaced with a vengeance as Jennifer ran, trying to escape herself.

Back upstairs, she quickly awakened the twins and left them dressing while she took a vigorous hot shower. With a towel wrapped around her head turban-fashion, she shepherded the children down to breakfast. After fixing them hot instant oatmeal, she checked their lunch boxes and book bags and kissed them goodbye for the morning. As she stood on the front porch watching them climb into the school bus, she was glad that it was a busy workday and that she would not have time to think about last night.

She was dressed and ready for work when Margo came down the stairs, smiling at her daughter. "My, you're up early this morning. How did it go last night with Race?"

"Fine, Mom," Jennifer said dryly, "if you think that total surrender is any way to win a war." Before Margo had a chance to say anything at all to that cryptic statement, Jennifer leaned down and kissed her mother goodbye. "I'll try to be back by six," she promised. "Want me to pick up a pizza for dinner tonight?"

"Sure," Margo said easily as Jenni disappeared out the door. "Total surrender," Margo mused, realizing what must have happened and hoping that Jenni was not going to be hurt again.

When the two dozen long-stemmed red roses appeared at Jenni's desk, she knew immediately that they were from Race, and she shrugged them off as his standard operating procedure. She told herself that she wasn't touched, but knew she was lying. "Bet the man has sent flowers to every lady he ever slept with. He probably owns stock in FTD," she argued cynically with the part of her that thrilled to his gesture. Unable to resist the fragrant, velvety flowers, she set them on one corner of her desk and tried unsuccessfully to forget last night. At least he lived up to his billing. He was a master at making love.

Race felt far from masterful later that morning as he received an emergency call from California. The people producing the film needed to see him—"yesterday," his agent insisted. Finally Race promised to fly out the next day and see what needed to be done. He refused to leave until he'd spent the evening, and hopefully the night, with Jenni. Race didn't want to think what she would imagine if she returned home from work to find him gone.

Jenni answered the phone around three that afternoon and was only faintly surprised to hear Race's deep, resonant voice. "Honey, your mom said you were going to bring home a pizza tonight. Would you and the kids rather come over and let Jameson and me cook?" When there was no answer right away, he continued, "Jen? Please. I barbecue a mean hot dog. I'll even share my last box of caramel popcorn with you," he offered in a light tone.

"Okay, mister, but I get all of the peanuts," Jennifer said, feeling lighthearted all of a sudden. Race didn't sound as though he were finished with her. It was going to be more than a one-night stand this time. "We'll be over at six."

"Earlier if you can make it," Race urged. "I miss you."

"I . . . thanks for the flowers," Jennifer told him before she hung up. *Before* she admitted that she missed him, too. What was she going to do? There was no going back this time. She'd given herself to Race, and it sounded as though he were not planning on letting her forget it. *So, lady,* she thought, *it seems as though you're going to have a love affair. So what? Doesn't half of the world have love affairs?* She was due this one. In fact, she owed it to herself.

After all, what sort of fool would turn down a love affair with the only man she'd ever loved, especially one as wonderful as Race? She could not turn him down. She'd take him for what he was. Let herself enjoy whatever time they had and hope that her heart would heal after he left. What choice did she have?

Feeling somehow freer for the decision she'd made, Jennifer made herself two promises. The first was to protect her children. The second was to maintain her self-respect. If she and the kids always remembered that Race was but a temporary part of their lives, they should all be able to enjoy the interlude. As long as she kept her pride, she'd make it—as long as she promised herself that when it was over she'd be able to look him in the eye and say goodbye without begging him to stay, without him seeing any tears. Those could wait for the long nights after he left. There would be time for the sorrow he would cause, more than enough time.

"Here we are," Jennifer announced a few hours later, strolling casually into Race's kitchen dressed in a pair of blue jeans and a short-sleeved nubby blue-and-white cotton sweater. "What's for dinner? Can I help you do anything?" she asked brightly, trying to ignore the sudden frisson of excitement that ran through her at the very sight of him. How did any one man manage to look so good? His dark hair was still damp from a shower, and his jeans were tight and low on his hips. Another V-necked sweater covered his broad chest, this one a gunmetal gray that matched his eyes. Closing her eyes briefly, Jennifer swore to keep it light as she gestured toward her children, who were running in circles on his lawn.

"Later," Race growled in a low tone. "Later you can help me with everything." His eyes raked over her body, claiming what was already his, fanning fires that still simmered. When he was satisfied that she was aware of his claim on her, he released her from his gaze and offered her a glass of iced tea.

"Jameson made some potato salad and a tray of raw vegetables. His feelings were hurt when I brought home all of that junk food. You wouldn't believe the hassle he gave me when he found all of it in the kitchen this morning. Do you know," Race said, getting slightly indignant at the memory, "he actually told me that I had to watch my weight. Can you imagine? I wear exactly the same size as I did ten years ago. Well, seven years ago," Race admitted with a rueful smile.

"Race," Jennifer said soothingly, biting back a smile, "go ahead and indulge yourself, at least this one time. Who knows how long it'll be before you get a chance like going to K-Mart again."

"What do you mean?" Race asked her, but he was sidetracked when the twins came racing up, tiring of their soccer game.

"What's for dinner?" Rick demanded as he trotted through the screen door that his mother held open for him.

"Can I have a drink, please?" Becca asked, flopping down in a chair dramatically. "I'm hydrated."

"Dehydrated, honey." Jen corrected her daughter gently. "Dehydrated means that your body is lacking in fluids." When she saw Becca's bright eyes look into hers with a slightly confused look, she tried again, explaining the word until she was sure that Becca understood.

Race brought out a pitcher of iced tea but soon turned around and replaced it in the refrigerator when the kids gave him a dirty look.

"Can we have soda? Please?" they both asked, looking to their mother.

"You know the rules, guys. Milk or juice at this time of day."

"All right. Milk, please," Becca told Race, and Rick nodded his agreement. Soon they had both drunk enough to satisfy themselves and were out the door, reminding their mother to call them as soon as their dinner was ready.

"They are incredible," Race told her. "Where do they get all that energy?"

"You should have seen them when they were three and four. I nearly collapsed in a heap every night. I swear I logged a hundred miles a day chasing after them. They were unreal," Jennifer told him, missing the twinge of anguish in his eyes as she sat back. Her face softened at the memory of the two children.

"Dammit all, you should have let me know," Race told her. "I missed so much of their life."

Resentment shot through Jennifer, accompanied by anger. Attempting to remain calm, she turned, pinning him with her coldest gaze. "You have no one to blame for that but yourself. I refuse to take any blame for your life-style. We've been over this before, and my feeling isn't going to change. Try to remember that you're Uncle Race and that your interest in their lives is temporary."

"What do you mean, temporary?" Race snapped as Margo entered the kitchen and told them to keep their voices down. Jameson emerged from the living room at the sound of Margo's voice as Race and Jennifer stared at each other in frustration. Finally Race said, "Later," and she nodded in agreement.

Dinner was a festive affair, despite the undercurrents that passed between Race and Jennifer. The twins were excited about the upcoming holidays and the Halloween party that their school was having. Now that they were relaxed with Race and Jameson, the twins were their usual rambunctious selves and kept the conversation going with their constant chatter. Soon enough they'd consumed two hot dogs each, plus a reasonable amount of potato salad and several raw carrots to keep Jameson happy. They both refused to touch the raw broccoli and cauliflower Jameson had set out, insisting that it was rabbit food.

Finally dinner was over and Jenni and Margo took the children home for their nightly baths. Jameson asked Margo if he could come over that evening to watch television with her, and Jennifer told Race that she would be back later.

Race waited on his back porch for Jennifer to come, wondering what he should say, trying to plan a strategy to bind her to him. He knew that telling her that he had to be gone again was the worst thing he could do, but there was no choice. Writing a score for a movie involved so many people and so much money that he could not justify holding up the production meetings any more than was absolutely necessary.

While he sat, calmed by the soft night and the quiet sounds of the nearby trees, Jennifer walked up to him. She slowly opened the screen door, then sat down next to him on the swing. "What's so serious, Race?" she asked him, reaching out a finger to trace the frown lines that were formed around his mouth.

"I've got to go back to Hollywood tomorrow," he told her without thinking. "They needed my input to decide what—never mind. There are some meetings I have to attend. Dammit, Jenni, I don't want to leave you. Not after last night." Turning to her, he swept her into his arms and captured her face against his hard chest. "Not ever."

"Hey," Jennifer told him lightly, "don't worry about it." Glad that her face was pressed to his chest, she put her arms around him. She closed her eyes against the pain and prayed that she would be as strong as she needed to be. She had hoped that they'd have longer than one or two nights.

"I know how complicated it is to make a movie, especially a big-budget one. I understand."

Hearing the distress in her voice, Race jerked back and forced her to look him in the eye. "No, you don't. You don't understand at all. I'm going back, but only for a few days. As few as I can manage. Then I'm coming back home. To you and the twins. Can't you believe that I love you?"

Jennifer tried to sound calm and collected as she answered him. "I believe you, Race. You think that you love me and the twins. And I'm happy that you do."

"What do you mean, I *think* that I love you? I know for sure that I do," Race bellowed at her.

"Come inside," Jennifer insisted, shocked at his loud voice. "Someone is going to hear us."

"I don't care if the whole world hears me. I love you, Jennifer Grange, and the kids, too. I want to marry you and go back to—"

Race stopped talking when he saw Jennifer shake her head and start backing out the door. Rushing forward, he grabbed her and held her to him. "I'm sorry. I'm going too fast for you, aren't I?"

"You're going too fast for yourself, Race," Jennifer insisted. When he started to contradict her, she put a hand on his shoulder and led him into the attractive living room. "Let me talk to you, please."

Unable to resist her request, Race sat down on the leather sofa, capturing her hands in his two strong ones.

"I know that you think that you love me and the kids," she told him softly, praying for strength and maturity. "You honestly do, I suppose, right now. But I think it's a momentary thing with you. A new experience, something different, a novelty. Maybe it's not," she told him as he shook his head vehemently, "but I can't let myself think anything else. Don't you see that? Nor can I let the kids' lives be interrupted. I don't want them to live as Race Hunter's kids, always afraid of kidnappers, photographers."

Getting up, she walked to the window and looked out over the golf course. This honesty was costing her more than she'd expected, but it was necessary for her survival, hers and the twins'. "I want to leave everything as it is now. You go back to your life and come here when you can."

"What about us?" Race asked her, stalking up to grab her from behind. "Was last night all that you'll offer me?" he demanded, pulling her tight against his aroused body. His hands trapped her as he began a slow circular action with his hips locked against hers. He reached down and feathered kisses across her neck and tantalized her ear with his lips and teeth.

"No," Jennifer gasped as she felt the now-familiar spire of excitement begin deep within her center. "I can't deny you. We can have an...affair. Very adult—" she started to say as he edged his hand up and cupped her breasts underneath the sweater that she wore. "Very wonderful," she murmured as his thumbs began rotating on her pointed nipples and her legs began to collapse underneath her. Race put his arm around her and led her quickly to his bedroom. Closing the door, he pulled her to him.

Race's hands went wild she leaned into his body. She felt his hands run over her body, rubbing, touching, tempting, deftly unzipping her jeans and pushing them to the floor at her feet. Soon his knuckles skinned her sides and she felt his hands, palms firmly over her hipbones, take control of her very being. As he nipped her ear he used his fingers to bring her to the point of ecstasy, and while she melted and burned in his arms he carried her over to his bed. There, in the cool light of evening's shadow, he pulled off his clothing, protected her and then taught her all over again the joy of being his woman. Tasting and touching all of her, Race showed her in a hundred ways that she belonged to him as she surrendered totally to his spell.

"I will be back, my love," he promised her later as they lay exhausted in his warm bed, legs twined together intimately. "I will always come back to you."

Chapter Nine

Jennifer knew that Race was really gone the minute she came home from work and took a look at her children's faces. The twins were sitting on the couch watching a rerun of their favorite cartoon, periodically kicking the furniture with their heels. "What's wrong?" she asked them as she caught a glimpse of their stormy frowns.

"Uncle Race is gone," Rick complained, and Becca added, "We wanted to show him our costumes and he wasn't home."

Forcing herself to remain neutral, Jenni sat down between her two children and pretended to pout. "Does this mean that I don't get to see them?"

By the time the twins returned, wearing their costumes and smiling happily, Jenni had unearthed her instant camera. "Why don't you guys choose the best picture from the batch, and I'll send it to Race?" she suggested. "That way, if he gets held up on business and can't be back for Halloween he'll see your costumes anyway."

Rick glowered in his Dracula costume and Becca posed with one arm on her hip, trying to look beautiful, while Jenni took several different shots. Soon the children were happily settled down to dinner, the latest crisis neatly avoided. Jennifer made a point of telling the twins not to count on Race's presence on any permanent basis. It seemed as good a time as any to let them get used to the truth.

"He's a very busy man most of the time," Jenni explained deliberately, "so it will be hard to say when he'll be here and when he won't. He won't be coming to Charlotte on any regular schedule. He was kind of on vacation when he was here the last few weeks," Jenni explained, thinking that once his next tour started he'd be lucky to get back to see the twins once a month, "and he still had to make a couple of trips."

When they asked her where he did live, she told them he had no real home because he traveled a lot. She did not like being less than honest with the kids, but she also did not want to glamorize Race's life. It would be too exciting to tell the twins the truth, that "Uncle Race" had several homes, in New York, Nashville, London and Hollywood. Seven-year-olds were not too young to be impressed by money and glamour. Or too stupid to figure out his real identity if they were given enough clues.

Later that evening, Jenni sat on the couch struggling with a review of the movie she'd seen that afternoon. Margo was out with her bridge group, and Jenni was alone. The movie was a touching love story that she would have enthusiastically reviewed no more than three weeks ago. She still thought it was a good movie, but Jennifer now viewed it with new eyes. Now she knew that it reflected only a pale shadow of what genuine passion could be. Race was so much more intense, so much more sensuous than the leading man who made love so coolly on the silver screen.

Even in his absence, her body recalled Race's touch and burned in memory. For the first time she could appreciate how difficult passion was to portray on film, with or without resorting to explicit scenes. After having experienced the real thing, she realized that she could recall very few movies that had managed to convey the actual sexual fireworks that were possible between the right man and woman.

The movie reviewer in her was valiantly trying to convince herself that that knowledge would help her in her future work, and Jennifer was laughing wryly at her rationalizations when the phone rang. It was nearly midnight, and her heart lurched as she wondered if Margo had encountered some difficulty on the way home. Leaning over on the couch, she grabbed the phone on its second ring.

"Jennifer?" Race's low, deep voice asked over the phone. "Is that you?"

"Yes, Race," Jennifer replied after a short pause. For some reason she had not expected him to call. He hadn't before. The sound of his voice was so totally unexpected that she'd tumbled onto the floor from her awkward position on the couch and needed a moment to catch her breath. "What's wrong?"

"Nothing. Are you all right?" he asked, wondering at her shocked tone of voice. "Are the kids all right? Margo?"

"They're fine." Jenni told him, deliberately making her voice cool. He'd surprised her, and she'd lost control for a moment. "How are you doing out there?" she finally asked, wondering why he was calling. "Did you need me to do something with the house?" Jameson had left a key with Margo, and Jenni wondered if they'd forgotten something.

"I don't need you to do anything," Race told her in exasperation. "Not long-distance, at least. I called to talk, that's all. I miss you."

"Oh," Jennifer said in a small voice. "We missed you, too," she told him automatically. "The twins finished their costumes this afternoon and wanted to show you." Then, worried that he'd think she was trying to complain, she rapidly added, "Don't worry, I took care of it. I took a picture of them and promised to mail it to you. I assured them that you wanted to see it."

"Jenni, knock it off! You don't have to be polite with me. I'm your lover, not some casual acquaintance," Race told her irately. "If you want to send me the picture, fine, send it. But I'm probably going to be done here in three days, so you may just as well keep it for me. Do you really think that I'm not going to come back to you as soon as I possibly can?" Before she could reply, Jennifer heard the sound of a door opening, and loud music blasted out of the phone. "Hang on," Race ordered as the receiver went silent.

A few seconds later Race came back on the line. Jenni noted in a light tone of voice, "Sounds like some party. How have you managed not to go deaf with all the loud music? One of your concerts is enough to affect my hearing for days."

Ignoring her attempts at small talk, Race went directly to the issue, explaining the noise that she'd heard. "I'm at the director's house, Jennifer. There is a party of sorts. It spilled out from a working dinner. I'm working." When she didn't reply, he went on, "It's only eight o'clock here. This is not a midnight orgy, just a few musicians relaxing after a hard day."

"Of course it is," Jennifer agreed with him in a perfectly reasonable voice. "I'll send the picture to your lawyer's address you left with Margo and tell the twins—"

"Stop telling me to go away," Race said. "Haven't you learned anything about me over the last month? It's business, nothing more. Think! Why would I call you in the middle of all these people if I didn't miss you? Can't you understand I'm done with this life? It's only my work, woman. You're my love," Race bellowed as the sound of music came over the phone again. "I'll call you tomorrow,'' he promised just before he hung up on her. ''You save that picture. I'll pick it up myself.''

Although Jennifer spent most of the next day telling herself to be realistic, Race's impassioned plea had made an impression on her. Worse than that, it had given her the merest splinter of hope. What if he was telling her the truth? He was staying with his lawyer and his wife this trip, rather than in a hotel. He could hardly be conducting any affairs out of Edward Kurray's house. What if he had changed and did want to be with her and the kids for more than a brief interlude? Calling herself every kind of fool, she sat by the phone the next night, hoping.

By eleven-thirty she was sure that she'd made too much of Race's promises. At midnight the phone rang, and she knew it was him. Race's velvet voice rasped in her ear as he greeted her. ''Did I wake you, love? I just finished dinner and decided to come back to Edward's to call you. I'm sorry about the interruptions last night, but—''

''I'm the one who's sorry, Race. I certainly don't expect you to explain your life to me,'' Jenni told him truthfully.

''No more sniping lady,'' Race warned. ''We'll start over. I'll say hello, and you'll say you missed me. Like a real couple,'' he ordered. ''I missed you today, Jennifer, and I need to talk to you. Is that some new kind of crime?'' he inquired in a softer, somehow more vulnerable voice.

When she heard him, Jennifer quit pretending that she didn't care and spoke honestly. ''No, it's no crime. I'm so afraid of your hurting me that I guess I forget that you have feelings, too. Can we start over? I'd like us to be friends, really friends, no matter what happens in the future,'' she told him sincerely. She cared so much, and she hoped she could fill a small part in his life permanently, even after their passion burned itself away.

Hearing the sincerity in her voice, Race gentled his own and responded tenderly. ''You will be my best friend, my lover and more, Jen,'' he promised her softly. When she sighed her acceptance, not wanting to argue anymore, they settled down to talk and Race began telling her about his day.

Sitting in the darkening room, Race confided his innermost thoughts with Jennifer, feeling as though he were talking to his own alter ego. "You know, this is a strange experience for me. I've been gone long enough that it almost seems like an alien culture. Everybody waits on me out here like I was some sort of god. Two beautiful girls, barely out of their teens, were hanging around the sound studio today before one of the younger guitarists let them in. And you know what, Jenni?" Race told her with a certain disbelief in his voice. "Either of them or both would have done anything for me. For me or any other guy who bothered to ask them."

When Jennifer didn't say anything, Race went on, talking more for his own sake than for hers. "You want to know what the worst part of this is? That it's always been like that and I never thought anything about it. In the beginning it was all such a tremendous ego trip. Then I realized that it wasn't me at all, but my fame, that they wanted, and I quit taking what they offered. But I never thought about it, really thought about what it meant until today. It was something to ignore, no big deal one way or the other."

Jennifer listened to Race with a real feeling of bewilderment. It disgusted her to think about his world and about his past, but it also puzzled her. Was his monologue of self-realization a sign of his growing maturity? Had he changed? And even if he had, would she ever be able to think of his past and not despise it?

With a cynicism born of despair and hurt, Jennifer asked him, "So why did you notice today? What's so different?"

"I am," Race admitted in a sad tone of voice, catching both what she said and what she meant. And not knowing how to make it any different. What could he say to her? He had been with girls like that before, women who'd wanted to be with the star, the great Race Hunter, not caring anything for the man himself. Why had he ever told her what he was thinking? Could she ever accept where he had been and how he had lived? Desperate to change the subject, he asked her, "How are Rick and Rebecca doing? Getting ready for Halloween?"

"Yes," she told him, biting her lip. "They're busy practicing for the second-grade play. It's going to be on Halloween day itself, since Halloween is on a Friday this year. They'd like you to come if you're back in time."

Race took her olive branch and breathed a sigh of relief. This was the first time she had given him any hope that she trusted him to come back at all. "I promise you I'll be back in time. In fact, I'm hoping to finish up here and be back before Friday. If things don't get any more messed up than usual. I've been keeping a pretty low profile."

"What has everyone said about your new look?" Jenni asked curiously. "Wasn't it a shock when you turned up clean-shaven and with short hair?"

A long silence followed until a sheepish Race told her, "Well, Jenni. Dammit woman, why did you have to ask me that? I've been wearing a cowboy hat, sunglasses and not shaving. I don't want any of those magazines to get a look at the real me and get my bloody picture plastered all over some cover."

"Oh," Jenni said, her green eyes dancing in amusement. "You're in disguise? That sounds quite sensible, Race," she told him, touched that he was trying so hard to protect their life from his other one. "Quite appropriate for the season."

"We need to talk when I come home," Race said abruptly, feeling frustrated by all the things he'd said and all the things he hadn't. When a knock came on his door, he swore and told Jenni, "I have to go. I've got a session at the studio tonight. I'll call you tomorrow and let you know when I'll be home."

Jennifer hung up the phone, feeling an odd mixture of pain and pleasure. What were they going to do? That she loved him was no longer in question. That he wanted her, for at least some time to come, was evident. Unfortunately, the solution to the problem was not as obvious.

For one thing, how would she ever be able to live with the gnawing, debilitating, resentment that she felt whenever she thought of Race's past and of all of the women who had paraded through his life. Sometimes she'd had a vision of him, his long legs pinning down another woman, many other women, sharing his body with them as he had with her, and she wanted to scream and cry from the anger and injustice of it.

If they were to fashion any sort of life together, she would have to overcome those feelings. Not only that, everyone's life would be drastically altered. Race would have to make some major changes in his life. The twins would be uprooted. Margo would again have to face changes in her life, just when she was finally recovering from the trauma of her husband's death. And Jenni would have to give up her career or start over in the shade of Race's fame. And the bottom line was that Jennifer didn't know if she could ever really believe that he could or would remain faithful to her. What if everyone did it all, made all the changes, and Race left after six months?

Sleep came no easier with Race gone than it had when he'd been home, for now Jenni was facing even more decisions in her life. Race continued to call every night. His visit was lasting longer than he'd planned due to some changes that the executive producers and the studio were arguing about.

He had shown true sensitivity to her needs. He'd even reassured her that he was using his private credit card to make the calls so that they couldn't be traced back to her. The press had been hounding him, he reported, but had no idea what he was doing with his life or where he was hiding himself to work.

Lately his calls had been much quicker and of necessity much less intimate. They chatted about minor occurrences, never drifting back to the important subject of their relationship. It was as if they both realized that only a long, uninterrupted time alone would serve to bring up topics that difficult again. It was enough that they had agreed to talk and were both filling time until they could be together once more.

Impatience drove Race as he worked in Hollywood. Luckily, most of his personal business was with Edward Kurray, his lawyer, whom he trusted implicitly. Edward had met him during his first few weeks in Hollywood and had helped guide him through the beginning of his success. Although Race refused to see or talk to Patti, he did sign final papers deeding her the ranch. Race also settled one more trust fund—for Jenni to ensure that she would never want for anything in the future.

His visit to his agent was much briefer and not as pleasant. Race told the unhappy man, Manny Feilderbelt, that he'd decided to quit touring permanently, and told him to cancel the tentative plans he'd made for a European tour next spring. Although Race had told Manny last July that he was done, the little man had still scheduled a new tour and cajoled Race into considering it. Now Race was absolutely unshakable, even when Manny told him that the plans were nearly set. When Manny protested vigorously, Race stood up and told him to stop complaining. He was done and that was that. If Manny didn't like it, he could always quit.

Jennifer had not told the twins of Race's promise to be home in time to see their play, and as Halloween day dawned she was glad she hadn't. There was no cause for them to be hurt, and she cursed herself for being disappointed. He'd called every night, promising that he'd be home soon, but he was still gone. This was the night of goblins and ghosts, and Jennifer was determined to enjoy herself, Race or no Race. She should have known better than to count on him.

That morning was a busy one. She double-checked the twins at the door, making sure that they had their costumes in bags, their lunches, their homework and the treats that each was bringing for their individual class Halloween parties. "I'll be there to see you soon," she promised as they rushed out the door for the bus. "Grandma and I wouldn't miss it for the world."

"Neither would I," a deep voice told her moments later as Race stepped from the shadow of the porch and pulled her into his arms. Reaching down to claim her mouth, Race clutched her body to his, fiercely reclaiming the woman whom he loved. The fiery passion that always sparked when they touched burst into full flame. For a precious moment they stood locked in each other's embrace, oblivious to the entire world.

As Race reached down to anchor Jennifer even closer to him, an amused voice interrupted their reunion. "Dears," Margo said for the third time, "you really must come in from the porch. The neighbors can see you two. You'll have half the mothers in the PTA quizzing you about Race if you don't come in soon."

"Oh," Jennifer muttered, blushing a bright red that almost matched her hair. Pulling back, she urged Race into the house and tried not to look into her mother's twinkling eyes.

"It's so nice to see you again, Racine," Margo said calmly. "Would you like a cup of coffee? You look rather frazzled," the older woman said, walking over to the counter and getting a mug from the cupboard.

"Yes, thanks," Race managed as he sat down at the kitchen table. "I've been flying for several hours and didn't sleep much," he explained. "I promised that I wouldn't miss the Halloween play."

"Race," Jennifer breathed, running her hand over his forearm to reassure herself that he was really back, "You didn't need to do that."

Looking her in the eye, he said, "Yes, I did. You're going to learn that I always mean what I say. And I'm going to teach you to trust me again." His deep voice filled the room, and Jennifer felt herself melting into his spell again.

"I'll go over and give the key to Jameson," Margo broke in, smiling at the two lovers, who had eyes only for each other. Margo remembered the early days she'd shared with her husband and hoped that her daughter would be as lucky with her great love as she'd been. "If he came back with you, Race?" As she thought of Jameson, she wondered if she was too old for a second love in her life. The man did have distinct possibilities.

"I'm sure he would like your help in reopening the house, but I insist you keep the key," Race told the older woman as he traced a finger down Jennifer's nose. "My house is your house."

"I've got to go to work, Race," Jennifer whispered. Pulling back, she deliberately moved from the table and his mesmerizing presence. "I'm taking the afternoon off already, for the play..." When Race didn't say anything, Jennifer went on, "Go home and rest. I'll be back at twelve and we can go to the school together."

"Okay," Race agreed, standing up. "I'll go and take a cold shower. But you won't get away so easily tonight."

"Nor will you," she whispered as he walked out the back door with his loose-hipped stride. He'd come back once again, but for how long this time? They were going to have to talk tonight and resolve some of her uncertainty. If that was possible. Jennifer felt her determination slipping. Each time he returned she loved him more, and finally she was being forced to admit the truth. Nothing she could do would ever change that fact.

Jennifer pulled her car into her driveway just before noon and had to laugh when she saw Race sitting on her back porch. He was wearing a too-large business suit with a hideous tie, and on his nose sat a pair of horn-rimmed glasses. He'd also had his hair trimmed into a conservative style.

"You almost look regular," Jenni told him with a giggle. "But do remember not to smile."

"Why not?" Race asked her, slightly peeved at her comment. He'd spent a lot of time trying to look like a suburban father and thought he'd succeeded admirably. He was slightly afraid to be seen in a large group of people, but he counted on the very banality of the setting to save him from recognition.

"Because you have the sexiest, most recognizable smile in the world. Without that, you might not be noticed too much."

"Okay. No smiling. Just poke me if I get too obvious, will you? I haven't been to a school play since I was in one. Are they still as bad as I remember?"

"Probably worse," Jenni told him as Margo came out and joined them. Mother and daughter decided to sit Race between them and to take their seats just as the show was beginning. That would give Race the least exposure and also save Jenni from answering questions about who he was.

The play was a roaring success. The parents applauded and laughed in all the expected places. More than enough to please the children and to make their teachers relax. Both Rick and Becca delivered their lines without any mistakes, and the entire activity arena was full of happy, excited children and proud parents.

When the children saw that Race had come to their play, they were overjoyed. Later, at home, Race brought over two huge pumpkins, and again the twins were excited. Race noticed Jennifer watching them with a camera in her hand. She asked if he minded her getting some pictures of him with the twins. "You're becoming an important part of their lives, you know, Race. They'll always remember you."

"They'll never have cause to forget me," Race told her in a serious tone. "Nor will you," he promised, looking deeply into her unsure green eyes.

"Yuck! Gross!" Rick and Becca were soon saying as Race had them pulling the insides out of their pumpkins. He was careful with the sharp knife he used to cut the tops off and promised Jen that he would do the actual carving while the kids did the hard work of cleaning out the inside and planning the faces they wanted. Soon there was a mound of slimy seeds and two happy, squealing children. About an hour later, Jennifer was summoned to the porch to inspect their handiwork.

Pronouncing the two pumpkins totally excellent, she found a small candle for each one, smiling as she watched them carefully position the masterpieces on either side of the front door. Race invited them over to an early dinner and offered to take them out trick-or-treating himself.

"Jameson can answer the door at my house and give out the candy. I'd love to take the children around, if you don't mind."

"No, lo—no, I don't mind." Jennifer told him, barely catching herself in time. She'd almost called him "love" in front of the children. She was in bad shape. And she knew from the twinkle in his eye that he knew it, too.

Eventually it was eleven o'clock, and the children were tucked in bed, exhausted, with huge bags of candy in bowls by their sides. Jen and Race had carefully checked the treats after the kids had come in, both regretting the change in society that made such an inspection necessary.

Finally they were alone, cuddled up on the couch in front of Race's fireplace. Margo and Jameson were playing a game of Scrabble at Jenni's house, and they were alone for the first time in nearly a week. Passion warred with their need to talk as they sat, legs touching, their feet propped up on the coffee table.

"So," Jenni finally said, fighting the urge to throw herself into his arms and forget the future. "You're back. How's the movie coming? When it's done, what will you do next?"

The dark man put his arms gently around her shoulders and pulled her into a close embrace. "It's coming fine. I expect to be done in another month or two. Then I'm going to write my new album."

Kissing the top of her head, he held his desire in check and went on. "I know this is too soon for you, Jenni, but I know you worry that I'll leave you. I'm not going to. I don't have the answers for everything, but I do know that I want you with me. I'll never quit hoping that I can convince you to marry me and move to California. You know that I love you."

"I love you, too," Jennifer admitted slowly. "I don't seem to be able to stop loving you. I just don't see how our life could work, that's all."

"We'll find a way," Race murmured as he dipped to tenderly kiss her lips and then to touch the tip of her tightening nipple with his mouth. As he closed his mouth over her pale silk blouse, Jennifer burst into flames. Frantically her hand sought his skin, fumbling to pull his soft shirt up.

Need and long-simmering desire burst into full flame as they strained toward each other. Pulling back, Race took Jenni's hand and led her to his bedroom. With a groan he took her into his arms again and kissed her long and deep. Suddenly they could wait no longer. Buttons and zippers eased, and their clothing fell from them. There Race paused for a moment, kneeling over Jennifer, his eyes worshiping her body, which glistened in the moonlight. As his hand reached out to trace the contours of her trembling body, sanity deserted them. They were driven by their need and their fear of losing each other to reach higher and higher plateaus.

Sparks rippled through Jennifer's body as Race reclaimed her, touching, tasting, guiding her closer and closer to the fulfillment that only he could bring. When he slipped inside her, she moaned in ecstasy. As her heated body welcomed him, Race lost control and drove them both to a peak that was high and rare, one where only lovers and fools found the most exquisite satisfaction.

As they drifted back to reality, Race cradled Jenni on his shoulder. He drew a cashmere blanket over their still-damp bodies and whispered into her ear that he loved her. She began to fall asleep, and Race watched her lovely face drift into slumber. He sadly knew that she would awaken at some time during the night and slip away from him. Nothing would make him happier than to wake with her in the morning, but he knew that Jenni was not ready for that. Not yet.

Saturday was a typical day in the life of a mother, with practices, a soccer game and a birthday party. Race ended up driving Becca to a friend's for the party and attending Rick's soccer game with Margo.

Later that night, Race and Jenni sat alone at dinner, much to their surprise. Both of the twins had elected to spend the night at a friend's house. Jameson had cajoled Margo into attending a local blues festival with him.

Race gently asked Jenni if she would spend the night with him and was pleased to see her accept with a shy nod. "You know, I've dreamed of waking next to you for weeks now, in my bed, where you belong."

"I've dreamed of it, too," Jenni confessed, wanting to be honest with him. Though she feared that they would not be able to work out their differences, she now trusted Race enough to believe that he genuinely wanted some sort of permanent relationship with her.

As they rested on the couch after dinner, Race took her hand and turned her to face him. "We've got all night, Jen. I think it's time we talked."

"I think so, too," Jennifer admitted. "I don't know what to say to you, Race. You know that I love you, but it's so complicated."

"It isn't, not really," Race countered. "It's actually quite simple. I want you to marry me and move to California.

You know that I can take care of you. The kids love me, and I love them. You can bring Margo. We'll buy a place big enough for us all. What's so complicated about that?''

"Everything. It sounds so simple to you. Well, it's not to me. You're talking about uprooting all of our lives. I'll have to give up my job. Mother will be faced with another decision about the rest of her life. And the twins! Not only would they have to move, to a new school, a new part of the country, but they'd be known as your children. We'll all be famous. Infamous, rather.''

"Some people would like all that attention.''

"Well, not us. I don't want my kids turning into rich brats with a father who's gone all the time.''

"We'll live somewhere in northern California where we can have a normal life. Other stars do it, Jen. They have normal lives. Look, if you want we don't have to announce to the world that the twins are my children, although they look so much like me it won't be much of a secret.''

His face lighted up with an idea. "We could say that we were briefly married years ago. A teenage marriage that wasn't ever mentioned in my bios. It would work, Jenni. You've always told that story to everyone here, so it'll check out. The children wouldn't be hurt that way.''

When Jennifer still didn't look up into his eyes, he slowly forced her to face him, putting his finger under her chin and gazing directly into her eyes as he asked, "Is that the real problem, or is it me? Do you think you'll ever be able to trust me, Jen? I promise you there will be no other women. I'll be home as much of the time as I can. I don't plan on touring anymore.''

Burying her face in his shoulder, Jenni at last confessed her real fears. "I don't know, Race. When you're with me, I feel we can have something lasting. I believe that you love me. But I'm just not sure it can last, stand up to the pressures of your life-style. I'm not sure you won't change your mind when another beautiful woman comes to you.''

Taking a deep breath, she asked, "How can I believe I'll ever be enough for you after all the women you've had? How can I ever forget all those women? I hate myself for caring about your past, but I hate that you've made love to so many others. I don't know if I can ever forget. Sometimes I close my eyes and see you, you and Patti, you and everybody. When I think about it, it makes me ache."

"Love," Race said comfortingly, his eyes full of grief. "I wish I could change the past. Erase all that meaningless— all the women who didn't matter. I swear to you that none of it meant anything to me. That you're the only woman that I've ever *made love* with. You are the only woman that I ever want to make love with again. Please," he murmured, "let me change your mind. I'll prove to you that no other woman will ever matter to me. No other woman has ever mattered to me. I love you and only you. I have never said that to another woman, never promised that to anyone else. Only you."

With that pronouncement, he pulled her to her feet and tenderly led her up to his room. There he undressed her and made love to her so gently and so profoundly that Jenni cried as her body melted and reformed itself in shudders of pure pleasure. "I love you, Race. Never leave me," she told him as he folded her into his arms and held her through the night.

As Race held her slender body close to his heart, he vowed that he would keep her forever. He had won half the battle already. She'd admitted that she loved him. Now he would prove that she could trust him.

Chapter Ten

Jennifer woke at dawn, feeling strangely disoriented. Opening her eyes, she realized that she was in Race's bed. His arm was firmly clasped around her waist, as though he felt the need to hold her to him even in his sleep. Smiling at the boyish innocence on his sleeping face, she gently moved from his grasp. Pulling on his discarded shirt, she walked over to the window, looking out at her own peaceful house. The twins would not be back until the afternoon, giving her several hours to think about Race and absorb what he'd said last night.

She was thoroughly sick of her own indecisiveness. This was the first time in her life that she'd wavered on the brink of a major decision for so long. She loved Race, and after last night she did not doubt that he loved her. Right now a good part of the problem was within her. She honestly didn't know if she would be strong enough to put his past out of her mind. Jennifer hated to think she was so petty that the thought of all his other women could ruin her life.

She didn't want to feel that she couldn't hold him. Jenni-fer plain didn't like what she saw in herself. Not liking it was not the same, however, as not admitting it was true. Slipping her clothes on, she quietly eased out of the house and walked back to hers.

This morning Race followed her, waking when he heard the bedroom door close. He found her sitting on her bed-room floor, cradling the scrapbooks she'd made of him and his women during her pregnancy. It was tear-stained and had obviously been through a lot.

Silently he walked back to his house, finally settling, as was his habit, on the shaded, screened porch that over-looked the golf course. Unwillingly he wondered if he would ever be able to get through to Jenni. He truly didn't know if there was any possible way he could make up for the pain he'd caused her. He didn't even know if it was reasonable of him to expect her to trust him again.

Scornfully Race admitted to himself that if the situation had been reversed, and that he knew his woman had been with scores of other men, he'd...he'd... Dammit, he didn't know what he'd do. He didn't know if he'd be able to ac-cept that any more than Jennifer could. With a touch of true rage, he wondered if she'd had any other lovers. Then he wondered how he dared to even wonder.

An hour later Jennifer had showered, changed her clothes and wandered back to Race's. She wanted to talk, to tell him that she was willing to try. When no one an-swered the doorbell, she walked around to the back porch and heard Race softly singing a new song, one that she'd never heard before. Haunted by the bittersweet melody, she paused in the shadows and listened to his tune.

Regret for lost love and past mistakes echoed through the lyrics of the sad song, and the refrain was clearly straight from Race's heart: "When the wild life is too empty, when the truth comes shining through, the lonely fool is left alone, with just the memories of youth. Love is lost for-ever, and regrets the bitterest pain of all . . ."

"Race," Jennifer murmured, walking up to his side, "that was beautiful."

"Hey," Race said, reaching out to pull her down next to him. Before she could speak, he put his fingers gently to her lips and asked her to hear him out. "I don't know what to say to you. I saw you this morning with your blasted scrapbook and it all hit me. Will you ever be able to forget my past?" With bitter honesty, he told her, "I don't know what I'd do if the situation were reversed. If you'd been with other men. Have you?" he asked, lost in a painful curiosity that was, he realized, not unlike hers.

For a second, Jennifer was tempted to lie and torture him, but she couldn't. She could not hurt him unnecessarily. At that very moment she finally acknowledged that she was strong enough to make it with him, mature enough to put the past behind them.

Taking his hand, she pulled it to her, brushing her lips across his knuckles, and told him the truth. "There were two other men, Race." As she felt his hand tighten into a fist, she soothed it with a kiss and told him, "Don't be jealous. Both were long ago, right after I graduated from college. The first happened because he looked like you. The second because he loved me to distraction and promised his love would heal me. It didn't. I guess I had to convince myself that there was only one passion in my life. You." After a moment she asked him, "Does that bother you?"

Race took a moment and honestly told her, "Fool that I am, it does. I hate it. The idea of you with another man makes my blood boil." Hitting the wooden railing with his fist, he turned to her with eyes too full of understanding. "If I feel like this, how terrible you must feel."

"Can you forgive me?" Jennifer asked, forgetting for the moment how ridiculously ironic her question was.

"There's nothing to forgive, Jennifer. I could never be angry with you." He paused and then went on. "The problem is me, love. Can you ever forgive my past, forget it enough to live with me?"

Taking a deep breath, she looked into his troubled gray eyes and said, "I've thought about us a lot, and I accept your proposal. I love you Racine Huntington—Race Hunter. I don't think I've ever loved another man, and I know I will never love another. I refuse to let our past ruin the rest of our lives. I'll marry you, if that's what you truly want."

"Oh, Jennifer," Race said, pulling her to him for a deep celebratory kiss. He sat his guitar to one side and pulled her onto his lap, her legs dangling down on either side of his. "Are you absolutely sure? Once we marry, I'll never let you go again."

"I'm sure, Race. I finally decided that I simply can't live without you. We both have to forget your past." Tenderly she traced the sides of his face with her hands. "Can you do that?"

"I promise you, Jennifer Grange Huntington," Race told her in a deep, solemn voice, "to be your husband, to be your lover, to be your best friend and to never, never touch another woman in my life. I swear it to you, my love."

As Jennifer felt his body hardening against hers, they both heard a car pull into Jennifer's driveway. "One of the kids is back," Jenni groaned, moving herself provocatively across his lap as she slowly got to her feet. "We'll have to finish this later."

"You temptress." Race groaned, standing up and holding her against him, effectively turning the tables. "We'll never be finished with this."

"No," she told him softly as she pulled free, "we never will. Do you mind if we wait a few days to tell the children? I still don't know what we'll do about that. We have a lot of things to discuss."

"Whatever you say, my love." Giving her rump a swat, he told her to go back to their children. "I've got an errand to run. Plan on going out to dinner—fancy. I'll have Jameson cook something for your mom and the twins."

"Okay," Jen called over her shoulder as she trotted back to her house. It would work. Somehow it would work.

Glowing, she went to greet her son and spent several minutes of idle chitchat with the mother who had brought Rick home. She found herself wanting to tell this plump woman that she was engaged. She, Jennifer Grange, was going to marry the most wonderful man in the whole world. She'd think I was crazy, Jennifer told herself as she walked into the kitchen with Rick, if I told her that Race Hunter was going to marry me. Margo was ready with lunch, her eyes asking a million questions as she noticed the irrepressible smile plastered on her daughter's face.

"Does this mean what I hope it does?" Margo asked quietly at the refrigerator door.

"Yes. But don't tell the kids yet. We have a lot of plans to make. I still don't quite know how I'll deal with his fame. Or what we're going to do. Whatever we decide, it will concern all of us." Giving her mother a hug, she added, "I hope you'll come and live with us. Race will buy us a house large enough, or perhaps you could have your own place nearby. I don't want to lose you."

"Oh, Jenni," Margo told her, her eyes glistening with happy tears. "Thank you for the offer. I'll think about it." Grabbing her daughter for a quick hug, she told her, "Oh, baby, I'm so happy for you. I think it's right this time, really right."

Jenni asked her mother to baby-sit that night and asked her if she'd mind eating over at Race's again.

"Not tonight," Margo said, her eyes sparkling. "Jameson and I are eating over here for a change. We'll be glad to include the twins in our dinner."

"Don't change your plans, Mom. I'll call Susie Ralston and have her baby-sit tonight."

Finally it was decided that Margo would cook for them all and that Susie would come over to sit with the twins at eight. Everyone was satisfied with the arrangement.

Smiling and in great good humor, Jenni welcomed Becca back and listened to her account of yesterday's adventures. Eventually Becca tired of talking to her mother and ran out to the back yard to play with Rick. Jennifer went upstairs and took a long, deep bubble bath. She wanted this evening to be perfect.

Race caught his breath as Jenni answered the door and drifted out of the house with him. She was wearing a deceptively simple dress of deep emerald-green silk that exactly matched her eyes. It was knee-length, with a slit up one side of its narrow skirt. The bodice fell in a deep V between her full breasts, making it impossible to wear a bra. Jennifer shrugged into an evening jacket, watching Race's eyes caress her tingling breasts and smiling at the effect even his gaze could have on her body.

"You are beautiful," Race announced, touching her tumbled hair with a finger. "I want to take you straight back to bed," he told her, running a finger along the top of her bodice and reaching down to kiss the wildly sensitive spot behind her ear. Taking a deep breath, he nestled his nose in the curve of her neck, inhaling the sweet perfume that was Jenni and only Jenni.

As she turned to him in agreement, more than willing to postpone dinner, he laughed at her and told her to wait. "We've got reservations at Frolmain's," he told her, naming one of the best restaurants in town. "I intend to celebrate our engagement in the proper way."

"So do I," Jennifer told him as she stood on tiptoe to nip the lobe of his ear. "The most proper way."

"Later, woman," Race told her, delighted by this playful creature. Her lack of restraint was convincing Race that she had truly committed herself to him. Taking her hand in his, he kissed it as he escorted her into the car. "I love you," he told her, his eyes shining with emotion.

Dinner was wonderful. They had champagne, the finest wine and a wonderful dinner of the restaurant's famous grilled shrimp with mustard sauce. All Jennifer remembered later of their engagement night was that Race never took his eyes from her and that during dessert he took her hand and slowly slid a ring on her finger. It was the most exquisite diamond she'd ever seen, a glistening golden canary stone that almost matched her hair.

Later that night, Race made love to her as though she were the most precious thing in the world. Slowly he touched and tasted every inch of her, slowly worshiping her body until she thought she would die from the beauty of it. Wordlessly they used their bodies to celebrate the deep and profound commitment they'd made to each other.

The next day they made it official and announced their engagement to the twins. The children were pleased that Uncle Race was going to be their father, and everything was going along smoothly. Except that Jenni and Race still hadn't told the twins his real identity or broken the news to them that they were going to have to move to California. Somehow Jennifer was reluctant to tell them that, and wanted to wait a few more days to get them used to the idea of a new father before they found out just how rich and famous their new dad was.

Two nights after their engagement, Race and Jenni were sitting in his living room, still grappling with the problem of how to break the news of Race's fame to the twins, when the phone rang.

"Manny?" Race answered. Putting his hand over the receiver, he told Jennifer, "It's my agent." When she started to leave, Race motioned to her to stay. "No more secrets between us. Never again." Pulling her over to him, he held the phone between them so that she could hear everything that was said.

As Jennifer listened to him, the reality of Race's fame began to creep up on her. Manny was calling to remind Race that he'd been booked several months ago to be one of the presenters on the most prestigious country music award show. It would take place in Hollywood in three days, and Race definitely had to be in town the day before the broadcast for rehearsals. Race swore for a moment and asked Manny if he couldn't skip it.

"Why did you wait so late to remind me about this?" Race demanded angrily. "I could have gotten out of it if you'd given me more time. You know how I hate these things. They're like animal parades."

When Manny reminded him that the television magazines had already announced that he was going to appear, Race gave in. "I'll fly in tomorrow, for the two days, and that's it." Just before he agreed, his voice deepened and he ordered Manny not to ever make any further commitments, no matter how brief, without clearing them with him first.

Jennifer heard Manny's voice impatiently asking Race when he was going to return to civilization. "You can't hide in that hick town forever. Someone's going to find you."

"I know, Manny. Don't worry, it's only for a little more time. We're moving back to California soon," Race promised his agent.

"Good. Good," Manny told him. "I hope you have that broad worked out of your system pretty soon."

In a cold voice, Race told Manny, "That broad is going to marry me, and if I ever hear you speak about her like that again you'll be looking for another job."

"Hey, it's okay. Sorry, Race," his agent said, his voice soothing and phony. "We'll talk tomorrow. I'll pick you up at LAX around noon. Ciao."

Turning, Race caught the look of distaste on Jennifer's face and told her. "It's no big deal. He always talks like that. I think he saw too many B movies when he was a kid. He's a nice guy, really, and one of the best agents in the business. I'll finish telling him that I'll be changing my lifestyle, and he'll do what I want. Don't worry."

Taking her hand in his, he urged her to join him on the trip. "Come with me. You can meet my people and we can start house hunting. They should have it narrowed down to a few choices by now," he told her, unconsciously revealing his plans.

When she questioned him, he sheepishly announced that he'd put some people to work looking for possible houses for them the last time he'd been back to L.A. "In case you would come to me, Jenni," he told her honestly. "I knew I loved you and wanted you. Don't be mad."

"I'm not." She laughed. She'd be a fool to get mad because he'd wanted her so much that he'd started house hunting before she'd agreed to marry him. Suspiciously she asked him about the ring and found out that it was indeed a special diamond that he'd ordered from Tiffany's a month ago and had waiting for her. It seemed to Jennifer that she'd fallen through the looking glass and that Race was trying to make up for all the past years in one fell swoop.

"Since you're in such a great mood, I should tell you that you're a rich woman. I settled a trust fund on you the last trip back. So you don't have to marry me for my money," Race said lightly, wondering how she'd take this last secret.

"Oh, Race," Jenni answered, touched to think that he had cared so much about her, had done so much without any assurance that she'd ever agree to marry him. "What am I going to do with you? You know I don't care about your money. I almost wish you didn't have any. Everything would be so much easier if you weren't famous."

Pulling her into his arms, Race rasped into her ear, "You don't know what that means to me. To be loved for myself, in spite of all the fame. Promise me that you won't change, that you'll keep me sane."

Holding him tightly, Jen spoke from her heart. "I can't stop loving you, even if I try. You're stuck with me, and once we're married, Mr. Superstar, I plan on keeping you with me every night in my bed. There won't be room for anyone else in our new life."

"Then come with me and start our life together now," Race entreated her. He didn't want to be separated from her. "It's only for two nights."

"No, much as I'm tempted, I can't leave everything so quickly. I have to give notice on my job, talk to the children's school. There's too much to do, Race. Besides, if I show up with you there's bound to be publicity. I don't want to tell the children about you until we're nearly all ready to go. They'll tell their school and the neighbors and we'll be inundated with people wanting to meet you."

With a quick kiss she looked into his eyes and said, "Go. I have to learn to trust you, you know. You'll be off now and again, no matter what we want. Why don't you arrange for us to go back over Thanksgiving to go house hunting? That's only three weeks or so from now."

"All right," Race agreed, knowing she was probably right. What could happen in two nights in Hollywood? Besides, knowing those award deals, he'd be so busy that they wouldn't be together at all. Actually, it was better that she not come. This was not the right impression he wanted to give her of California. The first time they went together, he wanted to be free to devote himself entirely to her and the kids.

He'd fly in, do the rehearsal one day and the show the next, and fly back the next morning. No sweat. He'd arranged ahead of time to stay at Edward's house, so there was no chance of Patti turning up in his bed again. Race hoped that once he was married, Patti would finally get the idea and disappear from his life forever.

Two nights later, Jennifer and Margo were sitting in their recreation room, their feet propped up, with a huge bowl of popcorn between them. For once the twins had cooperated and gone to bed early. "I'll be interested to see what Race does about his new look," Margo commented to Jenni. "Do you know what he's going to look like?"

"I think he's going to be himself. Whatever that is," Jenni replied. "I'm honestly not sure if he'll let his hair grow back long, but I'd guess he'll regrow the beard. Once we're out in California, he won't have to disguise himself anymore. I'll ask him when he calls later."

"I rather prefer the long hair and earring," Margo mentioned with a twinkle in her eye.

"So do I, Mom. Actually, I love him no matter how he looks. The only thing I don't like is the scruffy half-shaved look." The minute Race had known he was headed back to L.A. he'd stopped shaving, and he'd left town with two days' growth of beard. "It might look good, but it doesn't feel too great."

Margo reached over and squeezed her daughter's hand. "I'm so glad for you, Jen. I know Racine loves you and the twins."

As they watched the beginning of the show, with all the beautiful women in their sparkling gowns, Jenni turned to her mother and said, "I don't know what I've gotten myself into. I'm afraid that part of this new life is going to be a fantasy. It's a shame that I'm not more into glitter and glamour. I hope Race is right and we'll be able to live a regular life out there somewhere."

"You'll have to make a way for yourselves, dear." Margo told her. "I know that you can do it."

About an hour into the show, the announcer told them that Race Hunter would be among the next batch of presenters. Margo and Jennifer turned up the sound slightly and focused on the screen.

Jennifer almost spilled the popcorn when she saw Race walk out with his co-presenter, Patti Silk. The blond woman was stunning, dressed in a skintight sequined gown. She clung to a tuxedoed Race's arm like glue as they approached the podium together.

When Race, his face stern and controlled beneath his makeup, began to read the cue cards, Patti pushed herself slightly in front of him and batted her long, beautiful eyelashes at the camera. Wriggling her glorious body, she leaned over the microphone, exposing her ample bosom, and spontaneously announced, "I'm so excited, everybody, that I just have to take a minute to make an important announcement. Race and I are going to have a baby!" Turning to him and looking girlishly excited, she bubbled, "You're going to be a daddy in May, Race," before flinging her arms around him and giving him a deep kiss.

As Jenni felt her heart break into a million pieces, she froze, unable to look away from the sight of her fiancé and his other woman. "What?" Race said, shaking his head. "What are you talking about, Patti?"

Before he could say any more, Patti began to read the cue cards, apologizing prettily for the delay before she read off the list of nominees. Stuck, with the directors motioning them to hurry, Race swallowed his anger and announced the winner of the award. When the man proved to be absent from the proceeding, Race graciously accepted for him and grabbed Patti's arm.

They were immediately surrounded by photographers and reporters, all wanting the details about their reconciliation and the baby. "When is it due?" several of them asked. Patti smiled sweetly, ignoring the bruising grip that Race had on her arm, and answered, "In May."

An enterprising reporter asked, "Have you been off together somewhere? Is that the reason for Race's new 'straight' look? Everybody's wondered what happened to you, Hunter. You've been out of sight since your tour ended. Now I guess we all know what you've been doing." The reporter smirked.

"No, you don't know anything," Race snapped as he tightened his hold on Patti's arm and dragged her toward the back of the stage. Unfortunately, there was no place for them to talk, and Patti managed to slip away from him in the midst of the mob of well-wishers, reporters and other celebrities.

Race bolted from the crowd of reporters and ran back to his car, ordering the driver to take him back to his agent's house. Someone was responsible for this mess, and Manny was number one on his list. First, though, he decided, he had to talk to Jenni. He changed his instructions to the driver, asking him to find a private phone somewhere. Then he searched his pockets for some money. He had to call Jenni and explain. The stupid show was being broadcast live, and he knew that she must have been watching the whole fiasco. What a miserable mess. Cursing, he decided to kill Patti and Manny once he got everything straightened out with Jenni.

Finally the driver pulled up next to a public phone booth in a parking lot. Race shoved the quarter in the slot and got the operator. Desperately he wondered if Jenni would accept the charges and give him a chance to explain. She had to, that was all.

As a commercial faded onto the screen, Jennifer reached over and switched off the television. "Well, Mom," she managed shakily, "I guess Race has come out of the closet. He's not in disguise anymore. We found out the truth about him. Thank goodness it's not too late. At least we weren't already married...and the kids..." Pulling a pillow to her chest, Jenni collapsed into bitter tears. Like lava, the tears poured out of her eyes and ran in fiery rivulets down her cheeks. "You'd think I'd learn, wouldn't you?"

Standing up, she suddenly heaved the pillow across the floor, barely missing a lamp on an end table. "He was only gone for a few days in the past months. He must have slept with her during one of his business trips if she's due in May."

Shaking, and running her hands over her face in distracted gestures, she turned to her mother and stammered, "I—I'm going up to my room. I need to be alone." Anger warred with pain, and Jennifer's face felt as though it were going to self-destruct at any moment.

Margo looked at her in distress and gathered her daughter into her arms for a moment. "Maybe he can explain," Margo began, but stopped when Jenni pulled back.

"How could he explain? Unless Patti is lying about the whole thing."

"Maybe she is, hon. You know that she and Race were not together even when he was here in July. I bet she made the whole thing up to try to get him back. He'll call you. Wait and talk to him."

Hope battled with pain, and Jennifer wondered if she dared let herself ever believe again. He would call, wouldn't he? Jennifer asked herself as she stared down at the huge diamond that sparked so tauntingly on her left hand.

Finally the phone rang and Jennifer frantically answered it, barely hearing the operator ask if she'd accept the charges.

"Race," Jennifer said, trying to control her voice and not let him realize how upset she was.

"Jen, are you all right?" Race asked. Now that he'd gotten her on the phone, he was strangely afraid to talk. What was he going to say? How could he expect her to believe him after this fiasco.

"I take it you saw the show?" he asked hesitantly. When there was no reply except a small choked noise, he went on. "Look, honey. It was all a complete surprise to me. Somebody arranged the whole thing. Patti sandbagged me. I didn't even know she was scheduled to be on the show until the very last minute. Then she totally surprised me with that announcement of hers on the air. It doesn't mean anything. It's you I love, Jennifer. It's you I'm going to marry."

When he didn't say anything more, Jennifer asked the one question that she had to have answered—the question that Race had been praying she wouldn't ask.

"Is the baby yours?" Jennifer's voice demanded, sounding strangely hoarse.

"I don't know if she's even pregnant, for heaven's sake." Race argued truthfully. "It's all some sort of trick. She's perfectly capable of lying about something like that."

"Answer me, Race Hunter," Jennifer again demanded, changing the question so that he had to answer. "Could the baby be yours? If she's pregnant? Tell me, Race, did you sleep with her anytime in the last two months? You told me that you were not involved with her since last summer."

"Jen, I can explain. She— I don't know—" he started to say, and Jennifer hung up the phone. The dial tone echoed in his ear as he realized that Jennifer had disconnected. Cursing, he banged the receiver down and drove his fist through the booth's glass wall. Then he blankly stared at his bleeding hand in numbing pain.

Jennifer turned to her mother, her eyes bruised and full of pain. "He admitted it, Mom. Says he can explain." Laughing hysterically, she collapsed on the couch and started shaking. "How can he explain? 'By the way, hon,'" she said mockingly, trying to imitate Race's rich baritone, "'I just happened to sleep with Patti on my way to the grocery store. By the way, love, I just happened to sleep with a couple of groupies at the studio today. Hey, don't take it personally, it didn't mean anything.'" As the tears and laughter became confused, Jenni looked at her mother and whispered in agony, "How could I have been so gullible?"

"He fooled me, too," Margo admitted, feeling her daughter's pain as though it were her own. "He really fooled us both. I could have sworn on a stack of Bibles that he was sincere."

"He doesn't know the meaning of the word," Jennifer groaned. "Thank goodness it all came out before we moved to California."

As Jennifer really started to cry, Margo put her arm around her and walked up the stairs beside her. "Do you want one of my sleeping pills? It'll help you get through the night. You've got to think of the twins."

Trying to hold back her tears, Jennifer refused the pill and fell back onto her comforting bed. "I'll be better in the morning. I have to be better," she vowed as she slipped the diamond off her finger and put it in the small drawer in her nightstand. "He isn't worth it."

While Jennifer faced the unpleasant truth about Race, the driver of the limo rushed out, pushing Race into the car and speeding him to the nearest emergency room.

"Mr. Hunter, sir. Hold this on your hand," the young driver insisted, frightened by the look of total fury in Race's eyes and the total lack of regard the singer had for the blood trickling down his hand. "Man, you're bleeding all over my car," the man said, and suddenly Race looked down and realized that he'd sliced his hand open. Just what he needed, he sighed as they pulled up to the emergency room and someone helped him walk inside.

Swearing at the entire world, Race blistered the air with his cursing as the doctor sewed his hand up in the emergency room. He swore that he'd get to the bottom of this entire mess. He'd personally crate Patti and his agent up and carry them to Charlotte on his back. They'd explain everything to Jennifer. He absolutely refused to lose her now. Not when he'd had everything he'd ever wanted in his hands.

Stalking to the phone, he dared anyone at the hospital reception desk to challenge him as he dialed Jennifer's home number once again. The phone rang several times, and Race was about to hit something in frustration when Margo finally picked the receiver up.

"Margo? Please let me—" Race began, but the older woman interrupted him.

"You can't explain," Margo told him. "You slept with that woman at the same time you were here begging Jenni to forgive you. Swearing to her that you'd be faithful. How could you?" Margo asked. "Leave us alone. You've done more than enough damage."

"Let me talk to Jenni. I can explain," Race pleaded.

"She's asleep. Just stay away, Race. Stay away from us all," Margo ordered before she hung up.

When the phone rang again, Margo took it off the hook and went to bed.

Chapter Eleven

As day broke, Race wearily pulled into his driveway. Jameson tried one last time to convince the distraught singer to come into the house for a few hours' rest, but Race snapped at him, "You sleep if you need to. Just get into that house and stay by the phone. Edward promised to call me as soon as he tracks down Patti or Manny." His fists clenched in anger as he thought of the twosome.

"Look at your hand, mate," Jameson said, pointing at the fist that Race was making. Race looked at him in confusion. Jameson's English accent was becoming more pronounced as exhaustion and concern weighed him down. "Don't do that to your hand. The doctors said you shouldn't try to move it more than necessary for a day or two." He added dryly, "When we find the beggars you'll have to hit them with your other fist. Just leave the left one alone."

"Right," Race sighed wearily. "I'll keep that in mind."

After he'd left the hospital around eight last evening, he'd tried to contact both Manny and Patti several times before finally telling his driver to return him to his lawyer's private home. Edward Kurray and Race had discussed the entire unfortunate incident, from the surprise pairing of Patti with Race as co-presenter to her patently faked "spontaneous announcement." It had obviously not been a coincidence, and they reluctantly concluded that Race's agent had to be responsible for the setup. No one else would have been able to book Patti into a co-presenter's spot without his knowledge and permission or have dared to keep it a secret from Race.

Edward disclosed that Manny had been the one responsible for the investigation of Jennifer. The agent had insisted Race was making a big mistake after Race had told them about Jenni and his twins. Manny had deliberately ignored Race's decision to stop touring, and he'd really panicked when Race had moved to Charlotte. The anxious man had frequently pleaded with Edward to "talk some sense into" Race. Manny was convinced that Race's career would be ruined if he settled down with a wife and two children.

Race finally told Edward, in the strictest of confidence, about the episode with Patti. It was now clear that Manny must have been behind that incident, as well. Patti hadn't followed him to his hotel, as Race had originally thought. Manny must have given her the hotel and room number, maybe even provided a key for her.

Understanding Race's dilemma, the attorney promised to look into the legal side of things, although both men conceded there was no way that Race would ever be able to go into a court of law and prove that Patti had been the aggressor. Not with his reputation and their past history.

By the time Race was ready to leave Edward's home an hour later he had calmed down a bit, certain that at least one person in Los Angeles had his best interests at heart. Edward was holding a notarized statement firing Manny, effective immediately. He was also ready to start an investigation of Patti and her possible baby.

Right now, the important thing was to get to Jenni and explain. The singer ordered his pilot to take off immediately and fly directly to Charlotte, offering him a huge bonus as an inducement. It was just eleven o'clock, and they would reach the east coast by dawn.

It was pure luck that Race had been able to track down Jameson, who had taken the night in L.A. to dine with some of his friends, and that the man had been able to get to the airport in time to accompany Race home. For almost four hours the men had flown, one so nervous that he could barely sit still, one sympathetic and angry for his friend, the third kept alert by the huge bonus he was earning. Finally the jet had arrived in Charlotte just before six local time.

Moving one of the wicker chairs on Jennifer's back porch, Race sat squarely in front of the back door, waiting for his family to stir. He would explain it all to Jennifer if he had to tie her down and sit on her. He refused to have his life ruined because of manipulative schemers like Patti Silk or Manny Feilderbelt. Not now, and not ever.

At seven-thirty the children came down the stairs and let Race in. He urged them to be quiet and helped them get their breakfast, starting each time he heard a noise. As much as he loved them, he hoped that they would be off to school before he had his chance to confront Jenni. Cautioning the twins to whisper, he asked them where their mom was.

"She and Grandma are both asleep. Mom wouldn't wake up much. She told us to get Grandma, so we decided to get our own breakfast and then surprise her," Becca told him.

"Why don't I help you make it and get you ready?" Race suggested. "We'll let them both sleep. I know they've had a rough night."

The twins and their dad were nearly out the door when Margo came hurrying down, only to stop dead in her tracks when she saw Race at the door. "You—she started to say, stopping when she saw the huge eyes of the twins staring up at her.

"Dad's...Uncle Race's..." Rick started to say, trying to get used to the idea that this large man was going to be his father. On the whole, Rick seemed to like the idea but was still not sure what to call him. "He's going to drive us to school."

Staring daggers at Race, Margo agreed. "Okay, honey. Be sure you take your book bags. Do you both have your lunch money?"

When they nodded, Margo added privately to Race, "You'd better get straight back here. You and Jenni have a lot to settle."

"We certainly do," Race told her. "I'll be back in a few minutes."

"Why are you dressed so funny?" Margo heard Becca ask him as they walked over to the rented car in Race's driveway. Margo noticed that he was still wearing the black slacks and ruffled white shirt from the tuxedo he'd worn on television.

"What happened to your hand?" Rick asked, causing Margo to observe the bandage on his left hand, as well.

Deliberately listening, Margo heard Race explain that he'd had an accident last night and cut his hand. The children were talking about stitches as they got into the car, leaving Margo to wonder just what had happened after Race had talked to Jenni last night.

Putting on some coffee, she went to rouse her daughter. Jenni was going to have to face Race, and she would want to be as alert as possible.

Jennifer stepped into a cool shower five minutes later, still aching from last night. "He's here?" she asked her mother once again. Margo entered, bringing a cup of coffee, and said, "He took the kids to school."

"You let him go off with the kids alone? What if he tries to take them?" Jennifer demanded. Moments later Jenni's momentary panic subsided and her voice returned to normal. "Sorry, Mom," she said. "Just a gut reaction. You were right in letting him drive the kids to school. He wouldn't resort to kidnapping. He's obviously sure that he can explain everything to me, that I'll buy whatever story he gives and forgive him again." Vigorously shampooing her hair, she felt her strength return, fueled by pride and anger. "He's going to be one surprised country singer. It's too late for me to believe him again."

Taking her time, Jennifer blow-dried her hair, applied makeup to hide the ravages of last night's tears and dressed in her favorite and most flattering outfit. It was a good thing she hadn't given her notice at work. She was going to be keeping her job after all.

Strange noises drifted up to her window as she finished dressing. She looked out the window and saw what looked like a demonstration. There were people everywhere. Cars were parked up and down both sides of her street, one nearly blocking her car in the driveway. Margo came running toward the stairs as Jennifer walked down.

"What's going on?" Jennifer demanded, trying to catch her breath as she noticed Race standing at the kitchen table looking at her. She could not help but notice how tired he looked and that he was still wearing most of the beautifully tailored tuxedo from last night. With his stubble turning into a beard, he was returning to the look that she'd associated with him for so long. With his bloodshot eyes and the weary expression on his face, he looked as though he'd been out partying for hours.

"I think the press has found us," Race announced as he watched Patti Silk, clad in a skintight white leather suit, climb out of a long black limo, chat for a moment with one of the men with a camera and then settle herself on his front porch. "With Patti's help."

"Hadn't you better go and greet your guest?" Jennifer curtly asked, looking at the other woman. Even through the window at a distance of several hundred years, Patti Silk was breathtaking—tall, slim, busty and beautiful. "What are you doing over here in the first place? I thought you said it all last night."

Taking Jennifer's arms, he forced her to turn toward him and gave her a quick, hard kiss. Before she could do more than push him away, he spoke urgently. "I love you. It's all a nasty game that Patti is playing with the help of my agent—change that to my ex-agent. I swear that I was essentially faithful to you and that it's all a trick. Promise me you'll let me explain after I get rid of Patti."

Jennifer looked at him with scathing disdain and spit out, "*Essentially?* How can one be *essentially* faithful? Isn't that a bit like being a trifle pregnant?"

Race shook her slightly in frustration, wincing when he used the hand with the stitches. "Please, Jenni. I love you. It'll be all right. I really can explain everything."

Jennifer looked at him, weakening momentarily when she saw the pain and anguish in his eyes. She wanted to believe him so badly, even though she knew he couldn't be trusted. She knew she was a fool, but at this point it was too late.

It didn't matter, anyway. She knew she wasn't going to get through this without a great deal of pain. Race was going to insist on seeing her, and the sooner she got it over with the better. She'd listen to his explanations and then send him on his way. As much as she loved him, she could not live with him. Biting her tongue to keep from screaming at him that he was tearing her heart to pieces, she calmly agreed. "All right. You'll get your chance to explain. After you get rid of all those people."

"Thank you, love," Race said in the most grateful tone Jennifer had ever heard. She was going to give him a chance. "Right now, I'd like to get out of here before those vultures get over here. Manny knows about you, but I don't know if Patti does. Let me out one of the back windows, and I'll circle around over the golf course. If we're lucky, they won't know anything about you. Don't answer the

door, not until I get rid of them,'' Race ordered, rushing
through the house and crawling awkwardly out her bathroom window. "Remember that I love you," he told her as
he took off into the woods beside the house.

Carefully Jenni closed the curtains and called in to work,
grateful that her job had flexible hours. She failed to mention the crowd of newspapermen next to her house. No
doubt the *Charlotte Sentinel* had at least one of its members there, and she just prayed that it was not one of her co-
workers who knew where she lived. As a reporter she had
a duty to cover Race, but she was much too personally involved to even consider it. Jenni knew that she'd be in
trouble with her editor eventually but could only hope that
the man would understand her dilemma after she'd had a
chance to explain it all. It really didn't matter in the long
run. There was no way that she was going to join that crowd
on Race's front porch or take advantage of her unique position in his life.

Running one hand over her eyes, she felt the press of
tears. This should not be any surprise, she told herself. In
fact, it was something she'd expected all along. The last two
months of her life had been a fairy tale, with Race playing
the role of suburban father and wonderful lover. He should
take it on the screen and leave real life to those who had to
live it.

Race had been too good to be true, and a part of her had
known from the first moment he'd walked back into her life
that something like this would happen. Her dream had
ended last night. From that moment on, it was just a matter of trying to control the damage as best she could, especially for the twins.

Pouring themselves cups of hot coffee, Jennifer and
Margo moved over to the window, where they could view
Race's house from behind their semisheer curtains. So far
no reporters had ventured onto her lawn, and Jenni hoped
it would stay that way. Race's house was still surrounded,
and Jenni could see Patti, her hair gleaming in the sun, sit-

ting on the front porch. Suddenly they saw Race's front door open, and he stood there, illuminated by popping flashbulbs. Patti got up and threw herself into his arms. Although Jenni and Margo were too far away to see the expression on anyone's face, they could tell by Race's abrupt movements that he had little to say to the reporters. He dragged Patti inside and closed the door.

"Well," Jenni told her mother briskly, "it seems that...it seems that my life's a mess again, Mom. I have to decide what to tell the kids."

"You promised to listen to Race's explanation," Margo reminded her, "before you decide anything."

"I lied. What good will that do? Even if he can explain it, look at this circus. It was all a lovely dream, but it's over." She put her emotions firmly into a little part of her brain and packed them away. She could not afford to let herself feel anything just yet. "What do you think I should do with Rick and Becca? It's obvious they can't come back here for a while."

Swearing, Jennifer stalked over to the phone, berating herself for not having protected her children from all of this hoopla. "I should have run Race off at the very first," she muttered to herself.

"If I recall," Margo offered impartially, "Race bought the house without your permission. You've done the best you could to keep them safe." After a pause when Jenni merely shook her head, Margo offered to pick up the twins at school. "Maybe we can stay at Aunt Alice's again for a night or two."

"Mom, I'm afraid that someone will find them at school. If Race is right, and Manny had something to do with this, he knows all about the twins and me. So far the reporters are holding off, but there is too good a chance that it's only temporary. Would you be willing to take the twins down to Stephanie's for a week or so?"

Though Stephanie was not technically a sister-in-law anymore, it still felt as if she were, bonds of love and affection being as strong as those of blood. The immediate friendship between Stephanie and Jennifer had begun the day they'd met and had lasted nearly ten years, tested by tragedy and distance.

A couple of months after the automobile accident that had cost Stephanie her husband and child, Stephie had moved back to her own home town, St. Augustine, Florida, and begun to slowly rebuild her life. She now worked with troubled teenagers, trying to prevent more alcohol-related tragedies like the one that had blighted her own life.

Jennifer had often wished that Stephanie would try to meet another man and love again, but Jenni was rapidly changing her mind. Jenni had followed her own advice, and look where she was, hurt and betrayed. At least Stephie had a perfect four years to recall.

When Stephanie answered the phone, Jenni released a deep breath, grateful that she'd caught her friend before she left for work. Briefly Jenni outlined the events of the past few weeks and asked if Margo and the twins could visit her for a few days. "I hate for them to miss school, but this is an emergency. If Patti knows about me and the twins, it's just a matter of time until she directs someone over here. I won't have the kids exposed to this." Jennifer's fingers clutched the receiver as Stephie calmly agreed with all of Jenni's requests. Jenni arranged to call Stephanie from the airport and tell her the flight number of her mother's plane, then hung up.

Margo offered to return to Charlotte after delivering the twins to Stephanie, but Jenni would not hear of it. "I'm the one responsible for this entire mess," she said. "I'm the one who fell in love with Race Hunter, not once but twice. I'm the idiot who let him interrupt our life. Blast it all, why did I go to that stupid concert? I should have refused the assignment. I should have told Race to go back to California when he moved in. I should have—" Breaking down for a second, Jennifer turned away, covering her face with her hands, trying to erase the pain from her face, forbidding herself to cry.

"Regrets don't matter anymore. I can handle it. I can handle Race." Jenni turned to ask her mother, "Please, as a favor to me, take the children away so that I don't have to worry about them, too. I won't have their pictures on the cover of every cheap tabloid. If we're very lucky, it will not come out that Race is their father. That's the best we can hope for now."

Seeing the anguish and determination on her daughter's face, Margo agreed. As they prepared for the trip, Jenni reminded Margo that money was no longer any problem. It was ironic. Race was providing more than enough to finance their getaway.

He had been telling her the truth about some of his activities while he'd been in L.A. Her lawyer, Victoria, had contacted her only a couple of days previously about the twins' trust funds. The interest payments were going to start next month.

The cars were blocked in, so Jenni called a cab. When it finally came, Jenni and her mom ran out to the waiting car and were gone before the reporters got more than a glimpse of them. Three hours later, Jennifer got out of another cab and quickly walked up to her front door. This time the media people paid attention to her, making her think that Patti must have said something while she was gone. Reaching the door in time to avoid most of them, Jennifer ignored their questions and locked the door behind her.

The phone was ringing as she shut the door, and Jenni answered it without thinking. A reporter from a music magazine was on the other end, asking her if she cared to comment on the story that she was Race Hunter's newest lady. Softly she said she had no comment on anything and hung up the phone. It started ringing again immediately, and she fought the urge to pick it up and throw it. With rapid steps, she marched to the small back bedroom that she used for a den and found the telephone answering ma-

chine her mother had bought for her last Christmas. It was
turned off, as usual, and Jenni quickly disconnected it from
the phone in the den and carried it into the kitchen. There
she quickly reconnected it to the phone on the coffee table,
leaving the volume turned up so that she could hear the
identity of the callers without having to talk to them.

In between incoming calls, she placed a couple of calls of
her own, quietly taking a couple of days off from the paper, as well as promising them an exclusive if and when she
chose to talk. She called Victoria and got a few minutes of
support. Then she called Race.

"Jenni," his frantic voice said as soon as Jameson con-
nected her. "Where have you been? I've been calling you
for hours."

"I took the twins away from this circus, if you must
know."

"Thank goodness. I was worried about them. What did
you tell them?" Race asked slowly, not sure if he wanted to
know. "Did the reporters get to them? Do they know about
them?"

"You're asking me?" Jenni asked in disbelief. "That's
what I was calling you about. Those reporters are now on
my porch, asking about us, our relationship, so I assume
that someone told them about me. Exactly what has been
said and by whom? Do they know about the twins?"

Cursing fluently, Race took a deep breath and tried to
calm down. "It was Patti. Patti held another impromptu
press conference on my front porch as she was leaving and
told them that you were my new...woman." Race didn't
tell her the exact words that Patti used. They were so vulgar that he knew they wouldn't be quoted anyway. How
could he ever have fooled himself into thinking that he felt
anything for that woman?

"It'll be all right," Race said soothingly. "I think I got
rid of Patti permanently this time, but who knows? I
thought I was rid of her long ago. It's a real mess. She and

Manny were behind all this publicity. They're trying to break us up."

"Well," Jenni admitted dryly, "they seem to be doing a pretty good job of it."

"No!" Race said loudly. "Don't say that. It'll all work out, I promise you. What did you do with the twins, by the way? Are they over at Alice's again?"

"No, I sent them to Florida, to visit my sister-in-law. You remember Stephanie, Mike's widow?" Jenni asked him, bringing up another series of bad memories for Race. Stephanie wasn't going to be on his side, Race thought. The only time he'd met Mike's wife he'd been partying pretty heavily and had not made a good impression. Mike had left him with a few choice words of recrimination, warning Race that the world was not made exclusively for his own personal pleasure. That was the last time he'd spoken to Mike face-to-face and the only serious argument they'd ever had. They'd talked on the phone briefly when Mike, Jr. had been born, and he'd sent them a baby gift, but somehow Race didn't think that was enough to win Stephanie over, and especially not now.

"I haven't told them anything," Jennifer continued, unaware of the barely healed wound she'd disturbed. "I know I'm going to have to tell them something, but I think we had better settle our relationship first. And find out what the press is going to announce to the world. I won't lie to the kids, but I'd just as soon keep this as simple as possible. It's going to be hard enough on them as it is, since we already told them that we're going to marry. I knew we should have waited a while."

"What do you mean, hard enough? We're still going to marry," Race stated, anger and determination in his every word. "I'm coming over there right now. Stay put."

"Don't," she told the disconnected receiver. He'd already hung up, and she knew he'd be over sooner or later. Calmly she walked from room to room, making sure every drape and curtain was drawn. When she was sure of their privacy, she made a fresh pot of coffee and prepared herself for Race. It was only early afternoon, although she felt as though it had been more like forty-eight hours than fourteen since she'd seen Race and Patti on the awards show last night and Patti announcing her pregnancy with Race's child. That was the bottom line in this whole affair.

It was altogether too easy to excuse Race from this mess, to believe that he was an injured party. That certainly seemed to be the line of defense that he was planning to use. She knew that he'd try to play on her sympathy, try to do anything to get her back. Jenni paused, wondering at her own ego. Did she really think that Race was so enamored of her that he'd lie to get her back? Or was his ego so involved that he was going to have to make her forgive him before he walked away?

"Lady," Jennifer lectured herself, "you are one confused person. Make up your mind. Is he lying, or does he love you? Maybe both." Most likely, Jenni finally decided, Race's definition of love included having other women on the side. Of course, since it didn't matter to him, it shouldn't bother her.

Aside from her own feelings, she reminded herself, there was one other being to consider—the unborn child that Patti was carrying. No matter how Race felt about Patti, he was responsible for his own child. What that baby would mean to him was yet one more unknown factor.

All that would have to be resolved later. The first priority at this moment was to get rid of the reporters. Then she had to get rid of Race. Her heart protested as she decided that, but what choice was there? She had the twins to consider. Their young lives were her responsibility, and she had no right dragging them into a world like Race's—not to mention her own reservations about living in such a world herself.

An hour passed, interrupted only by the frequent phone calls and the infrequent ringing of the doorbell. Suddenly a commotion erupted outside her door, and she heard the sound of cars starting and feet running from her porch. Race must be leaving, she mused, wondering if it was worth the bother to get up and peek out the window to see. As she sat, holding a cold cup of coffee in her hand, she heard another noise, louder than before and coming from her own bathroom.

As she stood up, Race appeared in the room, looking even more rumpled and tired. He was holding his left hand with his right, an expression of pain on his lined face.

"What's wrong? Have you hurt yourself?"

"Do you think you have any spare bandages, love? I seem to have pulled this one off while I was climbing through your window. By the way," he added, "Jameson has temporarily lured the reporters away."

Jenni looked down at the stained bandage in his hand and ordered him to sit on the couch while she went for the first aid kit that she kept in the bathroom. She opened the large box and carefully took his left hand in hers. Unwrapping the gauze, she cringed when she saw the red, inflamed skin and the numerous small black stitches.

"What did you do to your poor hand?" she demanded as she took out a cotton ball and began to clean the wound with some hydrogen peroxide. As it bubbled, she looked up at him, insisting on an answer.

"I slammed my fist through a phone booth after you hung up on me last night." Silently daring her to say a word, he added, "It's no big deal. The doctors said I didn't injure anything permanently."

"Oh," Jennifer said, not knowing quite how to respond. This was more difficult than she'd thought it would be, sitting alone in the darkened room with the one and only man she loved. The man she couldn't trust. "I'm sorry."

"I'm the one who's sorry," Race told her passionately. "Let me explain. It's all a big setup, Jen. You were right about Manny. He wanted you out of my life, and he planned all of this to get rid of you. He and Patti were in it together. She's his client, as well as me. Knowing her, she must have worked on him to convince him that I wouldn't be worth anything if I settled down. Quit touring."

Recalling the long conversation he'd had that morning with Edward, Race tried to explain. "My lawyer caught up with Manny this morning and got the whole story. Apparently Patti wormed everything out of Manny right after I moved here and she lost track of me. She was sure that I'd come back to her after my tour, and went crazy when I just dropped out of sight. She finally got Manny to tell her that I was in Charlotte and what I was planning to do here. Patti worked on Manny's insecurities and had him convinced that if you and I married it would be the end of my career and Manny's big checks. Edward swears that Manny thought it was all for my own good."

"Maybe it is," Jennifer noted, trying to be objective. As she cleaned the wound and put some antibacterial ointment on it, she avoided looking at Race's face, concentrating on her task. Finally she wrapped the wound in new gauze and taped it into place.

"You're good at that," Race told her.

"Rick has had stitches two times," she said. "I've gotten pretty good at patching up errant boys."

"I'm no boy," Race replied, smoldering. He was becoming more and more aware that she was holding his hand in her lap. The back of his hand rested firmly on her thighs, and he slowly moved it up and down her leg as he went on. "I'm the man that you're going to marry."

"I don't think it'll work," Jennifer told him as he took his other hand and began to work his way up from her knee. "We can't—" Jennifer started to say before Race stifled her words with a kiss. The warmth of his hands felt as though it were penetrating her very bones, settling between her thighs, and Jenni stifled a moan.

Race saw the fire in her eyes and found himself caught in the smoldering green depths. As she leaned toward him, trembling with need, Race caught her to him and eased her down on the couch. With his right hand he pulled her to him, pushing up the soft velour top that she wore and struggling to remove his own clothing. His mouth devoured hers in a primitive, almost brutal caress, plundering with his tongue, almost challenging her to deny him and his claim on her.

Unable to resist his passion, unwilling to repress her own, Jennifer deliberately allowed herself to be swept into the flame. They had no future, but she could not reject their present. If there was but little time left for them, she would not deny herself the joy of the memories that they had or the few that they still had time to make. If she had to leave him, Jennifer vowed, he would always remember her. As she knew that she would always remember him.

"Come," Jennifer urged as she pulled herself to her feet and led him to her bedroom. When he began to speak, Jennifer silenced him with a touch of her lips on his. "Come with me," she urged, pulling him behind her.

Unsure of what she wanted, Race got to his feet and walked with her to the bedroom. "I love you," he told her as she closed the door and walked toward him.

Pulling her top over her head slowly, Jennifer answered him in a husky voice. "And I love you, Race." As she reached him, he pulled her to him, only to have her slip out of his grasp. "Let me," she urged, brushing her hand across the front of his now-bulging zipper. With feather-light touches and lingering kisses for the sweet flesh that she exposed, she undressed him, until he was standing fully nude, fully ready for her, in the middle of her quiet bedroom.

Pushing him back on her bed, she again told him to hush and moved away, just beyond his reach. There she proceeded to slowly remove the rest of her clothing, provocatively posing as she took each item slowly and temptingly off. She had never before felt as powerful or as sensuous. Something elemental burned within Jennifer, as if all boundaries of civilization had been peeled off and there was only pure woman, determined to brand her image on her

man for eternity. At last she, too, was naked, standing in his
hot gaze, feeling herself wanting him more and more.

This day, today, he'd always remember this one day,
Jennifer told herself as she walked over to stand above him.
Letting her own greedy eyes follow the lines of his masculine perfection, she slowly used one finger to trace a wan-
dering path down his muscular body from the top of his
shoulder to the top of his foot. Then she slowly followed
that path with her tongue as she traveled back up his body.

"Jenni," Race groaned, reaching for her, "come to me.
You're driving me crazy." His face was taut with desire, and
he marveled at the feelings that Jenni was causing to course
in burning rivulets through his body. All other women disappeared from his memory as he watched the top of her
head bend to caress him and move away. This one woman
was his entire being, the focus of his life. This one woman
had replaced all the others, burned herself into his very soul
so that woman and Jenni were synonymous, the very same
word. No other woman would ever do again.

"I'm trying to," she responded, moving from his grasp
once again. Over and over again she tormented him, with
little nips and small caresses, and finally she leaned over to
give him the deep, pulsating kiss that he so desperately
needed. Desire ate at her, calling her to stop this delicious
torment and end the exquisite pain with satisfaction. Jennifer fought herself, denying herself the pleasure that she
knew was to be hers. As her body trembled with excitement, she forced herself to pull back, to touch him lightly,
to caress him with the tip of her tongue.

Darting in and out, over and beside him, Jennifer pro-
longed their lovemaking until they both were aching with
need. Finally Race reached up to caress her face with his
trembling hand and asked, "Please, love, I need you so
badly."

When she heard that, Jennifer felt something break
within her, and she began to cry. The love and pain that
she'd felt were forgotten for a moment in the blaze of glory

that she felt as she lowered herself into Race's eager arms. His mouth caressed her aching breasts, and he drew one hard nipple into his mouth, where he sucked it strongly, causing ripples to form and converge. Moving her slender body over his, she lowered herself over his pulsing masculinity until he could take no more and anchored her with his strong hands.

Together they plunged into a frantic rhythm, hotter and faster than either had ever known, until their mutual joy exploded into a thousand bits of glittery rainbow crystals. Farther and higher than ever before, the two melded into one as they reached the peak together.

Slowly they descended, letting the warm aftershocks run from one to the other and back again. Jennifer rested her head on Race's sweat-soaked shoulder, wanting to melt into his body forever. If only, she sighed to herself, if only life could be this simple. All she ever wanted was to hold the man she loved in her arms and block out the rest of the world.

Sleep came, then, to them both. Neither had slept well the night before, and the combination of complete physical release with the hours of tense uncertainty was a more potent sleeping pill than any druggist could have manufactured.

Several hours later Jennifer awoke, aware that she was still lying on Race. She started to pull herself free, only to feel his hands surround her hips. The unmistakable stirring of desire surprised her, as did the sudden movement of Race's hands and hips. With a groan of desire he turned her over, trapping her between him and the sheets. All too soon they were thrown back into the inferno. Once again they were seared by the flame of their passion and made breathless by the joy they found in each other's arms.

"I love you, Jennifer Grange," Race told her tenderly as he kissed the damp forehead that rested against his shoulder.

"I love you too, Race," Jennifer admitted. "But this," she told him, gesturing toward their still-entangled bodies, "isn't going to solve anything."

"No, I realize that. But it certainly doesn't hurt," he said lightly, but then he saw the sad look in her eyes. Wanting to postpone reality for a few moments longer. Race noted that it was past nine o'clock and suggested that they get up. "Why don't I go down and fix us some food. We can decide what to do while we're eating."

"Okay," Jenni agreed. "We got sidetracked a few hours ago, but nothing really changed. You're still Race Hunter, and the house is still surrounded by reporters."

"We can make it," Race assured her, wanting to see a smile on her face. "Just give me a chance to finish explaining."

As she walked into the shower, she looked back over her shoulder and tried to hold back her tears. She was sure that he had some logical explanation. He always would be able to explain. This time, the next time, and the time after that, as well. He would explain as long as she was fool enough to listen.

Chapter Twelve

All the scrubbing in the world would not wash away reality, Jennifer reluctantly concluded a few minutes later. The hot water cascading down her back could only temporarily block the confusion and anguish from her mind. She let the soothing flow work its miracles on her battered psyche, giving her the serenity to do what had to be done. It was time to finish this chapter in her life.

Although it would have been easier and more comfortable to slip into a loose caftan or designer pajamas, Jennifer chose instead to dress in a pair of heavy blue jeans and a plain cotton blouse. There was no use in prolonging the fantasy that she and Race had any future at all.

Before she went downstairs, she walked into Margo's room to use the phone. She called the twins and talked to them each for a few minutes, making sure that they were all right at Stephanie's sprawling home and reassuring them that they'd see each other soon. The only time that her cheerful facade dropped was when Becca wanted to talk to her new daddy. Jennifer could barely keep her voice from quavering when she told her daughter that she would have to wait until later. As she replaced the receiver, she looked up to find Race glaring at her from the doorway.

"What was all that about? I heard you on the phone to the kids and came up here. Why didn't you let me talk to them?" he demanded, fear making his voice angrier and louder than he intended it to be.

"I—I was saying hello to the twins," she said, trying to put off the inevitable for a few more seconds.

"I gathered as much," he stated, waiting for an answer.

"I thought we should talk before you speak to them again. Things have changed, and I don't want them hurt any more than necessary," she told him, straightening up and walking toward the doorway. Race stood there blocking the way until she was within a foot of him.

"Shall we go down?" Jennifer asked, staring up into his hard gray eyes.

"I think we better," Race agreed as he moved to let her pass. "I thought we'd made up, that you'd forgiven me," he offered to her back as they walked down the stairs.

"Because we made love?" Jennifer asked him in a skeptical voice. "I hardly think that sleeping with someone is the basis of any sort of commitment."

"Well, it is, lady. Besides, we love each other. We were making love, not—" Biting back a vulgarity, Race stopped, trying to keep his temper in check. "I told you that I love you and you told me that you loved me back. What else is there?"

Laughing, Jennifer walked to the kitchen table and sat down, motioning him to the chair across from her. "For starters, the little matter of Patti Silk and your 'essentially faithful' behavior with her. Where is she, by the way? We sort of forgot to answer that question this afternoon. That one and many others."

"Didn't this afternoon mean anything to you?" Race demanded, not believing that this was the same woman who had ripped his soul apart only minutes ago and merged her very essence with his.

"Blast you, Race. Can't you ever talk straight? Can't you once answer a question without referring to something else? Stop playing all of your word games and answer me!"

After pausing a moment to think, Jennifer went on. "If you want the truth about this afternoon, I'll tell you." She stood up and walked over to the counter and put the teakettle on the stove. Although confronting the truth never got any easier, it became more and more important as she dealt with their relationship. She could not afford to keep any illusions, to be anything but brutally honest about her own feelings and his. "This afternoon happened because I'm weak. Because for some reason I lose all of my willpower and common sense whenever you touch me. Because I love you, *not* because you love me. There's quite a difference, you see, in our definitions of love."

"No, there isn't," Race said, looking away from Jennifer's hard stare. It was his turn to get up and move away. Finally he spoke, in a low voice that Jennifer had trouble understanding until she walked closer to him. "I was with Patti only once in the last five months," he told her quietly. "Look, I'm not so sure that you'll believe me," he said as he turned around, startled to find her standing so close to him.

"Don't tell me that she took advantage of you, Hunter?" Jennifer said tauntingly watching with amazement as a deep red color flushed Race's tan cheeks. "You're putting me on," she commented sarcastically, but she could see that Race was genuinely upset about this. Backing away, she caught his eye and asked in a gentler tone, "What happened?"

As Race haltingly explained the one night that he might have gotten Patti pregnant, the drinking and then his awakening to find himself in bed with her, Jennifer held back all comment. She honestly didn't know what to say.

Finally she asked him what he planned to do if Patti *was* pregnant.

Turning away, Race told her that his lawyer was prepared to deal with the matter. He was willing to take blood tests if and when the child was born and then to provide sufficiently for the child if it did turn out to be his. "I'll be the best father I can be," Race told her. "I know it's not the fault of an innocent baby that his mother is a—" Race stopped, seeing no point in belaboring the obvious. "I will have nothing more to do with Patti personally. Ever again."

Race turned around to face Jennifer and found her sitting on the couch, trying to suppress a smile. Incensed, he stalked stiffly over to her. "What in the world is so funny?" he demanded angrily, "I'm spilling my guts out to you and you sit there smirking."

"It's not really funny," Jennifer told him with pain-filled eyes. "It's just so ironic. You, Race Hunter, of all people, getting seduced against your will, not remembering anything about it in the morning. I know it's not funny, it's just so, so... appropriate."

"Please believe me, love," Race said, taking her into his arms. "It wasn't my fault. I don't remember anything. I've never felt as angry or disgusted as I did that morning when I found her in my bed. Not only with her but with myself. If I hadn't gotten so drunk, I would know for sure what happened. Hell, if I hadn't been drunk she would never have been anywhere near me."

"What happened to Patti? Where is she?" Jennifer asked, her voice muffled by Race's shirt.

Feeling Race's chest tighten, Jennifer automatically rubbed his shoulder to soothe him while she felt the rumble of his voice through his shirt. "She's gone. Back to Hollywood, I suppose. We had a long talk today. Patti wanted me back, for some reason or other. In fact, she swears she filed that dumb suit to get my attention in the first place. When that didn't work, when I totally disappeared, she convinced Manny that she had to see me in person as soon as possible. She made Manny promise to call her the next time I was in town."

With an ironic twist to his beautiful smile, Race continued, "Manny called her, and then she harassed me until I agreed to meet with her. When I didn't buy what she was offering and walked out on her, she intimidated Manny into revealing my hotel. I was stupid enough to be drunk when she found me, so she decided to win me back the only way she knew how. She tells me that I cooperated. I plain don't remember anything. All I remember is wanting to kill her when I woke up."

Groaning, Race ran his hand through his hair and continued, "After that episode, she got truly desperate. I still don't know if she's really pregnant, or whether she got pregnant by someone else and is determined to make me the father. She didn't change her story, not even after all the browbeating I did. I suppose if she is really pregnant we'll all find out if I'm the father after the baby is born.

"Anyway," he continued, stroking Jennifer's lustrous hair as he held her to him, "she's mostly responsible for everything. She talked him into this award show idea as soon as she found out I was scheduled to appear. Manny fell for it. When I freaked out she got this address out of him, promising that she could fix everything if we could only be alone for a few hours."

"What about the twins? Does she know about them?" Jennifer demanded in a worried voice. "Manny knew about them, didn't he?"

"She doesn't know that they're mine," Race said soothingly. "Patti knows that you have children, but that's it. Manny had at least one grain of common sense left. He told her about you, but not that your children are mine, also. Edward, my lawyer, cornered Manny this morning and straightened everything out. Manny will keep quiet about the twins, and I will not blackball him in the business. He's fired, but that's it."

When Jennifer started to protest, Race continued talking. "I think he'll keep it a secret. It's one thing to have me as an ex-client, quite another to have me as an enemy. If anyone knows what clout I could get together, it's Manny." When Jennifer looked up and saw Race's naked fury, she agreed with him. She didn't want Race to hate her, just to leave her alone. Stifling a sigh, she burrowed into him for warmth, ironically taking strength from him in order to leave him.

"So, do you forgive me?" Race asked lightly, his voice belying the serious look in his eyes and the intense expression on his face.

"Yes, I forgive you," Jennifer told him sadly, running a tender hand under his jaw. "Why don't you go home and get some sleep?"

"Why can't I stay here?" Race asked. "Nobody's home except you and me."

"I don't want the reporters to find you here, Race. Especially after Patti told them about us. I assume she did, or they would not have been calling me. What exactly did she say, by the way?"

Translating Patti's vulgar language as he went along, Race interpreted Patti's snide comment that Race and some hometown girl were "making it." "Patti implied that you were a one-night stand when I passed through town on tour last summer and that you were blackmailing me into living near you."

"What?" Jennifer exclaimed in disbelief. "Blackmailing you into living next door to me?"

"Don't worry, it sounded so absurd that none of the sensible reporters took her seriously. Her story didn't make any sense. Nobody blackmails someone into moving next door to them. Or into changing their appearance. I denied it all, anyway."

"What did you tell the reporters?" Jennifer asked. "The sane ones who didn't believe Patti? I suppose we'll be seeing what the insane ones write in the national tabloids next week."

"Nobody believes those rags," Race told her sincerely. "We'll be right next to the story that aliens kidnapped me and made me bleach my hair platinum and dress like Marilyn Monroe," Race quipped, trying to tease her out of it. "I told the responsible reporters that we were good friends and that the major reason I moved here was to escape the glare of publicity for a while and work in peace. I implied that finding you my next-door neighbor was a pleasant surprise, nothing more."

"If they investigate your buying out my neighbor, they'll know it isn't true," Jennifer commented. "I'm sure the Harrisons would be glad to tell anyone about the silly person who offered them twice what their house was worth to move out in a hurry."

"No, they won't. Part of the deal was that they would conceal the terms of the sale. Don't worry, it's all covered. We can announce our engagement anytime now, and everything will soon blow over."

"Race," Jennifer said, pain choking her throat and making it virtually impossible for her to speak. "I can't marry you. I'm sorry." Pulling free, she got up and walked to the kitchen.

"Why not?" Race shouted, bounding off the couch to follow her and catch her in his arms. "You promised to marry me. We have the ring to prove it."

"I can't marry you. Because of the twins. Because of who you are. I can't live with your fame. Even if you're telling me the truth, what's to stop other women from doing the same thing? How many Patti Silks are out there waiting for you? And what's to stop people from using Rick and Becca, for money, for fame, for everything. I can't let them grow up where love is a four-letter word and people only exist to use others."

"Jenni, don't say that. Don't think that. We can find some way to make it right," Race said, his heart filled with cold dread.

"No, we can't. Don't you think I wish we could? That I don't wish you were someone else?" Jennifer pleaded, tears in her voice. "Don't you know how much I'd like a regular life with you?"

"Too bad! Too bloody bad! I'm not someone else. I'm the man that you love, and I'm not going to lose you because you're afraid of some stupid reporters. I'm not letting you go!" Race told her, standing up and looking down at her. Rage and fear turned his voice harsh, and he fell back for a moment into his old role, the man who always had what he wanted, when he wanted it.

"You can't stop me," Jennifer told him, relishing the fury that took over—anger was better than anguish.

"I will. You agreed to marry me, and I'm going to announce the engagement tomorrow. Once the press knows about it, it'll be too late. Then you won't be able to use that as a flimsy excuse to run away from me."

"Flimsy excuse?" Jennifer hissed at him. "The privacy of the twins is no flimsy excuse! They are the most important thing in my life!"

"You were willing to risk it before. What's changed?" Race demanded as he felt his anger changing into sorrow. "Is it because of Patti? I swear it meant nothing."

"It's not Patti. It's nothing and everything," Jennifer told him. "I never really imagined it like this, the house surrounded by reporters, cameras going off, the phone ringing and ringing. Questions that are no one's business. I didn't let myself think too much about it because I wanted you so much.

"Selfish," Jennifer explained sadly, to herself, as well as to him. "I was plain selfish, Race. I deluded myself, let us live in a dream world. I didn't want to admit the truth, that we'd all be hounded by the media. I'd have to put the twins in private schools, deal with having chauffeurs and bodyguards around all the time. I'd have to tell them about you, about women chasing you, throwing themselves at your feet."

Whirling, she went on, "What do you think all their friends would say? Would they ever have any more real friends, or would it always be hangers-on like your staff? People who care for money and fame and nothing for human values.

"Good grief," she almost shouted, "you lived with a woman for almost a whole year who thought nothing of using you, in the most intimate of ways. What does that say for your values?"

"Not much," Race admitted. "But that was before." When he saw the look on Jennifer's face, he went on. "I have changed. I was discontented, already sick of Patti and her games when I saw you last summer. I was sick of the partying, the booze and the drugs. I'd stopped it all before I met you. *Before!* Then, when I met you, everything clicked into place. You and the twins are everything that I want." Then he added tenderly, "I love you."

An icy feeling slipped over Jennifer as she listened, really listened, to Race's words. "No, Race Hunter. You don't love me, you love the idea of me, the idea of a different life. You don't need us to make you into a different person. You've been using me and the children all along, trying to turn yourself back into a normal, everyday man. Well, you're not. You're a famous performer and you are going to have to deal with that all by yourself. You alone are going to have to come to grips with how you got where you are and what you want to do with the rest of your life. I was right last July," she said bitterly. "It is a midlife crisis, not real love."

"Don't tell me what I think and what I feel," Race replied, frightened that some of what Jenni had said might hold more merit than he wished to admit. "I love you, Jennifer. I have never felt anything like what we have when we're together.

"I think you're just scared," he told her bluntly. "Scared that you won't be enough for me, that somehow you're not good enough to hold me. You've been so safe here in Charlotte, using the children as a shield." When Jennifer started to interrupt, Race silenced her with his hand and went on. "It's your turn to hear me out. I've listened to you and your reasons for long enough. I may be a country singer, but I do understand people, too. You're plain scared to face me and my life. To take a chance and love me again."

"Well, you can hide here forever, use the twins as an excuse until they're grown and in college. Do anything you please. I'm going back to Hollywood for a while and let the publicity die down. You are wrong about me and what I feel, but I won't fight you."

With a deliberate stride, Race crossed the room and took Jennifer in his arms. Slowly and expertly he kissed her, drawing sensation after sensation from her. At first unwillingly, then with a desperation born of need and fear, Jennifer responded to his touch, unable to resist the lure of his body, unable to resist the sensations that overpowered her each time Race kissed her. Finally he drew away, breathless and as aroused as she.

"I'll be in touch, my love. You think about us and decide if you can live without me." Kissing her again, Race backed off far enough to gaze deeply into her troubled green eyes. "Please, for my sake and theirs, don't tell the twins that we're through, not yet. Tell them who I am and let them get used to that. Let them think the wedding is postponed and that I'll be back. That's the truth, no matter what you say. We're going to be married, sooner or later."

"Oh, Race," Jennifer moaned as she allowed herself to collapse against his firm chest. "It won't work."

"It will if you want me enough. If you're brave enough to try living again," Race insisted. "Even if it doesn't, I will maintain some sort of relationship with my kids."

"Okay," Jennifer murmured against his warm chest. "I won't tell them that it's off. Not yet. I'll let them lose you gradually. They'll forget you after a while. When you forget us."

"Thank you, love," Race whispered into her hair. "But never think that I'll forget you, or my family. Never. I won't let it end, not now, not ever. You think about that while I'm gone." With a final long kiss, he moved away from her and was gone before she knew it. Shaking herself loose from the sensual lethargy that Race's touch had led her into, she saw him disappear out her kitchen door.

Three days after Race left, Jennifer flew to Florida and brought the twins back home. Margo, Rick, Becca and Jennifer had a long, serious talk before they returned to Charlotte. Jennifer was as honest as she felt she could be, and broke the news to the twins carefully that the man they knew as Uncle Race was also known as Race Hunter, the famous country singer. Although they were excited, Jennifer was relieved to find that they were still too young to be truly awed by his fame.

The hardest part was explaining that Race was not going to be a part of their lives anymore, at least not in the near future. Although Jenni did not come right out and tell the children that she and Race would not marry she told them that some problems had come up and that she and Race needed a lot of time to think about their relationship. Jennifer admitted that part of the problem was that Race was so famous. Because of that fact, she felt obliged to reiterate her normal warnings about talking to strangers.

Although the twins were disappointed, they did not take the news as badly as Jennifer had feared. They seemed almost indifferent or unbelieving. Jennifer was so happy about that reaction that she didn't think about it.

Within a few days, everyone was back to normal. Jennifer had stonewalled at the paper and downplayed her relationship with Race. The twins were back in school, with nothing worse to show for their unexpected vacation than

a golden tan and some make-up work. Margo was busy
with her bridge club, and it seemed as though the interlude
with Race had never happened.

Everyone seemed to be doing fine, back in their old rou-
tines, except Jennifer herself. Although she told herself that
their separation was inevitable and that there was no way
that they could ever have had a trusting, loving marriage,
Jennifer missed Race. She missed him with every fiber of
her being. Not a night passed that she didn't long for his
touch. Not a minute passed that she didn't curse him for
coming back into her life and herself for wanting him.

Nights were the worst. Margo would often come down
late at night to find her daughter sitting in the dark, staring sadly at the empty house that had been Race's. Jennifer lost weight and, worse than that, her joy in life.

Margo worried about her, the twins worried about her,
even her colleagues at work worried about her. Inevitably
she responded to them all with the same message. She'd be
all right in a little while.

Finally Jennifer came face-to-face with herself. She was
not as virtuous as she'd thought. Jennifer had to admit that
she truly did love Race, despite all the women and despite
his past. Much of what had been bothering her was her own
foolish pride and insecurities.

As the days passed and Thanksgiving rapidly approached, Jenni finally admitted the truth. Race had been
right. She had been using the children as an excuse. They
were not the real problem. She was. She had turned him
away because she was afraid. Afraid that she was not
woman enough for him, afraid to trust again. Now he was
gone, and Jenni wondered, despite his promises, if he
would ever be back. This time she was the one who had run
away from love.

Chapter Thirteen

The day before Thanksgiving dawned bright and cheerful. The cheer, however, did not extend into the Grange house that particular morning. After a series of frustrating mix-ups and delays, Jennifer was commandeered to drive the twins on a field trip. Margo had originally been scheduled as their escort, but had awoken that morning with an upset stomach and had reluctantly asked Jenni to take her place. By the time it was all settled, Margo insisted that it was too late for the kids to go to school. The only sensible thing to do was for Jennifer to drive them directly to the airport and catch up with the class there. She handed her daughter a hand-drawn map, directing her to hangar 7A.

"What is this, anyway?" Jennifer wondered, giving the older woman her full attention as she scrambled for her purse and car keys. "I thought the class was going to Discovery Place."

"Not this morning. This is a field trip to the Air National Guard headquarters." Margo explained rapidly. "Discovery Place is the field trip for next month's science class. This is a social studies trip. The twins are studying emergency rescue services and are going to see a real medivac helicopter."

"That sounds interesting," Jenni commented routinely. "Are you sure you'll be all right alone? Do you want me to come back after the trip and take you to the doctor?"

"I'm not that sick, Jennifer. Some mornings these old bones just don't feel quite up to par, that's all," Margo explained. "Don't be mad at me, honey."

"Mad?" Jennifer asked her mother in surprise. "I may have been a bit preoccupied lately, but I haven't gone crazy. Why should I get angry because you're sick? I'm just very grateful that you've been able to help me with the twins." Reaching over, she gave her mother a hug and added, "I don't tell you that I really appreciate you often enough, Mom."

"Remember that," Margo instructed her as Jen and the twins hurried out of the door.

The twins sat in the back seat, oddly silent except for an occasional giggle during their ride to the airport, but Jennifer was still not aware of anything out of the ordinary. Finally they reached the airport and pulled up to a large metal hangar with 7A painted on the side of it.

They were waved inside by a mechanic standing on the tarmac waiting for them. "I hope this is the right place," Jennifer said nervously. She looked around inside the cavernous building and didn't see any other cars or any other mothers or any children at all. Just as she was about to panic, the door of the small jet beside her opened and a familiar figure stepped out.

"Hello, Jenni," Race said calmly, as if it had been two hours instead of nearly two weeks since they'd seen each other. As his eyes caressed her tense face and noted her hands clasping the steering wheel, the twins tumbled out of the car and ran over to him. Exuberantly he picked them up, one in each arm, and gave them each a warm and tender hug.

"You guys did it," he congratulated them as he twirled them around. "I didn't know if you'd be able to keep our secret." He hugged them tightly to his body, then lowered them to their feet as he told them fondly, "I missed both of you rug rats."

"I missed you, too," Becca said shyly, hugging him tightly.

"Me too," Rick added, holding back for a moment but then joining his sister in hugging the man they had grown to love. "I thought you'd never come back for us. You sure took a long time."

Jennifer had moved out of the car by now and was glaring at her two offspring with angry, disbelieving eyes. "What is all this? Did you two know Race would be here? You both tricked me!" Jennifer said in a low, angry voice. "Grandma must have been in on it, too," she added, crumpling the directions she clutched in her pocket.

"Of course, Mom. Uncle Ra—Dad told us all about it before he left town. He told us that you and he were having problems and we'd have to wait for him to make it better. He drove us to school that morning and told us that we were going to have to be brave and wait for a long time. He said it'd be hard but that he promised to come back for us and to fly us to California in his airplane if we could keep it a secret from you. And we did, didn't we?" he asked proudly, looking up at his father's face, gray eyes connecting with identical smaller ones.

"You two are absolutely wonderful at keeping secrets. You trusted me to come back. And I did, just like I told you." Race gave them each one last hug, then patted them on their bottoms and suggested, "Why don't you get onto the plane and look around. I think Jameson is in there somewhere with a new video game that I just installed in the back."

"Wow!" Rick yelled enthusiastically scooting over to the steps and racing into the plane. Rebecca followed more slowly, peeking inside and seeing Jameson before she ventured aboard.

"What is going on?" Jennifer requested furiously as another car pulled up behind hers. To her amazement, Margo got out and matter-of-factly unlocked the trunk for the man who came up from behind the car. In dazed silence, Jennifer watched her mother direct the man to unload several suitcases and start taking them aboard the plane.

"What in the world is happening?" Jennifer demanded. For the first time in several years, she was tempted to start swearing again—a habit she'd given up when the twins were old enough to repeat her every word.

"What is going on?" she demanded in an even louder voice as she watched Race direct the men to bring the rest of the luggage past her and onto the plane.

Her mother walked past her, patting her shoulder. Margo stopped only long enough to remind her of the words of appreciation and love she'd murmured in her ear less than an hour ago.

"That, dear Mother," Jennifer muttered, "was before you turned into Benedict Arnold."

Suddenly Jenni stuck her fingers into her mouth and gave a very loud whistle. "Now, tell me what in the hell is going on!"

"We're going house hunting, my darling," Race explained blithely as he pulled her after him toward the silver aircraft. "Remember? We planned this back a couple of weeks ago."

"This is kidnapping," Jennifer announced as she let Race lead her into the small plane. When she didn't struggle or protest, Race directed her to a seat, buckled her in and told someone in front to get going. Before she could comment further, the twins raced back, sat down in two seats opposite her and were joined across the aisle by Margo and Jameson.

Rick announced happily to his mother, "See, we're all here."

"You can't do this," Jennifer protested weakly, feeling obliged to object but knowing that she really didn't want to stop him. She knew that if she stood up and demanded to leave, she could. And she knew that Race realized that, too. This was her decision. Whether to run away or to give their love one last chance. Full of apprehension and determined not to be swayed by his fantasies, she decided to see what he had planned. She refused to be the coward Race had been so many years ago.

Race reached over to take her hand, and she stopped thinking, period. All she was conscious of was the warm hand that clasped her own. All she knew was the joy that bubbled through her at the mere sight of him. She'd thought she'd never see him again, never touch him again. Now, as she felt the back of his hand on her thigh, she wondered how she had ever managed to live without him.

"I've already done it," Race told her cheerfully as she noticed the plane beginning to move. Stooping down, he brushed her cheek with his mouth and whispered in her ear, "Don't worry, love. It'll be all right. I told you that I'd be back for you, didn't I?"

Jennifer sat back in her seat as she watched Race lean forward and help the children buckle their seatbelts. The twins were bubbling over with excitement, asking him to explain everything as the jet taxied out onto the runway. Patiently he started answering their questions, affection and pride shining from his eyes.

Jennifer viewed him as though he were a stranger. He looked nearly the same as he had eight years ago. His hair had been trimmed and was a trifle longer and fuller, but still only brushed the back of his shirt collar. He looked beautiful to her.

Tears formed in her eyes as she stared at him, drinking him in as though she could not get enough. This crazy gesture explained so many things that had puzzled her over the past two weeks. This was the reason the children had so easily adjusted to Race's departure—because they'd expected him back.

Suddenly she grew impossibly angry and pulled Race back to her. "How could you do this to the children?" Jennifer challenged him. "They are going to be devastated when we go back home."

"No, they won't," Race declared confidentially, "because we are going back home now. We're going to be together from this day forward."

"Race, I told you that it won't work. I can't live with the uncertainty and all the publicity that comes with you and your life-style. I just can't," she repeated, growing desperate to convince him.

When tears of anger glittered in her beautiful green eyes, Race touched her softly on the shoulder and pleaded with her, "Give me my chance to prove to you that we can have a life together. We fit so well together in Charlotte. If you would not mind finding another job, I know we could have the same thing, be together the same way, only better, out in California."

With a crooked smile and his most coaxing tone, he went on, "You promised that we'd all try California over Thanksgiving vacation, and I'm holding you to that promise. If it doesn't work out, I'll fade away. I will never lose contact with my children, but I promise I'll be a friend to you. Is it a deal?" he asked solemnly, offering her his strong hand to seal the bargain.

Jennifer looked up to see several pairs of hopeful eyes watching her. Both of the twins started begging her, and Margo quietly added her own encouraging advice to the twins impassioned pleas.

"All right, all right," Jennifer agreed, putting her hand in Race's. "You've got this weekend to convince me that we can have a life together. But," she added in a loud voice, looking directly at the twins and then at her mother, "I don't think it's possible. There are a lot of things that are hard for children to understand, Becca and Rick. Grown-up things that even grown-ups can't understand very well. I know it doesn't make any sense to you while you're so young, but even if people love each other, there can be reasons why they can't live together. I promise you that you'll be able to see Race whether I marry him or not. Beyond that, we'll have to wait and see." Looking directly into the twins' slightly subdued faces, she asked them, "Do you understand?"

She stared at them until they both reluctantly nodded their acceptance. "All right, then. Let's have some fun while we're living in the lap of luxury. Show us around your big toy," Jennifer suggested, indicating the airplane with a wave of her hand. "Is it yours or did you borrow it?"

Laughing, Race told her that he did neither. He leased it by the year. The flight progressed smoothly from that point on. The four adults chatted casually among themselves and passed the time entertaining the twins. The small refrigerator in the miniature galley fascinated the entire Grange family, and they all agreed that traveling with the rich and famous was certainly better than traveling tourist. Just being able to walk around a bit was sheer bliss. The trip seemed shorter than it actually was, and they were all pleasantly surprised when the pilot's voice ordered them to sit down and buckle up for landing.

Jennifer didn't know what to expect when they landed, but it certainly wasn't the chauffeur-driven limo that picked them up right at the plane and whisked them out of the airport before she had time to think. They were driven leisurely through the city, with Race deliberately highlighting the sights and sounds that were the best of his chosen city. Finally they cruised slowly down Rodeo Drive and saw the surprisingly small, exclusive area that was so famous.

They eventually stopped at a lovely shaded home that reminded Jennifer of a New England colonial. Oddly enough, it did not look out of place in Beverly Hills, surrounded as it was by a huge hedge and a perfectly kept lawn. When Race saw her curious eyes, he turned to her and whispered, "This is Edward Kurray's home. Remember? He's my lawyer and friend. His wife came from Connecticut, and she decided long ago that if she had to live out here in California she'd bring a little piece of New England with her. This is probably one of the few homes that I know that doesn't boast a single palm tree or hibiscus bush."

Raising his voice slightly so that everyone could hear him, Race announced, "We'll be staying the night here. Edward has plenty of guest rooms, and he insisted that we stay with him."

Race dared to look directly at Jenni and took his first deep breath in a long time. She was nodding easily and wasn't going to fight him. He knew then there was a possibility that she'd come to him. He'd planned and schemed for two weeks, getting this outing ready, aware that it was his last shot at winning her back, praying that she would allow him this one last chance. He knew in his heart that their life could be wonderful together, but he wasn't sure that Jennifer would let herself take the risk. With his past record, Race didn't know if he'd have enough courage if the situations were reversed. It was all up to him to prove to Jenni that he could be everything she needed.

Race smiled as the kids clambered out of the car, amused that the chauffeur wasn't fast enough to get the door open first. His dignity intact, the driver opened the other door for Margo and Jameson while Race helped Jenni out himself. They rang the doorbell and soon a tall, moderately plump, distinguished lady in her mid-fifties opened the door.

"How good to see you, Race," Sharon Kurray said, then turned with warm, knowing eyes to Jenni. "You must be Jenni. I've heard so much about you."

Graciously Jennifer acknowledged the introduction and motioned first her mother and then the twins forward to meet their hostess before thanking Mrs. Kurray for her hospitality.

They all spent the rest of the day by the large outdoor pool behind the spacious colonial home and then enjoyed a surprisingly cozy dinner. Jennifer was surprised to discover that Sharon Kurray reminded her very much of her own mother. In fact, Margo and Sharon got along so well that they were already planning on staying in touch. The twins, tired from the long day and the four-hour time difference, ate quickly and soon were asleep in the one guest room that had twin beds.

Race called Jennifer into Edward's study later that night and closed the door behind them. "I want to tell you something I've done," Race started to say as soon as Edward had poured the three of them brandy. He moved over to lean against the fireplace, holding his glass tightly in his hand. "I had some papers drawn up that show that we were briefly married and divorced, early enough to make the twins legitimate. They're Mexican papers, totally legitimate in their own way. I'm sure that they will convince anyone who will ever want to embarrass you because of your—your connection with me."

"You forged a marriage certificate?" Jennifer asked incredulously.

"Nothing quite so dramatic. Actually, Edward found a sort of justice of the peace in Mexico City who was willing to marry and divorce us and predate the papers a bit. Look, Jenni," Race told her, his hand raised in defense of himself, "I know that the possibility that the media will find out that the twins are illegitimate has been bothering you. I don't blame you. I'm no more eager for the fact to come out than you are."

"These papers," he told her, pointing to a packet of legal documents on Edward's desk, "will at least take care of that one worry. I'm not saying that you have to use them, or lie to the twins, but they're there if you ever want them. Just flashing them at the media, if they question you, should help. I don't want to ever hurt you or our kids. If you want any more details, ask Edward," he said. "I'll be in the garden if you want to talk to me. Otherwise, I'll see you in the morning."

As Race strode out the door, the attorney came over to sit beside Jennifer. "He wanted me to assure you it would have absolutely no effect at all, except to perhaps prejudice the judge against him, if he were to try to use them in a custody dispute involving the twins. In fact, I have another packet of papers prepared to swear that this first batch is a forgery. For your use only. I promise you have no need to worry about Race in that way. It's really quite harmless, my dear," he said, patting her hand softly, "The only thing it does is leave Race open to several lawsuits from you claiming his money."

Pulling her hand away, barely aware of the fact that she no longer even considered worrying about Race wanting custody of the children, Jennifer turned to glare at the older man. "I would never do anything like that—" she started to say, but the other man interrupted her.

"I know that. I was just pointing out how much the man loves you. How much he trusts you. I know I'm an outsider in this matter, but Race has been my client for nearly ten years now, and I think I know him as well as anybody." He gazed seriously into Jenni's wide green eyes and spoke honestly. "He was a wild one, I'm not denying that, but never one of the crazy, mean kind. This town can eat you up if you're not very strong, especially if you're as phenomenally successful as Race is. He really cares for you and his children, Miss Grange. I'd swear to that in a court of law." After a pause, he looked at her consideringly. "I don't know if I'm out of line or not, but I want to tell you

that in my opinion Race was truly innocent in the matter of
the Silk woman.''

Standing up, the distinguished man moved to the door
before Jennifer could frame a reply. He opened the door
and turned to wish her good-night. ''I'll see you in the
morning, then,'' he said quietly, leaving a beleaguered
woman on his sofa, absently sipping the brandy in her
glass.

Again Race had surprised her with his quixotic behavior. It was the kind of crazy, wonderful thing he'd done for
her as a child, she realized, remembering their years of
friendship before he'd left Charlotte. Once he'd taken the
blame for a broken car window that had been her fault,
suffering the punishment that rightfully should have been
hers.

Memories of their childhood overwhelmed Jennifer as
she tried once again to reconcile the adult Race Hunter with
the man-boy Racine Huntington. She loved them both but
was still not quite sure that she could trust the man who had
grown from the boy.

Finally Jennifer stirred and carefully followed Race's
path out of the room. She found him sitting in a gazebo in
the middle of the shaded lawn. He was staring out into the
night, his hands clasped behind his head as he leaned
against one of the supports.

''So,'' Jennifer said awkwardly, ''you've been quite busy
since you left. Too busy to call, but not too busy to plan this
elaborate charade.''

''No charade, Jennifer. The truth. I'm going to show you
what we can have together. You've already seen the worst
of it, now I want you to see the best. You know that I want
you to marry me, more than anything I've ever wanted.
Don't answer me now,'' he told her as she started to open
her mouth. ''I want you to be sure.''

Walking over to where she stood in the shadows, Race
pulled her into his arms. Tenderly he traced the outline of
her lips with his fingertip. ''I love you,'' he whispered as his

mouth descended to claim her own. Parting her lips with his tongue, he demanded entrance. As always, passion flared when they touched, and Race captured her mouth with his own, letting the fire burn them both as he explored and reconquered every bit of her.

They stood locked together in each other's arms for several precious minutes, need growing and expanding until it filled both their bodies and souls. With a great effort, Race finally pushed slightly away from her. Putting his head on top of hers he held her tightly until the tremors of passion subsided and the fierce wanting ebbed to a less demanding ache. "This is real, my love. This is forever," he told her before he forced himself to release her and walk briskly to the house. "I'll see you in the morning."

As she prepared for bed a few minutes later, Jennifer cursed herself for not knowing what to do. Indecision had never been a problem in the past, but this situation seemed so unsolvable. Love versus trust. Her own needs versus the needs of the children. Once it became known that Rick and Becca were Race Hunter's children, there would never be any anonymity in their lives, regardless of her own relationship with Race. As her body reminded her of the pleasures that she was denying herself, she fought with her conscience and her better judgment. She loved him so much. He could hurt them so badly. If only she knew what to do.

Jennifer barely had time to greet her mother the next morning before Race insisted that she and the twins climb into a brown Mercedes station wagon with him. Margo and Jameson were going to follow them, he explained as they took their leave of the Kurrays. They were to have their Thanksgiving dinner in a very special place.

"I've got something I want to show you," Race told her enthusiastically as they pulled onto the freeway and headed north. They had been driving for well over an hour when Race slowed down and turned toward the coast. A few minutes later he pulled into a driveway and drove up to a breathtaking multilevel modern house. It was perched on the cliffs overlooking the ocean and had a magnificent view.

The sea breeze filled the air as Race got out of the car and led Jennifer and the twins up to the front door. With a flourish he unlocked it and led the way inside to a wide panorama of blue sky and crystal-clear ocean. Wall-to-wall, floor-to-ceiling windows embraced the view. Natural wood and brick walls blended together to create a wonderful feeling of comfort and welcome in the huge room. The furniture was spare but attractive, mostly in leather and fine wood.

"It's incredible, Race," Jennifer told him as she walked over to the windows. Becca stood by her mother, staring out the window at the wide blue sea while Rick rushed to look down the stairwell.

"You guys can look around," Race told them. "Don't go outdoors, though."

Minutes later, Margo and Jameson drove up behind them, the trunk of their car filled with several baskets of food. Everyone helped carry their dinner into the house. The odors of turkey and all the trimmings floated from the baskets as they put everything away. Soon Margo and Jameson joined the twins in exploring the building, leaving Jenni and Race alone once more.

"What is this place?" Jenni demanded, looking around at the rooms that led off from the kitchen area. "Who lives here?"

"I hope it'll be our home. I put down a deposit on it last week, subject to your approval." Before Jenni could interrupt him, he went on enthusiastically. "It's got seven bedrooms, eight baths, a great kitchen. Anything that you don't like we can fix. The schools are really good. I asked the realtor when she showed me the place. There are enough wealthy people in the area that I swear we won't be bothered. There's a separate cottage over to the left that could easily serve as a home for your mother, if she'd like to stay." Walking up to her, Race looked her in the eye. "It was as close as I could come to the home that you said you dreamed of by the ocean. Will you share it with me?"

"I don't know," Jennifer told him, torn between hope and terror. "You know that I want to, but how can you be sure that you won't change your mind in six months?"

Race exploded. "Dammit, Jennifer, I'm not the light-weight country singer that you think I am. I'm thirty-two years old, but somedays I feel like I'm fifty-two. You think my life is so exciting and glamorous that I won't be able to leave it? Come with me."

Stepping forward, he took her arm and led her down the stairs. "Margo, will you please mind the children for a while? Jennifer and I are going down to the beach." Without waiting for her reply, he led Jennifer out the sliding glass doors that faced a large, sloping backyard.

Race led the way down a set of wooden steps that were cleverly set into the rock cliff, and in a few minutes they were down on the deserted beach. Leaving his shoes on the last step, Race rolled up his jeans, waiting impatiently for Jennifer to do the same.

"Maybe I should have been honest with you long ago, Jennifer, but I didn't want to make myself seem any less desirable than you already thought I was. I cannot stand for you to think that you are some impulse in my life, some crazy midlife crisis that I will eventually get over. I've been sick of this life for a long time—three, maybe four years, at least. Touring is a grind, nothing more. Performing is great, but the rest of the time is less than wonderful. Rotten food, sterile rooms, loneliness. Yes, real loneliness, Jenni, even though there are people everywhere. All of them want something from you, want to use you. They want a piece of the glory, or money or a break. Nobody cares about who you are, only what you do. You could be evil, a murderer, as long as you get up on a stage."

Striding along so rapidly that Jennifer almost had to jog to keep up with him, Race continued. "You don't know it, but it's hard to say no when you're on the road, and for a while you know that I didn't. I was everything you thought I was. Nothing seemed to matter, and after a while I just didn't care, about me or anyone else. Then, three years last May, Kelsey Ross—remember him? He was my drummer when he OD'd." Stopping in midstride, Race turned to her and said, "It was in all the papers, you must have read it."

"Of course I remember. I'm sorry," Jennifer said quietly, trying to understand all of what Race was saying. "Was he a good friend of yours?"

"The best, nearly as good a friend as Mike was. He was with me all the way from college. You even met him once, if you remember. I brought him home with me my freshman year, over Easter, I think." Without pausing, Race went on, driven suddenly by the need to tell Jennifer everything. "Kelsey ran himself deliberately into a tree while he was snowed under. Coke, cocaine," he explained further.

"I've never done many drugs myself," Race added, knowing that she would be wondering. "I never was able to enjoy being so out of control. But don't think I was any saint. I drank way too much, way too often. Alcohol was always easier and safer.

"Kelsey wasn't so lucky, or so smart. He got so messed up on coke that he killed himself. I found the note later."

"I'm sorry, Race," Jennifer told the tall man who was revealing an unhealed wound to her, knowing that it left him vulnerable. "It wasn't your fault. Edward told me that this town could make or break a man. I'm only glad that you were strong enough to make it."

"I'm not so sure I did very well. After that, after Kelsey died, that's when I took up with Patti. She was fun and she made me laugh, and I was so bloody sick of fast affairs. I tried to convince myself that I cared for her, that she was different than the rest, but in a few months I saw that she'd been lying to me, too. She only wanted the famous singer, not the real me. I broke it off with her before this last tour started.''

Running his hand through his hair, he admitted, ''The fact that Manny already knew that I was finished touring only helped Patti convince the man to help her in that little charade of theirs. I had already told everyone that I was pretty sure I would quit touring soon, that I was going to find something else to do with my life. Maybe it will be producing or composing. I don't know yet. I already had the deal worked out to score the movie when I saw you and everything came clear.''

''Dammit all, you want honesty, then you're going to get it. I had been thinking of you long before I came to Charlotte. I was moving my stuff out of the ranch when I found that old song that I'd written during that night. After I played it, I remembered you so clearly that it hurt. I was haunted by that song, and I had to record it.''

Race came to a stop and looked directly into her eyes, willing her to believe him. ''I didn't admit it to myself until I was there, but I know I took that gig in Charlotte in the hopes of seeing you again. When you showed up at the concert, I sort of lost it. I was so afraid it was all a dream that I let my image take over. Maybe I was trying to impress you. I'm not so proud of myself, Jen, but I do know what I think and what I feel. And this is love. It might have started out as remembered love and surprise about the twins, but it's way more than that. You're the best friend I've ever had, the only one who always tells me the truth, the only one I can be true to myself with. Please,'' Race told her, directly from the heart, ''at least believe that I truly love you. I need you more than I can say.''

Jennifer stood, stunned by the depth of his feelings. For the first time she saw him exactly as he was, facing the brutal truth that Race was a man, not a superstar, a man with needs and wants and fears. Joyously she realized that he was speaking the truth, the truth that she needed to hear.

The truth that she would count on for the rest of her life. He needed her. Every bit as much as she needed him. Her insecurities and fears faded into nothingness as she finally accepted their past and their future. Nothing was as important as their love and the trust that flowed from it to envelop them both. Together they would build a good life for themselves and their children. Nothing would keep them apart ever again.

"I love you, Race Hunter," she told him carefully as she stepped into his arms and into his life, "and I'll be honored to be your wife."

Epilogue

Well, Mrs. Huntington,'' Race whispered against his wife's shoulder as he reached over to nibble on her ear, ''I think that it all went very well.''

''What went well?'' Jennifer asked him as she lazily ran a finger down his throat and along his collarbone.

''Our family's reunion,'' Race groaned as she followed the path of her finger with her tongue.

Momentarily sidetracked, Jennifer paused to agree with him. ''Your parents were so sweet with the twins. I'll never forget your mother's face when she saw Rebecca and Rick for the first time. Why didn't you warn your folks that the twins take so much after you and your youngest sister? You realize that your sister and my daughter looked more alike than any other two people in the entire family. It's almost eerie.''

''It sure is. I didn't realize the resemblance was quite as dramatic as it turned out. My sister and Becca look almost like twins themselves, with a twenty-year age difference.

Seeing is believing, I guess. Mom did look a little faint there, didn't she? Right there in the beginning. She recovered fast, though," Race added, "and she had a wonderful reunion with your mother. Can you believe that they both had the nerve to say that they knew we'd marry years ago?"

"Nothing would surprise me anymore," Jennifer admitted, gazing into Race's glowing gray eyes. "My life has been turned upside down ever since I saw you again."

"Speaking of upside down," Race said, making a grab for Jennifer.

"Speaking of recovering fast," she teased him, moving quickly and pinning him down on the waterbed. When she felt his body responding against hers, she reached down and stroked his silken strength tenderly. "Fast recoveries seem to run in your family."

"Oh, love," Race moaned as he moved to claim her mouth again, "I will never get enough of you." Slowly now, since their first rush of passion had already been satisfied, Race drew the satin sheet back from his wife's lush body and gazed possessively at her. "You belong to me," he murmured, his voice raspy, as he lowered his head to tantalize her rose-tipped breasts.

Jennifer looked up at the mirror over her head and was scandalized to find that she enjoyed the look of his strong male body bending over her paler, more fragile one. She moaned as he moved to caress the hardened tip of her nipple with his tongue and slowly drew it into his waiting mouth. Strongly he sucked on first one crest and then the other, rhythmically creating a need that centered and grew deep within her.

She saw her own hand reach around to touch his shoulder and then reach down to caress his muscular back. As she watched, he moved down her body, kissing and caressing her until she could stand no more and pulled him back to her. Suddenly he rolled over and joined their bodies with a single powerful stroke.

Momentarily stunned by the absolute perfection of their union, Jennifer lay quietly on Race's strong body for a second, absorbing him into her very being, feeling totally complete.

Soon, too soon, the throbbing presence within her body demanded more, and they moved together toward a satisfaction greater than either had ever known.

As they lay together afterward, flat on their backs and partially covered by the red satin sheet, Jennifer looked up and smiled at Race. Their hands joined as they locked gazes in the mirror above them. When Jennifer began giggling, Race turned to smooth her deliciously wild hair away from her face and asked her what was so funny.

"This looks like a scene from my imagination," she explained.

"You imagined yourself in a waterbed with mirrors?"

"No. I imagined you in one. I thought that you probably lived in a house that looked just like this. That must have been why I trapped you here last summer. It seemed just your style."

"Did you ever imagine that we'd be honeymooning here, in the very same Blue Panther Motel?" Race asked. "I admit that the last time I was here, making love was the farthest thing from my mind. All I wanted to do was get out of here and throttle you. You certainly were a jolt to my ego, honey."

"Oh, love," Jennifer sighed, "I hope that it will be all right."

Sitting up, oblivious to everything, Race took Jennifer in his arms and demanded, "What do you mean? We're married and nothing will ever change it. You can't change your mind now."

"It's been so fast, Race. Do you realize that I agreed to marry you just three days ago?" Jennifer asked, still amazed at the whirlwind of activity that Race had initiated the minute she'd accepted his proposal.

Once Jennifer had agreed to marry him, Race had lost no time. After a long, satisfying kiss, he'd grabbed her hand and rushed her back up the steps. From that moment on, they'd been on the move. First they had told the good news to a pair of very happy children and a smugly pleased pair of older adults.

If Jennifer had had any doubts about the twins' accepting Race, that emotional session had totally dispelled them. She had wanted to wait until they were older to tell the twins that Race was their natural father, but matters had been taken out of their adult hands by the eager questions of their two small offspring.

In the manner of children everywhere, Rick asked the question as it crossed his mind. "You're our real dad, aren't you?"

Race looked down at his son, took him into his arms and told him, "I'll always be your dad."

Rick had persisted, however, and finally the adults understood that he was asking if Race was their biological father, as well as their "new father." When Race had answered, the boy had thrown his arms around his father's neck and held on for a very long time. Soon Rebecca joined her brother on her father's lap. They all talked after that, answering questions and sharing feelings. From that moment on, they were a true family. That Thanksgiving Day was the most moving and meaningful any of them had ever experienced. The feast that they ate in their new home marked a beginning for them all.

Within two days everything was arranged and they were flying back to the east coast along with the Kurrays for the wedding. Together, Race and Jennifer decided their marriage should take place back in Charlotte so that her friends could be invited. His parents had been flown in, along with all three of his sisters and their families. Stephanie had come up from St. Augustine to witness their vows.

Before they left California, Edward finalized the purchase of the house and, more importantly, found out the real truth about Patti. She wasn't pregnant. When Edward told her of Race's imminent wedding, she confessed they had not made love that one night. She sent a message begging Race to forgive her, vowing she'd done it all out of love. Neither Edward, Race nor Jenni believed that, but they were all glad to be finished with Patti Silk for good.

Jennifer felt totally enchanted that Saturday morning when she walked off Race's plane and was whisked to her house to prepare for her wedding. A selection of dresses waited for her, complete with all accessories. Within hours of getting off the plane, she and Race, the children, and their friends and relations were all together in a small chapel. After the touching ceremony, they returned to Race's home to find a cake and champagne awaiting the newly married couple. Everything had been perfect.

Looking from the image above her head to the real man beside her, Jenni commented idly, "Do you realize that I haven't even told the newspaper that I'm quitting?" She held up their joined hands to admire the wide wedding bands that encircled the third fingers of both their left hands. She had been touched and grateful when Race had insisted that he wear a wedding ring as a symbol of their commitment to each other. Sighing slowly, she stretched and rolled over to lay her head on his shoulder. "You know that they still think that I'm on vacation?"

"We'll deal with it all on Monday," Race promised. "Think of the exclusive story that you can have." With a playful swat on her delicious behind, he said, "I knew that the only way I'd get you into this bed was to give you a story. You newspaper people will do anything for a good byline," he said, reminding her of their first encounter last summer. Jenni was still struggling with the problem of Race's fame, but she knew it would work out. Finally secure in his love, she realized that she could handle anything that came their way.

"Are you sure that you won't miss working on the paper?" Race asked once more. He had been worried that

Jenni would miss her job, but they both realized that it was impractical to think that Jenni, as Mrs. Race Hunter, would be able to remain a reporter. She would be too much of a story herself to be effective.

"I realized that what I enjoy most is writing," Jenni said. "I've wanted the time and leisure for years that I'll have now. I can free-lance articles and start a book. If you approve, I think I'd like to start writing a biography on Kelsey and the dangers of drugs."

Crushing her to his chest, Race inhaled the sweet perfume of her hair and thanked his lucky stars for this woman. "That would be wonderful," he finally whispered. "I know Kelsey would have liked that."

Race promised that they would have a long honeymoon alone as soon as the twins were settled into their new surroundings. They could vacation in London, Paris, Tahiti, anywhere Jenni wanted. Smiling, Jennifer told him that it didn't matter to her as long as they were together. Tonight, their first night as a married couple, Race had insisted that they return to what he deemed the scene of the crime.

Jennifer lay back, smiling languidly. Now, suddenly, everything seemed possible. Tomorrow their new life together would officially start. Tonight was theirs. Tomorrow they would all start out again for California. Tonight would be spent in the manner of honeymooners the world over.

Margo and Jameson were seeing to the details of the move, and Jennifer had been pleased to discover that Margo's relationship with the Englishman seemed to be turning into something more than friendship. Margo had agreed to live in the cottage by the main house and was looking forward to a new chapter in her life, as well.

Jennifer turned to her husband, thrilling at the thought that he was hers, and asked him one last question. "Are you sure that this is what you want?"

"Surer than anything in my life, Jennifer Grange Hunter," Race promised as he looked down at the woman who was now his entire world. "For now and forever."

"Does that mean," Jennifer teased, "that you would consider getting a mirror above our bed in our new house?"

"Anything you want," Race promised. "Anything."

*   *   *   *   *